FIRST COMES
MARRIAGE

T0244938

Laila Rafi has dabbled in a few industries but realised that her real calling was putting pen to paper, or more accurately, fingers to keyboard and getting lost in the world of happily ever afters. So now that is exactly what she does. Her debut novel was shortlisted for the RNA Katie Fforde Debut Romantic Novel Award.

Laila lives in the heart of London with her boisterous family and when she's not writing or reading romance, she can be found watching almost any sport – preferably Formula 1 – or working on her latest crochet project.

Also by Laila Rafi

From Fake to Forever

FIRST COMES MARRIAGE

Laila Rafi

ORION

First published in Great Britain in 2024 by Orion Fiction,
an imprint of The Orion Publishing Group Ltd,
Carmelite House, 50 Victoria Embankment
London EC4Y 0DZ

An Hachette UK company

1   3   5   7   9   10   8   6   4   2

A CIP catalogue record for this book
is available from the British Library.

ISBN (Paperback) 978 1 3987 1644 5
ISBN (eBook) 978 1 3987 0995 9

Typeset by Born Group
Printed and bound in Great Britain by Clays Ltd, Elcograf S.p.A.

MIX
Paper | Supporting
responsible forestry
FSC® C104740

www.orionbooks.co.uk

For all my readers – thank you.

And for me – for being brave and making my
dream my reality.

I

Zafar

'Let me get this straight.' With the strongest of holds on his reflexes, Zafar stopped himself from rolling his eyes. The last thing he wanted or needed right now was his father talking to him as if he were a belligerent teenager – he was thirty-three not thirteen.

Nasir Saeed puffed out his chest, ready to launch into a self-indulgent monologue. As if he hadn't got himself straight twice already, albeit using different words each time. 'Reshma went to Mombasa ten days ago for Ruqayyah's daughter's wedding and you didn't go with her.'

Like he had twice already, Zafar nodded, taking a fortifying sip of his coffee. He wanted to lean back and savour the caffeine boost, but if he did that, his father might well blow a hole through the ceiling, thinking that he wasn't taking this conversation – read, telling-off – seriously.

It wasn't often Zafar found himself on the receiving end of a verbal pasting from his father. He was the model his father frequently used as a yardstick for his younger brothers and there was an implicit expectation that he would lead his brothers by example. Being at the receiving end of criticism from his father – or anyone else, for that matter – was such a rare occurrence that Zafar didn't know how to act. Was he supposed to stand up or stay seated? Make eye contact or look down into the dark depths of his coffee?

He decided to stay where he was and switched between making eye contact with his dad and breaking it, while they sat in the room designated as an office in their family home, where his father was catching up on all he'd missed over the past six weeks while he'd been holidaying in Canada with his wife. He'd landed yesterday, while his wife was due back next week, after spending a bit more *husband-free* time with her family.

'Why? What were you thinking, son?'

In all his blustering, this was the first time his father had actually asked him for a reason. Zafar took a deep breath and put his mug down in front of him.

'The hotel deal is at a crucial stage, Dad. I need to be available for it and I can't afford any distractions.' The chances were that Reshma was probably happy that he wasn't there, giving *her* a chance to have some *husband-free* time with her family while she enjoyed the various wedding celebrations taking place. She hadn't said as much, but the thought appealed to his conscience. She got to spend time with her family without him and he got to focus on his work. A win-win scenario.

'This is not acceptable by any stretch of the imagination, Zafar.' His father smacked his hand on the table. 'You've not been married coming onto thirty-five years where you can do things like that. You've only been married for a year. It's the first time she's gone for an event on her family's side since her own wedding and her husband's nowhere to be seen. How do you think that reflects? On you? On her? And, most importantly, on the Saeed family name and our reputation? We've been family friends of the Mirs since my late father and Reshma's late

2

grandfather's childhood. Just under a century. That's not something to be ignored.'

Zafar squirmed in his seat. His father wasn't wrong, if a bit dramatic.

But Zafar had different priorities. He had promised his grandfather that he'd take care of the family business just like his grandfather had. That promise preceded all of this – a wedding in the Mir family, his own marriage and relationship with Reshma, keeping up appearances with his in-laws. It even preceded any feelings he might have, which, at that point in time, told him that he knew what he had to do and there was no reason to feel guilty about it.

The door to the study had been left ajar and as it moved open a bit more, Zafar turned to find his grandmother in the doorframe. The menace had probably been standing there the whole time, listening to his dad chew him out and waiting for the right moment to come and interfere.

She swanned in, bringing a wave of her floral perfume in with her. His grandmother, Mumtaz Saeed, while small and dainty, packed a punch enough to fell the greatest of giants. She held the strings of the Saeed family in her little hands and knew exactly when to tighten her grip and when to loosen it.

She walked towards him and dropped a kiss on the top of his head. She could only manage the gesture when he was sitting and she was standing. He succumbed to her affection and then stood up, letting her have his seat, and she took it like a queen taking the throne.

'Did you not say anything to him, Amma?' His father addressed his mother. 'I expected better from him.'

That twisted the knife for Zafar, but he didn't let it show on his face as he moved towards the faux fireplace and leaned against the mantel, swirling the dregs of his coffee.

'I did, sweetheart, but Zafar said that his work was at a stage where he couldn't leave it and so I didn't push. Perhaps I should have. In fact, I've decided that he needs to go to Mombasa after Reshma.'

Zafar straightened at that. Daadi's voice held a note of steel he seldom heard. It brooked no argument and he had a slim-to-none chance of getting her to change her mind when she took that tone.

'I've also decided that I'll go with him. It'll be better if there's another family member there. I was familiar with Reshma's grandmother – even if we didn't always see eye to eye – and I'm fond of the Mir children. Well, at least two of them.'

His father sat back in his chair, his steepled fingers resting against his lips, very Bond-villain-like as he regarded him for a moment before lowering his hands to grip the chair's armrests and looking at Daadi. 'Yes, Amma. I agree. I think you going with him will add credence and show support from the head of our family.'

Zafar pushed away from the mantel and took a few steps towards the desk, regarding first his grandmother – who smiled at him warmly – and then his father – who scrutinised him with a pinched mouth and raised eyebrows. 'Very well. I'll book tickets so we can make it for the wedding and the reception. That'll give me some time to sort things out on the work front.'

'No, no. There's no need to do that.' His father shook his head. 'You'll take the first available flight and stay there for as long as the wedding events are running. Leave the visas to me, I'll sort them out. And as for work, you seem to forget, young man, that while I might be semi-retired, it doesn't mean I've forgotten how to do the job which I taught you alongside your grandfather. Have some faith in your brother, your best friend and the people we've recruited to work with us. I can always step in to help as and when needed. You need to be in Mombasa as of yesterday.' His tone brooked no argument.

'Nasir is right, my angel,' Daadi said, looking at him solemnly. 'It's only right that you take out time and spend it with Reshma. She's such a treasure, does so much for all of us, so it'll be nice to do something with her on her side of the family, yes?'

Another twist of the knife.

Knowing there was nothing for it, Zafar excused himself, leaving his father and grandmother to talk. He made his way to the kitchen and found his youngest brother wrestling with the oven. He put his mug in the sink and then turned and leaned back against the worktop, watching Haroon, who adjusted the shelves in the oven and turned it on.

'What are you making?'

'A Sunday roast. I was craving roast potatoes. But then they're nice with gravy. And then I thought that I might as well do some meat with the gravy and before I knew it' – he clicked his fingers – 'I was doing the whole thing. There's enough for everyone. I don't know how to cook for just one person. It's a dinner party or nothing for me.'

Zafar laughed because he understood that logic perfectly. Haroon had only ever cooked on a scale that fed the entire family, so he only knew how to cook for six or more people. Thankfully he didn't cook too often.

Contrary to popular belief about big, joint families, theirs had a positive dynamic – most of the time – and they all fitted together like puzzle pieces. Unique in their own way but a part of a whole. There was Daadi and his parents. There was him and his four brothers – Ashar,

Ibrahim, Rayyan and Haroon – and since last year there was Reshma, his wife.

Reshma.

The woman after whom he was supposed to fly to the tropical destination of Mombasa, Kenya, and be a part of her cousin's wedding celebrations. Celebrations which he was sure would go just as well without him. His hotel deal, however, wouldn't go just as well without him, but he had no choice now. He'd have to go to Mombasa and that was that.

He didn't mind going as such. It was more the fact that the timing was off. But given that he hadn't taken more than a week off for his own wedding last year and hadn't taken any time off since, he wasn't sure that excuse would wash.

'Why are you frowning? Did you know that if you frown like that, you'll get permanent frown lines?' Harry said as he observed him, a tea towel tucked in his apron pocket and oven gloves in his hands.

'I've got work coming out of my ears, so much that needs my attention and now I have to go to Mombasa for a wedding because Dad and Daadi have said I have to.'

Harry blinked at him, taking a few moments to process what he'd said presumably, before a slow grin spread across his face. 'You're going to Mombasa? When? Can I come? No, wait. I can't come. I told the guys I'd go away with them for a break. Maybe I can join you there.'

'Stop thinking so hard, mate, you'll hurt yourself. I'm not going holidaying. I'm going for a wedding. Dad wants me there yesterday, so I'll probably be leaving tomorrow, unless he finds a flight for tonight.' Zafar said it sarcastically, but it wasn't outside the realms of possibility. 'Feel free to come out there if you want. Though I'm not sure what

6

the accommodation set-up is yet. Maybe let me get there and see how things are.' He'd never say no to having one of his brothers there with him.

Harry turned back to the worktop and started preparing a salad. 'Hmm, I probably won't. It doesn't make sense to go there but not take part in all the wedding events. That's the whole fun of it.' He and his brother had very different ideas about what constituted *fun*. If only they could swap out. 'Reshma will be happy to see you. Tell her I miss her.'

Harry and Reshma got along like a house on fire, bonding soon after Zafar had got engaged to her. 'Well, I'm going upstairs. I need to pack and make sure I squeeze in a catch-up with the others before I have to go. Are Murad and Ibrahim around for lunch?'

'I think so.'

Zafar hoped so. He needed to bring his friend and now business partner and his brother up to speed as much as he could before he left. He hated having to do this. He had wanted to be here every step of the way for the hotel deal and having to leave it midway like this wound him up. If Reshma hadn't gone and . . .

He paused that train of thought before it gathered momentum. He wasn't being fair here. None of this was on Reshma. It was just the hand they'd been dealt and the best thing – the *only* thing – he could do was get himself there, see the visit out and come back so he could pick things up where he was leaving them. Who knew, maybe it wouldn't be so bad.

2

Reshma

A gentle breeze ruffled her hair as warm water rushed over her feet and ankles, and Reshma breathed a soft sigh of contentment. Since coming out to Mombasa, walking along the shoreline had become one of her favourite parts of the day, imbuing her with a sense of peace which she'd felt had eluded her for some time.

In these moments, with just nature for company, she felt as though all was well with the world. Perhaps she was deluding herself, but it beat the alternative of fixating on things she couldn't change and had zero control over. Like the fact that her marriage hadn't turned out anything like she'd dreamt it would. Or that rather than come out to Mombasa to her cousin's wedding with her – and make a short holiday of it – her husband had chosen to stay behind in London and carry on working, much like he had for the entirety of their one-year marriage.

She huffed a sigh of frustration. So much for feeling content in the moment. Inevitably, her thoughts always veered to the same territory and led to her going through a spectrum of emotions. Well, she wasn't going to let that happen today. She'd do what she had set out to do before coming out for a walk and that was to focus on her latest work project.

She was working on a new website for a small band that were starting out and she was hopeful that if they were happy with her designs, they might well hire her to work on their new album cover too. She'd love to have some variety in the kind of work she did as a freelance graphic designer. She enjoyed the freedom of being able to set her own hours and location of work and being here in Mombasa, with her family, the beach and uninterrupted sunshine, she'd found that she'd been more productive than she'd expected.

She'd moved further along the beach, brainstorming different ideas and making brief notes on her phone when she heard a shriek which had her looking sharply to the left.

A man had his arms wrapped around a woman's waist from behind as he swung her up and spun around in a circle. The woman shrieked again, but there was mirth in her tone, which had the sense of alarm Reshma had first felt dissipate as she smiled at the scene unfolding before her.

They were obviously together, given the familiarity between the couple and the affection with which he was looking at her. Reshma felt a pang in the region of her heart at the sight. What would it feel like to be looked at like that? As though all his attention was solely for her. To know with absolute certainty that you were wanted, cherished and loved by a person just by the way he looked at you. Touched you. Held you.

The pang in her chest made its presence felt anew. Shaking her head at the futility of her thoughts, Reshma turned and started making her way back towards the villa, where she was staying. There was absolutely no point in letting her thoughts wander down that particular road because there was nothing but potholes of misery and chicanes of disappointment lying in wait for her. Because the truth of the matter was that if *he* had wanted to be here with her, he would have made the effort to be.

'Reshma?' She looked up to find her cousin, Saleema, a few metres ahead of her, panting slightly with her hands on her hips. She moved her arm in a come-on gesture. 'Hurry up. We need to start getting ready and you promised me you'd help me with my hair.'

'Yeah, come on. I was on my way back anyway.' She linked arms with her and they both started walking as Reshma tried to banish the thoughts that had clouded her mind moments ago to focus on the present moment and making the most of being in Mombasa with her family for her cousin's wedding.

'Surprise!'

Reshma froze on the bottom step, grateful that the loud cheer hadn't caused her to lose her footing in her high-heeled sandals. She blinked a few times in . . . well, *surprise*, as she took in the sight in front of her, slowly cataloguing everyone's bright smiley faces, her own face sporting both a frown and a smile. It wasn't a great expression, but that's what confusion looked like on her.

It wasn't her birthday and she was pretty sure there was no big achievement worth celebrating recently, so she had absolutely no idea why she was being *surprised* like this.

And then her eyes landed on him.

It was Zafar.

Her husband. The man she had left behind in London. Or rather, the man who had *chosen* to stay behind and work rather than spend a few weeks with her.

She blinked a few more times, unsure if she was seeing things or if he was really there. He was the last person she had expected to see that evening. Or at all during this trip, really. Hadn't he made his feelings about coming with her crystal clear?

He lifted one eyebrow before a corner of his mouth slowly turned up, very much *there*. She wasn't seeing things after all.

He looked as handsome as always, immaculately dressed in dark trousers and a light grey shirt, his jaw was clean-shaven and his hair was neatly styled in short layers. His grin broadened a fraction as he tilted his head to the side ever so slightly and Reshma felt a spark of joy light inside her at the sight of him as her tummy did a little somersault.

Zafar was here. He'd actually come.

Those two thoughts circled in her mind a couple of times before coming to a standstill as she processed them fully.

Zafar was here?! Why?

The small spark of joy she'd felt seconds ago metamorphosised into uncertainty, slowly engulfing the joy she'd experienced until it was entirely gone. She was sure the change in her reaction was visible on her face because she saw the shift in his expression before he turned and looked pointedly down at the person standing beside him.

Reshma moved her eyes that way too and was surprised anew when she saw his grandmother standing beside him, her face wreathed in smiles as she slowly lifted her arms and beckoned Reshma to come forward.

'Daadi?' This time, there was definitely joy in her reaction and she let it spill forth, ignoring her bewilderment momentarily as she stepped forward and hugged Daadi, inhaling her signature floral scent.

'Hello, sweetheart. How did you like our first surprise?'

Reshma eased back and held onto Daadi's hands as she took in her sweet face. 'I'm over the moon to see you.' Which she was, it was no lie. She couldn't say exactly the same about her grandson, but she also couldn't say as much to his grandmother.

When Reshma had spoken to Zafar about coming to Mombasa for Saleema's wedding, he'd refused to even entertain the idea. He'd told her how important his work was and how he couldn't afford to leave it and 'go off to some destination wedding with her'.

She'd stewed on that for quite some time, going through various thoughts, and at the end of all that thinking – and a blinding headache because of it – she'd come to the conclusion that his refusal had bothered her and it wasn't just about going to Saleema's wedding. It was more than that. So much more than that. But the invitation to Saleema's wedding had ended up becoming a catalyst for her. It had sparked Reshma into thinking very carefully about Zafar, their marriage, her place in his life and his home and, most importantly she supposed, it had forced her to think about herself. About who she was, where she was and where she wanted to be. Of course, there were additional *hows* and *whats* that could be included and answered, but the point was that she'd had some choices and decisions to make. Was she going to simply accept Zafar's refusal and choose not to attend Saleema's wedding in Mombasa or was she going to do something else?

Given the fact that she was standing in the front courtyard of a complex of villas her aunt and uncle had hired for their daughter's wedding, in Mombasa, she had chosen to do something else.

What didn't fit the narrative, however, was Zafar's sudden appearance. It really was a surprise and then Reshma remembered Daadi's words.

She glanced around her and behind Daadi. 'You said first surprise. What's the second?'

'Surprise!' Reshma turned to look behind her as the sound of her uncle Jawad's voice boomed across the space, drowning out the voices of his immediate family who stood beside him. She wasn't expecting them to arrive until the following week.

She beamed at them as she made her way towards them, hugging her two cousins and aunt before she was enveloped by the arms of her beloved uncle. He squeezed her against himself and Reshma rested her head against his broad chest, heaving a sigh of contentment. It didn't matter how old she was, this was the one place where she felt most at peace.

They eased away from each other and he smiled down at her. 'We managed to get early flights and brought Auntie Mumtaz and Zafar along with us to surprise you. Happy?'

Reshma looked at all the faces around her, their attention solely on her and her reaction. She jerked her head up and down in a nod and heard a collective 'Aww' from everyone. What could she have said anyway?

I'm happy to see you Uncle Jawad, the family, and Daadi. But Zafar?

It wasn't that she didn't want him there.

She did, very much so, that's why she'd asked him to come in the first place, but after his blatant refusal to even consider the idea of coming here with her, she couldn't understand what had prompted him to change his mind. She was truly baffled by this turnaround.

Her aunt Ruqayyah – her father's sister and the bride's mother – chose that moment to step forward.

'It's been so hard to keep this secret from you since yesterday, but worth it. Are you happy, my darling?'

Reshma looked at the exuberance on her aunt's face and smiled back at her as her cousin, Khalil, moved forward, throwing his arm across her shoulders before she could respond to her aunt.

'Everyone got a hug. But poor Zafar, who has come all the way from London to be here with you, barely got a nod. Don't be shy on our account, cuz. If you would prefer, we can all look the other way.'

Reshma felt her cheeks warm.

'Behave yourself, Khalil, and stop embarrassing them.' Auntie Ruqayyah – *thankfully* – stopped her son from making things any more awkward and addressed Daadi. 'Auntie Mumtaz, we've been invited by Saleema's fiancé and his family for dinner tonight. I told them that you and Zafar and Jawad and his family will be with us too, but I was wondering if you'd like to have a bit of a rest before we leave? I'm sure they won't mind us getting there in two groups.'

'No, no, Ruqayyah, please don't change your plans, and certainly not on my account. I'm actually feeling fine to come along, especially after that little rest at your place just now while we waited for the girls to get ready. We can all leave together as you'd originally planned to.'

Reshma was about to move off when Khalil's arm, which was still slung over her shoulders, tightened. He lowered his head and whispered to her out of the corner of his mouth. 'The adults are distracted. You should use the opportunity to—'

'Go away.' She pushed him away and he staggered back, laughing. 'I don't need you meddling, thank you very much. Especially if you don't even identify as an adult, even though you're creeping closer to thirty with each day.'

Before he could respond, his father called him away and Reshma turned and faced Saleema, who had come down the steps with her but, at just the right moment, had raced ahead and now Reshma knew why.

'Your expression was priceless.' Saleema opened and closed her mouth three times in succession, presumably imitating her, and her cousin Haniya – Uncle Jawad's daughter – laughed.

'You're the world's biggest traitor, Saleema. You knew! You too, Niya.'

They simply grinned at her.

'Yes, I knew and, like Mum said, it was super hard to keep it a secret, but, boy, am I glad I did. Uncle Jawad called to tell us that they would all be coming today, including your mister and his grandmother.' She waggled her eyebrows when she referred to Zafar. 'Papa needed to arrange the airport pick-up and they got here a little while ago, but we decided to time your surprise for just before we left. It gave them all time to change and have a breather. It was actually Uncle Jawad's idea to surprise you. Didn't you see Papa recording the whole thing on his phone just now?'

'I'll get both of you back for this.' She pointed at her cousins in turn who continued to smile at her, completely unrepentant. She would deal with Uncle Jawad in due course, though she was happy that her family was with her.

'Oh, please. It was such a cute surprise.' Haniya looked in Zafar's direction, as did she and Saleema, watching as he hovered around his grandmother, presumably trying to get her to take Auntie Ruqayyah up on the offer of a rest. He was the perfect example of a helicopter grandson.

'I'd be so chuffed if my fiancé did something like that for me. Come all that way just to surprise me,' Saleema added dreamily, both her and Haniya looking like they were about to melt on the spot as Reshma frowned.

'Yeah. OK.' She knew she sounded a bit churlish, but she didn't know what to say or how to react in a way that didn't give her true feelings away. She didn't want to bring that all out in front of everyone, but she certainly wanted some clarity from Zafar at some point. She felt a sense of nervousness as he made his way towards them. Everyone else seemed to have gone towards the cars, ready to leave.

Zafar came to where she was standing.

'Hi. I'm Saleema. This one's cousin.' Saleema canted her head towards Reshma, before opening her arms towards Zafar for a hug. She sounded like an overexcited child meeting Mickey Mouse for the first time. Though to be fair, she was meeting Zafar for the first time. She hadn't come to London for their wedding last year, only her parents had.

Ever the consummate gentleman, Zafar gave Saleema a megawatt smile before returning her hug, towering over her. 'Hi. I'm Zafar. This one . . .' he cleared his throat though his voice was laced with amusement, 'Reshma's husband.'

She just about stopped herself from rolling her eyes.

Very funny.

Except she seemed to be the only person not amused. Zafar, Haniya and Saleema were all smiling away quite happily.

'I believe congratulations are in order,' Zafar continued.

'Thanks. I'm so pleased you came out here for my wedding. Reshma said that you had loads of work to do and that's why you didn't come with her. But I'm glad that—'

'Saleema? Come on, guys. I know being late is the bride's prerogative, but I'm starving,' Khalil called out.

Saleema rolled her eyes and shook her head. 'We'll catch up later.' She linked arms with Haniya and they walked towards the cars, leaving Reshma behind to follow them as Zafar fell in step with her.

'Hello, Reshma.' His voice was low and slightly gravelly as he spoke.

'Hey.' She looked up at him and he smiled at her, his hands stuffed into his pockets as they reached the parade of cars in the driveway.

Her uncle, Imtiaz, stood beside the open door of the third car in line, the first two cars already full. 'You and Zafar come in this one, Reshma. No sense in squashing in with the others when we've got the cars and drivers at our disposal. We'll see you at the restaurant.'

Reshma nodded at her uncle as she slid into the back seat. Zafar went around to the other side, and after a few minutes, the driver moved off.

Aside from the low hum of the engine, there was silence around them as they drove out of the gates and then Zafar spoke. 'Still not talking to me?'

'I never really stopped talking to you.'

Except she kind of had.

After he'd refused to come with her or even discuss the subject any further, she'd backed off and said even less than she usually did to him, though part of the reason for that had been because she'd been in her own head, trying to make sense of the myriad thoughts vying for attention.

Their relationship as husband and wife was . . . different. Their marriage had been arranged by family members and while they'd been married for a year – thirteen months, to be precise – they still felt like strangers. Zafar treated her like a stranger, or an acquaintance at best.

For her part, Reshma knew she'd tried. She'd made the effort to try to get to know her husband and while she'd begun to, it wasn't because they spent time together. What she had was the kind of understanding one developed after living with another person for a period of time, learning their traits and habits, their likes and dislikes – the obvious ones at least.

She'd tried to fit into his established family set-up and had been successful on many fronts. But she couldn't say that her relationship with him was any stronger than it had been this time last year when they'd been married for just a month. He was never unkind, but she sometimes got the feeling that he simply wasn't interested.

The scent of his aftershave made its way to her, the cedarwood and sandalwood comfortingly familiar, a feeling which added to her confusion about him because this was the same man who had refused to come here when she'd asked him to and was now sitting here as though being here had always been the plan. As though she had gone through all the frustration she had since then for nothing.

She looked his way in question. 'Was it . . . was this your plan all along? To come out here and surprise me?'

In the soft light of dusk, she could see the twin dark pools of chocolate that were his eyes, looking straight at her with an intensity she wasn't familiar with from him. There was a small nick on his chin where he'd probably cut himself while shaving and she could see faint lines of tiredness bracketing his eyes and mouth. She curled her tingling fingertips in towards her palm, resisting the urge to reach out and touch him.

He was still looking at her intently and she saw his eyes moving from her hairline to her eyes, across her face and then down to her lips. On instinct, she wanted to run her tongue across them but held it firmly behind her teeth, swallowing instead as goosebumps rose on her arms.

His eyes moved down her, presumably taking in her purple sari. She wondered if he remembered it. She'd worn this sari at Daadi's birthday party last year and had taken her time getting ready and making sure everything was on point, only for Zafar to have his eyes glued on his watch when he'd come into the room to tell her it was time that they made a move and then walked straight back out of the door.

She'd been pretty miffed but hadn't said anything. Maybe if she had . . .

There she went again, on the same thought journey she had been on since he'd refused to come here with her when she'd first asked him to.

Maybe if she had said or done things differently, then their relationship wouldn't be where it was right now.

But surely the onus wasn't only on her to make a success of their marriage, was it?

'Huh?'

Reshma's eyebrows lowered as she regarded him, trying to bring her thoughts back to the moment. 'I asked if this was your plan all along. To surprise me.'

He gave her a small smile but shook his head. 'No,' he said quietly, his voice a low rumble. 'It was decided after you left.'

3

Zafar

With a will of iron, Zafar stopped himself from squirming in his seat. The look of patent curiosity paired with an earnestness he found disarming was directed towards him and there was nowhere to hide and nothing to distract Reshma from this line of questioning.

He had known to expect it. He knew that at some point she would ask him what he was doing in Mombasa and he'd have to give her some answer. And, to be fair, it was a perfectly valid question because when she'd asked him to come with her, he'd refused.

With work being the primary focus of his life for the past four years, putting it aside was something he found almost impossible. Because if he wasn't being consumed by his work, then guilt would rear its ugly head and take its place. He'd allowed work to become his all in the past four years, giving it everything of himself because it helped keep his demons at bay. He'd not even allowed Reshma to distract him.

Coming out here without any link to his work – thanks to his father practically confiscating his work gear as though he were a recalcitrant teenager – meant his time was his own and he had no idea what he was going to do to fill it, aside from joining in with the various wedding celebrations.

He knew he ought to tell Reshma the truth, but now wasn't the time for that. He didn't want any potential upsets between them to cause any disruption to her cousin's wedding, even a small one. He didn't know how Reshma would react. She might take it all in her stride, or she might be unhappy. It made sense, therefore, to have this dinner and then he could tell Reshma how he had ended up being there at his father's say-so at a more appropriate time.

He could still feel the heat of the disappointed look his father had cast his way when he'd found out that Zafar hadn't accompanied Reshma. His grandmother had gone straight for the jugular and used the D word. *I have to say, Zafar sweetheart, I'm disappointed.* He'd not felt that uncomfortable in a long time.

They weren't exactly wrong, especially when his grandmother had pointed out the lengths Reshma went to for *his* family. From day one, she had made an effort with everyone and – aside from his mother's slight antagonism towards his wife, simply for the reason that she thought Reshma wasn't good enough for him and she had wanted Zafar to marry her best friend's daughter – she got along pretty well with them.

Reshma always went above and beyond for his family, especially his grandmother, who doted on Reshma. She'd never made him feel like doing anything for him or his family was a big deal, but that was exactly what he had done to her and he didn't feel all that great about it. What made it worse was the fact that he still hadn't come here of his own accord, he'd been made to by his father and grandmother.

That thought settled in his gut like a lead balloon as he looked at Reshma, whose confused expression had been replaced with a tentative smile.

'Thank you. Both for coming and for surprising me. It's actually really sweet.'

Oh, boy.

He swallowed the guilt that was now lodged in his throat and smiled back at her as best as he could. 'Don't thank me. I should have come when you first asked me to.' Which – while being true – was easier said than done.

'I do appreciate how hard you work, Zafar. I know it couldn't have been easy for you to leave everything to be here.' She covered his hand with hers and gave it a soft squeeze and Zafar felt his chest squeeze in response.

He hadn't appreciated until now how hard it was going to be to come clean with her about how he came to be in Mombasa. She looked so happy. The last thing he wanted was to hurt or upset her. He knew he wasn't a contender for a 'Husband of the Year Award', but he cared for her. He wanted a relationship of mutual respect and maybe even some level of affection between them and he hoped that when he told her the truth, it wouldn't widen the chasm that had been between them since they'd got married.

'How's your time here been so far? Been enjoying yourself?' he asked in an attempt to move away from the difficult conversation and feelings it was engendering.

'I have.' A broad smile broke out on her face and her eyes sparkled. 'It's been really good. The last ten days have flown by. I've been working, but I've also helped with some last-minute wedding stuff. I've had the chance to spend some quality time with my aunt and cousins after ages. And now everyone else is here too, so I'm really happy.'

The driver pulled the car into a bay, bringing their conversation to a natural close. Everyone gathered on the pavement before Reshma's uncle led them into the restaurant. The top floor had been reserved for their party, with two long rectangular tables set up in the middle of the room. A group of people were standing off to one side and as they saw the bridal party approach, they came to the doors to greet them.

Reshma's aunt made all the introductions for those who weren't familiar with her daughter's fiancé and his family.

Zafar saw his grandmother with another one of Reshma's aunts. She was in her element as the people gathered around her hung on her every word. She was familiar with most of Reshma's family before they had got married through the long association the two families had. Despite that though, he had only met Reshma when his father had made the introduction with a view to arranging their match.

Reshma's cousin – Khalil? – called them over and all the cousins and siblings sat at one table with the bride- and groom-to-be. Their parents, aunts, uncles and grandparents sat on the second table. Zafar knew some of her relatives, but in that moment, he felt like the new kid in the class who watched all the action around him, not sure where he fitted in. He felt a bit out of place.

He had a fleeting thought that this was probably how Reshma had felt when she'd joined his family, but he couldn't dwell on it for long because one of her cousins called out to him.

'You have to tell us, Zafar, because your wife won't spill any beans, how miserable life with her really is. And don't hold back. We've known her since childhood and are well aware of what a nightmare she's capable of being.'

Zafar looked between Reshma and her cousins, unable to hold back his surprise at the exchange between them and let out an unexpected laugh when Reshma stuck her tongue out at one of them. She faced him abruptly and he saw a rosy flush fill her cheeks, though she didn't say anything, just grinned sheepishly. He'd never seen Reshma like this and he found himself fascinated.

★

23

The meal was exquisite, with brilliant company. Reshma's cousins didn't spare a single chance to have a dig at each other and he was surprised to see Reshma join in with them just as ruthlessly. It reminded him of how he bantered with his brothers. In the short time he'd been there, he'd seen a different side to Reshma he hadn't even known had existed and he was intrigued by it. There was more he didn't know about the woman next to him than he did and he thought that, if nothing else, he'd get the opportunity to find out more about her while they were here.

By the time the evening came to a close, he felt quite relaxed, though physically tired after the day of travelling he'd had. On the way back, Reshma gave him an explanation of her family tree when he asked her how they were all related. 'Uncle Jawad is the eldest, followed by Auntie Ruqayyah and then my . . . my father.' She went quiet for a moment but Zafar didn't say anything.

He knew Reshma didn't have a good relationship with her dad, but he didn't know what had caused the rift or why it was still ongoing. He knew she'd been raised by her uncle Jawad and his wife Bilqis after the death of her mother when she was a child and that was it. They'd never had a conversation about it and he'd never thought to ask.

'You already know Shoaib and Haniya – Uncle Jawad's kids. Khalil and Saleema are Auntie Ruqayyah's children and Uncle Imtiaz is her husband. That's the immediate family. The others who'll be joining us over the coming days are distant relatives and family friends. I'll introduce you as and when we meet them. But the ones I've told you about are the important ones.'

When they got back to the villas, Reshma's aunt met them outside with Daadi and led them to a villa a few metres from hers.

'We thought this was the best option of being together but also being able to have our own space and make the most of this glorious location,' Auntie Ruqayyah explained. 'You have access to the private beach, an on-site gym and a pool behind your villa. It's all serviced by a small team who take care of all the villas, so if you need anything, just alert a staff member. Reshma knows.'

They were left to settle in and all Zafar wanted to do was to drop face down on a bed and sleep.

'Why don't you go upstairs? I'll help get Daadi settled in the bedroom downstairs. Auntie Ruqayyah said all our luggage has already been moved for us,' Reshma suggested as they walked through an open-plan living area.

Zafar didn't need to be told twice, and after bidding his grandmother a good night, he made his way towards the stairs.

The staircase led to an internal balcony which overlooked the living area downstairs and there was just one door along the whole wall, which led to the bedroom.

Zafar went into the exceptionally large bedroom which took up the entire width of the villa and found a huge bed dominated the space on one side of the room and a small seating area was set up in front of one of the walls that was made entirely of glass. Beyond the glass, he could see furniture on a balcony. There was a bathroom and an adjoining dressing room on the other side of the room and in there he saw his and Reshma's luggage.

He grabbed a pair of sleep shorts and made his way into the bathroom.

By the time he had finished his shower, there back was still no sign of Reshma, so he went to the bed and decided to wait for her there.

He wanted to talk to her sooner rather than later because the longer he left it, the worse he was feeling about her misunderstanding his sudden appearance. He lay back, checking his watch to find that it was just gone midnight.

Zafar turned over, slowly opening one eye and seeing shafts of sunlight hit the wooden floor. He closed his eye and turned the other way, only to jerk his eyes open and look around the room. Daylight streamed in through the gauzy excuse of a curtain covering the glass wall as he slowly blinked the remnants of sleep out of his eyes. He glanced to his side and saw that while the space was empty, it had been slept in.

He heaved a tired sigh. He'd fallen asleep. Without talking to her.

Reshma had probably come up and seen him sprawled on the bed like a beached whale, out for the bloody count, and when she'd woken up, he'd probably been in the same position. Travelling never had agreed with him.

Argh, shit.

He scrubbed his face as he sat up and looked at the time. Ten-thirty.

'Oh. You're up.' He looked at the doorway and saw Reshma framed in it, dressed in a bright orange dress and looking like she'd been up for a good few hours. 'How are you feeling?'

'I think I was knocked out.' His voice was croaky.

She laughed softly. 'Yes, you were. You didn't hear me come up last night or get up this morning.'

'I wanted to talk to you last night.'

'Mmhmm.' She came into the room and sat on the corner of the bed. Her face was open and smiley and Zafar felt the words he needed to say lodge in his throat. He rubbed a hand along the back of his neck.

'Dad was back from Canada when I left.'

'Yeah, Daadi told me last night. Did they have a good trip?'

'Umm, yeah. Yeah, I think they did. Mum was still there, although I think she's due today.'

She nodded.

Why was this so hard? It was a simple enough thing to do. All he had to do was say that his dad had thought it would be better if he joined Reshma and that's why he was there.

'Daadi was up early this morning, and after breakfast, Auntie Ruqayyah came and took her to her villa. She said she wanted to show her some of the clothes and jewellery she's got. I think they're just going to spend the morning having a bit of a catch-up with Auntie Bilqis. I'm sure copious amounts of tea will be involved.'

'How was she this morning? Not too tired?'

'No, she did better than you. She was bright-eyed and bushy-tailed. Ready for the day,' she said cheekily, her nose stud sparkling in the morning light as she smiled at him. It was like he was seeing a different version of her, more relaxed and cheerier than he'd seen before. It made him more certain that when he told her the truth, her happy bubble would burst.

4

Reshma

'Saleema made plans for us to go and get our nails done, so I'm about to head out for that, but we should be back before lunchtime.'

Zafar didn't respond. Reshma couldn't put her finger on why, but she had a feeling that something was troubling him. He seemed distracted. Last night, she had thought it might be tiredness and being around lots of new faces, but this morning he seemed more so.

'Are you feeling all right?' She lowered her eyebrows as she asked him. When she'd come up to bed last night, he'd been fast asleep, not moving even an inch as she got into bed beside him. This morning had been the same as she'd got up and got ready. Assuming he must be really tired, she'd not woken him and left him to sleep it off.

'Huh? Yeah' – he cleared his throat – 'just a bit groggy, I think. Jet lag perhaps.'

'Well, maybe a shower and some breakfast will help. There are plenty of things in the kitchen downstairs, so help yourself. There's a coffee machine too and there's a card beside it with instructions on how to operate it. You've got the villa to yourself, so just take it easy and I'll see you in a bit.'

Reshma smiled at him, and after a moment, he smiled back and nodded. 'Yeah. Have fun.'

She collected her bag and made her way downstairs, wondering if it was more than just jet lag affecting Zafar. She picked her phone up off the island and saw a message from Saleema.

Running a bit late. Will come and get you in about 15. xoxo

Reshma shook her head. Classic Saleema.

Oh, well.

She put her bag and phone on the island and her eyes went to the coffee machine. She decided that since she had time, she'd make Zafar a coffee to save him from struggling with the machine on his first day here. He looked like he could do with the pick-me-up.

She put a selection of croissants and pain aux raisins on a plate and a large mug of coffee on a tray and carried them upstairs. The bed was empty and she could see that the bathroom was empty through its open door.

'Mum, slow down. Just hear me out.' She heard Zafar's voice from the other side of the curtain and saw that the patio door was open and he was standing just outside it.

'No, you listen to me, Zafar.' His mother's voice came through loud and clear on speakerphone in the silence.

Reshma didn't want to intrude and decided to turn back, but her mother-in-law's next words stopped her in her tracks.

'If I had been here, I'd never have let your father force you to go there. I'm barely away for a handful of days and I come back to find out that he's sent you to Mombasa after that girl.'

Force you? Sent you?

Was Zafar's mum saying what Reshma thought she was?

She lowered the slightly shaking tray onto the table beside the sofa before she dropped it.

'Her name is Reshma, Mum. Please stop referring to her as *that girl*, it's not nice. I've told you before.'

His mother huffed. 'Fine. But my point still stands. If she'd gone by herself, then that was her choice. I don't understand why your father insisted that you go after her. You hadn't planned to go with her, otherwise the two of you would have gone together or you would have joined her there of your own accord. When I told him as much, he started talking to me about the family's reputation, for God's sake, asking me what the Mirs would think if no one else from our family was there. I'm not sure why it's not good enough for him that you didn't want to go.'

'Mum, stop stressing about this, please. All Dad said was that it doesn't look good if Reshma is out here by herself and that I should be here with her. He's not wrong. It's really not so bad and it's only for a couple of weeks.'

Reshma sucked in a shuddering breath, feeling it sharply in her chest, like she was slowly being stabbed with an icicle, the cold spreading from the centre of her chest throughout her body despite the tropical temperature.

Zafar wasn't here because he wanted to be. He hadn't come here to be with her. He was here because he'd been told to . . . No, *forced* by his father. She'd misunderstood his appearance because her family had decided to surprise her and he'd allowed them to. He'd allowed her to believe that he was there because it was where he wanted to be, and like the fool she was, she'd thought he was there for her. She'd wanted it so much that she'd gullibly believed it to be true.

'Reshma?' Zafar was standing on this side of the patio door now, his phone in his hand by his side and confusion lacing his voice. 'I thought you were going out?'

Reshma shook her head as she slowly lowered herself onto the sofa, nearly missing it but righting herself in time.

'I'm such an idiot.' Her voice started out as little more than a whisper. 'I should have known. You said no to coming here. But I let myself get caught up in the moment when everyone arrived. I should have known.'

'Shit.' She heard him mumble. Then he spoke a bit louder. 'I was going to tell you, Reshma. That's what I wanted to say this morning, but it's not . . .' He ran a hand through his hair, the strands sticking out at all angles. 'What part of that conversation did you hear?'

Reshma looked up at him, her shock slowly giving way to an emotion she hardly ever felt, believing it to be one which never served any purpose but left a person feeling drained of energy and hollow.

Anger.

At the situation. At him. But more than that, anger at herself. When was she going to learn?

Every moment in her life in which she had felt let down, an afterthought or unimportant flashed through her mind's eye as she sat there, feeling numb but also acutely sensitive to all the feelings that were giving her an emotional bashing.

Her father not stepping up to his responsibility to care for her – his only daughter and the last link to his deceased wife, who he had claimed had once been the love of his life.

Her maternal grandparents rejecting her because she reminded them too much of the daughter they'd lost.

Her father promising and then failing to ever live up to any promise of being with her and ultimately showing her that there was no place for her with his new wife and children.

She closed her eyes, trying to even her breaths which were sawing in and out of her, but all that did was intensify each and every memory of moments that had left an indelible mark on her. It was strange how, even now, she could feel like that child her father had left with his brother, except this time, she wasn't feeling like that because of her father.

But because of Zafar.

The man she had chosen to marry after her uncle had suggested the match, but the man who had never made the effort to forge a relationship with her. In the thirteen months they'd been married, it had always been her who made the effort, only to be met with a lacklustre response. He was always civil and polite, but wasn't there more to marriage, even an arranged one? Didn't she deserve more?

It was clear to her that he didn't want to be with her. He had only married her because she had been his father's and late grandfather's choice, the man she knew Zafar revered above all others.

He never did anything with her because he *wanted* to. It was always because he had to or because it was perceived to be the right thing to do, like coming to Mombasa. What had his mother said? Oh, yes. Family reputation. Something that meant a great deal to Zafar.

She was pleased to hear that her voice was devoid of all emotion when she opened her eyes and responded to his question. 'Enough to know that you're not here because this is where you want to be. You're here because your father told you to be here and being the model son you are, you did as you were told to.'

He took half a step forward and then stopped. 'It's not just that, Reshma. I can see that it was the right thing to do. You do so much for me and my family, it's only fair that if you want to—'

'So, it's payback then, is it? You think you owe me one?' Her anger bubbled to the surface.

'What? No, that's not it. I just . . . This isn't how I wanted to have this conversation.'

Reshma scoffed. 'I don't think you were going to have this conversation at all, otherwise you would have told me the truth yesterday. You told me it wasn't your plan to come here and surprise me, but you never said that you were here because your father made you come. *Forced* you, in fact. You didn't say that had it been up to you, you would not be here at all. Because, the fact of the matter is, Zafar, that you don't want to be here with me. I'm not important enough, I'm not your priority. You do things with me because you have to or they're expected of you. Nothing is ever forthcoming from *you*. And, like an absolute idiot, I actually thought you were here because you wanted to be, when that's never been the case before.'

'That's not true, Reshma. You are important. And I really was going to tell you about Dad encouraging me to come. I wasn't lying when I said I had a lot of work to do and didn't think I could afford to take a lengthy break from it.' His voice had an urgency to it, but it was completely lost on her.

She couldn't believe how stupid she'd been. She'd actually thought he'd wanted to be here. That he'd realised that fact after she had left. He'd discovered that he did want to spend time with her and had followed her out here. But how wrong she had been.

She would never be his priority. His choice.

Any forlorn hope she'd had of having anything more with him shattered to pieces. There was never going to be any such thing between them and the sooner she accepted that fact, the better it would be for her. She needed to realise that what hadn't happened in twenty-nine years of her life wasn't going to happen now. She wasn't suddenly going to become someone worth doing something for.

Reshma shook her head, though whether she was shaking it in denial or disbelief, she couldn't say for sure. She pressed her fingers to her chest and then her forehead, trying to hold the pain at bay.

Her mind went back to the day before, when, in her naivety, she'd celebrated Zafar's arrival – thanked him for it, *for God's sake* – but had been completely oblivious to his true motive, and she covered her face with her hands, feeling the sting of tears prick the corners of her eyes. Really, when *was* she going to learn? What would it take for her to stop having expectations of people who were never going to live up to them?

She'd been with Zafar for long enough for him to have shown her that she was an important part of his life and he hadn't. What more proof did she need? She'd seen him up close and knew how he was with those he cared about, but he'd never connected with her in a way she had always hoped for. Like a true partner.

She had never expected declarations of undying love from him, she knew how far-fetched a dream that was. But she had expected honesty from him. Honesty and perhaps friendship. But the only thing she seemed to have was cold civility. Maybe even indifference. While she, in all her naivety and gullibility, had fallen for everything he represented.

And what did she have to show for it?

She had one more person proving that her existence in his life, or lack thereof, was one and the same thing and he had only shown up because he'd been asked to. To keep up appearances.

'Reshma? Look at me, please. I swear to God I was going to tell you what led to me coming here. I was just waiting for the right opportunity. I've never lied to you before and I wouldn't start now.'

Reshma moved her hands away from her face, glad that the tears that had threatened to fall hadn't. She didn't want to show Zafar any more evidence of the hurt he'd caused her. She took a few deep breaths before she looked at him, his expression sombre.

'I'm sorry that this is how you found out. I was just waiting for the right time to tell you. And I'm glad I'm here, honestly.' A corner of his lips lifted but she wouldn't call it a smile.

She had no idea what to say or do in that moment. Her mind was both full and empty, and nothing made any sense to her.

She didn't know how long they stayed in the same place, her sitting on the edge of the sofa and Zafar standing there awkwardly, the only noise in the room coming from the humming of the air-conditioning unit.

The doorbell rang three times in succession and Reshma swung her gaze to the bedroom door, as if that would tell her who was there.

'You were going out with your cousins, weren't you?' Zafar asked as the doorbell rang again.

It was probably Saleema and Haniya, finally ready to leave.

Reshma internally laughed at the irony of the situation. If her cousins had been ready on time and if she hadn't decided to be considerate and bring Zafar breakfast, she would have been none the wiser and would have carried on with her day, blissfully happy in her little bubble for a bit longer.

If 'ifs' and 'buts' were candy and nuts, we'd all have a merry Christmas.

Reshma got up, pushing her thoughts to the back of her mind. 'That's probably Saleema and Niya. I'm not sure if that coffee is still warm enough to drink. If not, feel free to make yourself another cup.' She walked to the door and paused, turning to face him. 'And feel free to book your flight back to London. You don't need to be here, certainly not for me. Go back home, Zafar. I'll let my family know that there were important things that needed your attention.'

And with that, she left the room and made her way downstairs, grabbing her bag and phone before she left the villa on wooden legs.

5

Zafar

It wasn't often Zafar turned the air blue. He was usually calm and composed, choosing to deal with situations practically and logically. The introduction of emotions tended to affect a person's ability to make sound decisions and he'd been trained to be a damned good decision-maker, keeping feelings out of the process. Cold hard facts couldn't be argued with and he always ensured he had plenty in his arsenal, something he'd learnt at his grandfather's knee.

But this morning he'd been caught completely off guard. First by his mother's phone call and then finding Reshma standing there looking like she'd seen a ghost. Not only did he have nothing in his arsenal, he'd not even been able to defend himself well enough to warrant a conversation with Reshma.

She'd told him to leave and had walked out of the room without looking back.

To be fair, it wasn't any more than he deserved. He should have plucked up the courage and just told her what he had to when he'd woken up. Or, better yet, he should have told her everything in the car yesterday on their way to the restaurant. None of this would have happened then.

He spotted the tray on the table. There were pastries and a mug of coffee, and when he touched the side of the mug, he could feel that it was still warm. A hollow pit opened up in his gut at the stark difference between him and Reshma. She'd brought him coffee and pastries before leaving and he'd made her feel like an inconvenience. *Unimportant* was the word she'd used.

Running out of expletives, he sat next to the spot she had just occupied and picked up a pain au raisin. It was sweet and flaky, a perfect accompaniment to the rich coffee, but it might as well have been cardboard for the enjoyment it gave him in that moment.

He felt like crap on so many fronts, but none more than the fact that he felt like a failure as a husband. He'd seen evidence of that, crystal clear in Reshma's eyes as the spark in them had gradually dimmed to nothing in seconds. Gone.

He finished the coffee and made his way into the bathroom, hoping that standing under a blast of hot water would help fire up his brain cells enough to come up with a plan of action. Sitting there and ruminating wouldn't get him anywhere.

After a quick shower, he got into a pair of shorts and a T-shirt and made his way downstairs. The villa was silent as he looked around it, taking in the place properly in the morning light. He could see a small corridor leading to the room Daadi was using and on the opposite side was a kitchen, separated from the living area by a big island. The open-plan seating area was bright and airy, decorated in warm, earthy tones, and the back wall – much like it was upstairs – was made of glass, overlooking the pool and beyond that was a view of white gold sand and the Indian Ocean.

It looked tranquil and inviting and Zafar followed the pull of it and decided to sit by the pool after fiddling with the coffee machine and making himself another cup of it.

What was he going to do now? That was the big question on his mind.

He'd been practically dismissed by Reshma, given leave to go back home and get on with what it was that had kept him there in the first place. But he had to consider the fact that if he *did* go back, his father would demand an explanation as to why he was back and his wife was still out there. It would defeat the objective of coming out here in the first place.

If he put both those considerations to one side and asked himself what *he* felt was the right thing to do, then the answer was simple. He needed to stay, not because his father had instructed him to and not because his grandmother had cajoled him to. He needed to stay because that's what a supportive partner would do. Something Reshma did a lot better than him and something he needed to make a better effort to do.

He leaned back against the sunlounger, putting his feet up as he took a sip of the coffee, nowhere near as good as what Reshma made.

She managed to take care of so many details which were easily overlooked, but if he paused for long enough, he could see how she discreetly smoothed things every step of the way. And not once had she lorded it over him.

He hated that she'd found out the truth the way she had and was upset as a result. It was the last thing he had wanted. He needed to talk to her. She'd said so many things earlier and they alluded to hurts beyond him coming here because he had been forced to.

The sad thing was that despite over a year of marriage, he didn't know a great deal about his wife. What were those hurts and upsets? Those deeper wounds of hers that he'd got a glimpse of this morning?

The ringtone of his phone interrupted his thoughts and he put his coffee down, seeing his friend Murad's name come up on the screen.

'Please tell me my business is still in one piece,' Zafar answered.

'You know, Zaf . . .' Murad went quiet and Zafar heard a creak and then a slurp. 'I feel like I ought to be offended by how little faith you have in me. But then I remember that I'm working with your brother, and your dad has been in the office since yesterday too, so if you can ask that question with them around, then what chance do I have? I mean, I am only your childhood friend. We've only known each other since we were in nappies.'

'You missed your calling, you should be on stage in the West End.'

'Funny. How's Reshma? Happy to see your sorry mug?'

Zafar picked up his coffee and took a silent sip of it, buying time rather than being dramatic like Murad.

They had been friends since they'd been in nursery together. They had bonded over the moment they'd both decided that their teacher's mustard woollen coat wasn't the colour of their school uniform and had painted it green to match their sweatshirts. The earful they'd got, plus the heavy reduction in playtime, had meant that they'd never been caught in such shenanigans again, but they'd remained firm friends since. Murad had spent many holidays with the Saeed family and Zafar had spent similar chunks of time with the Aziz family. Needless to say, they knew each other very well.

'She was, until she wasn't,' he said, part resignation, part frustration.

'Huh? What's that supposed to mean? Did you piss her off or something? Mind you, she doesn't strike me as the kind of woman who can ever get pissed off. She's as easy-going as they come. If only she'd met me first.'

'She was chosen for *me*, not you,' Zafar said sharply, Murad's words bothering him, even though he knew his friend was joking.

'Maybe that's your problem.'

'Meaning? I wish you wouldn't speak in riddles, Murad. I'm really not in the headspace for that shit right now.'

'Why don't you tell me what's happened? Because I can tell from your tone that you're not relaxing and sunning it up on the beach.'

Zafar debated saying anything to Murad. His friend knew that his marriage to Reshma had been arranged, but they'd never had a conversation about the details of his relationship before. Though someone intuitive like Murad didn't need to be told much to know when something was troubling someone. He had this innate ability to know when something was bothering Zafar and often had a nugget of wisdom to share alongside a big fat side of his own brand of nonsense. He was a complete romantic at heart.

Heaving a sigh and taking another fortifying sip of his brew, Zafar went on to tell Murad what had happened. He told him about his father's blustering, Reshma and her family's reception at his arrival, his mother's irate phone call and then Reshma finding everything out the way she did.

'Jesus Christ,' Murad huffed.

'Tell me about it.' Zafar had finished his coffee and spun the empty mug in his palm. 'I wonder if I should save us both the grief and just come home.' He still wasn't entirely decided on what he would actually do.

'Don't be daft. This whole thing happened because you didn't go in the first place.'

41

'And you would have? Knowing we've got that new hotel project to get under way?' His frustration had him sniping at Murad.

'Yeah, I would have. Nothing would be more important than my wife.' He said it with utmost conviction, as though there was no question about it.

'Is that why you don't have one?' He knew his friend had been in love, but whenever the subject came up, Murad skirted around it and moved onto something else or just shut the conversation down. Zafar didn't even know who it was that had claimed a hold on his friend's heart. Murad knew that whenever he was ready to talk about it, Zafar would listen.

'We're not talking about me here, Zaf. We're talking about you and how you're going to get out of the situation you're in. For what it's worth, I think you should start at the beginning.'

'What do you mean, start at the beginning? Did you miss the part where we got married last year?' Zafar got off the sunlounger and made his way back into the villa. He headed to the kitchen, placed his mug in the sink and filled a tall glass with water.

'Ha ha. I mean give your marriage and your wife the time you never did in the first place. I remember you being back at work three days after your wedding and I don't think you've taken any chunk of time off to spend with her since then, have you?'

'You above all others know what I've had going on, Murad. That hotel was my grandfather's dream and now that I'm this close to realising it, I don't want to cock it up.' It was too important a project for him. It was his chance to fulfil his grandfather's unrealised dream.

'For crying out loud, Zaf. Spending time with your wife doesn't mean you'll fail in all other aspects of your life.

You need to get that kind of thinking out of your head. I know your grandfather advocated such thoughts, but you can't seriously believe—'

'Let's not go there, Murad.' He didn't want to have that academic discussion just then when there were other things that needed his attention, like the situation with Reshma.

He heard his friend sigh on the other end of the phone and took a deep breath of his own.

'Give Reshma and your relationship a chance, Zaf. Give it time and attention. All the things you haven't in the past year. And see if you can surprise yourself and us by actually having some fun while you're there.'

'I know how to have fun.'

'Yeah, OK, grandad. Anyway, as much as I love playing agony aunt, I actually called you for a completely different reason. Two reasons, actually. Firstly, your dad cracks me up. I'm waiting for Ibrahim to snap and tell him that his *meetings* can easily be emails. Secondly, this hotel deal . . .'

They spent the next ten minutes talking business, even though his father had forbidden him to do so while he was away. Murad knew that there were certain things his father wasn't in the know about and it was more a matter of expediency than control, given that Zafar knew the details of this hotel deal inside out.

'Oh, and, Zafar?'

'What?'

'Don't forget the simple gestures. They speak volumes.' And with that, Murad ended the call.

Zafar decided that the best thing to do would be to try to talk to Reshma when she got back. Hopefully they'd be able to come to a better understanding and move on. It wasn't like her to get annoyed and not even listen. It must have just been the shock of finding everything out the way she had.

With that plan of action in mind, Zafar decided that with nothing else to do until she got back, he'd use the pool.

Zafar had just got out of the shower for a second time in the space of three hours when his phone rang again.

Reshma.

He swiped the screen. 'Reshma, I'm—'

'Uh, uh, uh, before you say anything more that's meant only for your wife's ears, I'd like to tell you that it's me.'

'Daadi?'

'Yes. I left my phone to charge in my room, so Reshma let me borrow hers. I thought I'd let you know that we're all at Ruqayyah's villa, so you can join us. We'll be having a late lunch shortly.'

'Yeah, I'm coming.'

'See? He said he's coming.' She was obviously talking to someone else. 'Reshma was sure you wouldn't come.'

Well, all the more reason to go, then. He had some making up to do, so it was best to get started sooner rather than later.

He ended the call and after closing the villa up, he made his way to the main one. It was almost double the size of theirs, with probably four or five bedrooms. The front door was already open when Zafar got there so he headed inside, the cacophony of noise hitting his ears after the last couple of hours of near silence he'd had.

This villa had a separate kitchen in which he could see staff members working away, Reshma's aunts, Ruqayyah and Bilqis, overseeing all the action. On his left was a large room dominated by a TV, with kids sprawled on the sofa and the floor. He went down two steps into a large open-plan area which overlooked a pool and the beach.

The patio was open and he could see Uncle Jawad sitting outside, along with a few other familiar faces.

He spotted Daadi sitting with another elderly lady on the sofa in the lounge area and when he made his way towards them, Daadi introduced her as Reshma's Uncle Imtiaz's mother. They'd only just met, but by the look of them, it seemed as though they were already the best of friends. But then that was his grandmother in a nutshell – easily befriending anyone and everyone. Zafar greeted them both and Daadi urged him to go outside and have fun.

Outside, Uncle Jawad bellowed his name across the pool, making everyone turn and look at him. 'Come here, son. We've been waiting for you to arrive.'

Zafar waved at him, looking around the space to see if he could spot Reshma.

Bingo.

She was sitting on a swinging bench with her two cousins, a few others sitting around them. One of them spoke and the rest of them all laughed, though Reshma only smiled. She caught him watching and her smile faltered.

He decided to take Murad's advice and make more of an effort with her.

Zafar walked to where she was sitting, and as soon as he got there, Haniya stood up and told him to take her place next to Reshma, who barely looked his way.

'I'm not here to break up the party. I thought I'd pop over and say hello.'

Saleema introduced her friends to him. 'And this is Reshma's husband, Zafar Saeed, and you guys have to hear about how he came here to surprise her. *O-h m-y G-o-d.*' She elongated the last three words.

Zafar caught Reshma's expression and saw the same

45

hurt reflected in her eyes as he had that morning. God, it felt like ages ago, but it had only been a few hours. There was no softness on her face, something he'd never seen before. Reshma was always ready with a smile or an open, approachable expression. This closed-off vibe was completely new and he was the cause of it and it made him feel dreadful.

'How was your morning, ladies?' he asked in an attempt to be engaging.

'Sooo good. Look.' Haniya splayed her hands for him to see an array of colours on her nails, each fingernail sporting a different colour.

'Nice.'

Saleema showed off her pink nails.

He looked at Reshma, who stood up. 'I'm just going to go and see if they need a hand in the kitchen.' She moved to walk past him and he blocked her path.

'Did you have a good time this morning?'

She looked up at him, her eyes glowing with annoyance. She glanced over her shoulder, but her cousins were busy talking a mile a minute with their friends and weren't paying them any attention, so she looked back up at him.

'I did, thanks. Despite hearing what I did.'

6

Reshma

Reshma tried to move past Zafar, but he was big and quick and blocked her move again. Thankfully, they weren't in earshot of anyone where they were now standing. To any onlookers, they probably looked like a couple having a moment together. *What a joke!* Little would they know that she was doing her best to stay calm and not push past him.

The atmosphere in the garden was happy and party-like and she didn't want to be the one to poop it. As it was, she'd had a hard time trying to be excited and coming across as though she was having the time of her life when she'd been out with Haniya and Saleema, whose friends had joined them afterwards too.

She wasn't worried about Saleema, but Haniya knew her better. They'd grown up together and once she caught the scent of something, she didn't let go until she'd investigated every single angle she could. There was little Haniya didn't know about Reshma, except her recent discovery of the reason behind Zafar's *surprise* arrival.

She and the girls had grabbed iced coffees and then made their way to the nail salon where they'd had manicures and pedicures. Thankfully, Reshma's technician's station had been a bit further from the other two – who were side by side – and she'd got away with it. She didn't want them finding out what was going on.

'Look, Reshma, I know I handled this morning badly, and I'm sorry for that.'

'It's fine, Zafar. There's really nothing more to talk about. I get the picture.' And she was done with this conversation. She wasn't even sure why he was still there.

'How can you if you won't even give me a chance to explain myself properly? I was caught off guard by Mum and then suddenly you were there and—' He ran his hand through his hair, something he'd done more of in the last twenty-four hours than she'd seen him do before.

'And the truth came out. I know. I was there.' She didn't know where the sudden sarcasm was coming from, but she let it. It was better than allowing her true feelings of hurt to come out.

He sighed as he shook his head. 'I don't want to be at odds with you, Reshma.'

She laughed softly at that. 'We can't be at odds, Zafar. One's got to be in sync in the first place, in agreement with a person. We've never been in sync.' Reshma felt her suppressed anger from earlier start to simmer again but was mindful that this wasn't the time or place to be having this conversation. She was feeling an array of emotions and the last thing she wanted was for any of them to spill over with everyone around her. It would cause her aunts and uncles – and Daadi for that matter – undue worry and she didn't want to sour the atmosphere for Saleema or the others, who were together after a long time, enjoying themselves.

Besides, how was she supposed to explain the fact that it wasn't so much about him turning up at his father's behest as it was a build-up of . . . everything.

'That's because we've not had the chance to.'

She looked at him in disbelief. 'No. That's not true. We've had a year, longer if you include our engagement. In that time, *I* have made the effort. It's you who's never bothered, but you know what? I'm not having this conversation with you right now. It's neither the time nor the place for it.'

A collective *aww* had both her and Zafar looking to her right, where she saw a cousin from Saleema's dad's side of the family with his wife. They were sitting with a small group of guests, who chuckled as the couple blushed.

Reshma suppressed the pang in her chest and instead scoffed, loud enough for Zafar to look away from the happy couple and back at her. 'That's what being in sync looks like, Zafar. Not this.' She waved her hand between them, and after a fraught pause, she moved away from him again, though this time he didn't stop her and she was glad. She didn't want to lose the little control she had on her cool and for there to be a falling-out. She went into the villa, not bothering to look back at where Zafar was or what he was doing. She was going to avoid him as much as she could and for as long as she could. At least until she could put her thoughts into some semblance of order and figure out what she was going to do. Only then would she be able to work out how to move forward.

Later that night, after she'd got into her comfiest pyjamas, Reshma grabbed her e-reader and sat on the sofa in the bedroom, hoping to immerse herself in a fantasy world because reality wasn't worth her time right now, only to get up five minutes later in restlessness. She opened the patio door and stood leaning against the frame. She could smell the salt on the ocean breeze and hear the soft lull of the waves in the distance.

Today had, without a doubt, been one of the harder days of her adult life. She'd managed to avoid Zafar for the better part of the day and sensing that she wasn't in the mood to engage with him, he'd kept his distance from her. It had been easier after their late lunch because the guys had naturally gravitated towards sitting together outside and the women had gone into the villa to relax and socialise where it was cooler.

Food and drink had been free-flowing well into the evening and by the time everyone was ready to say good night, the mood was comfortable and mellow. A vast contrast to how Reshma had been feeling.

When she'd seen Daadi stifle another yawn, she'd seized the opportunity to make her escape with her and they'd left Zafar sitting with her uncles and cousins as she and Daadi went back to their villa. He'd made a move to join them but Uncle Jawad had urged him to stay.

Daadi was settled and Reshma had taken the opportunity to have a long soak in the massive claw-foot bathtub, bubbles and all, to try to ease the tension she'd felt thrumming through her body since she'd overheard that conversation that morning. They did say that no good came of eavesdropping, though that was not strictly what she'd been doing.

She hadn't come to any grand conclusion since then, but what she had decided was that she was done with pretending everything was OK between her and Zafar – at least between themselves. If she was brutally honest, their relationship had been stagnant since soon after they'd got married. So, there was no point in her just smiling or making small talk or trying her best with him, waiting for him to respond. Waiting for him to *see* her. She was going to stop pretending that they were in a good place and she had all the patience in the world to wait for things to be how she'd dreamt they would be, in all her naivety. She'd had enough lessons in life to tell her that things rarely worked out like they did in fairy tales, books or films. It was all make-believe.

She rested her head against the frame, closing her eyes as she turned so her back was resting against it too.

Thoughts and memories that had been hidden in the deep recesses of her mind had surfaced today after she'd discovered Zafar's real reason for coming. Some of those memories were so old, that when they'd resurfaced, they'd felt alien, until she'd realised that they were her own. Like the memory of her mother's parents being so full of grief for their lost daughter that they had little to no affection for their granddaughter. Or when she'd learnt that her father had found someone and was planning to get married. She'd thought he might finally be ready for the responsibility of a daughter with his new wife, though she'd been torn between wanting that acceptance and leaving Uncle Jawad and his family, who had embraced her as their own. Of course, nothing had come of that. Her father's new wife hadn't wanted the responsibility of a twelve-year-old girl and neither had he, which was rich because they'd gone on to have three children.

A soft click had her opening her eyes and she found Zafar standing beside the closed bedroom door, his hand on the doorknob.

He looked at her, his expression inscrutable, and Reshma turned the other way as she swiped at her cheeks, brushing away the errant tears that had fallen.

Thankfully, he didn't seem to have seen them.

'Hey.' He stepped further into the room, his hands in his pockets.

'Hey.' She responded over her shoulder and then turned to look out the patio door, not that she could see much in the dark. The sliver of moon that was supposed to be in the sky seemed to have taken cover under the clouds and she couldn't see any stars. It was kind of poetic how it reflected her mood.

'Can we talk?' He sounded closer, but she didn't turn and look his way.

'There's nothing to say, Zafar.' Her voice sounded heavy to her own ears.

She heard him sigh before he spoke. 'We didn't manage to talk this morning and you didn't want to talk in the garden this afternoon and I didn't push, but I don't want to leave things like this.'

She turned to face him at that, finding him standing a metre away from her. His brow was furrowed and lines bracketed his mouth.

'What is there to say? I told you, you don't have to stay, feel free to go back to London.' She stepped into the room and closed the door behind her. She moved past him to make her way towards the bed when he stopped her with a warm hand on her arm.

'I'm not going back to London, Reshma.' He said the words so vehemently, she was tempted to believe him. But she was done with being gullible.

'Why not?' She pulled her hand away and faced him. 'It makes sense for you to. You don't want to be here and I'm telling you that you don't need to hang around on my account, so what's the issue? Or is it the fact that you'll disappoint your dad by going home early without me?'

'It's nothing of the sort, Reshma.' There was a lace of annoyance in his words as he said them through gritted teeth, before shaking his head as he looked down. He looked tired and deflated, something she'd not seen before. But then she'd always seen Zafar in his element, being his brilliant self all the time, as though failure was a foreign concept to him. 'I was wrong. When you first asked me to come here for the wedding, I should have agreed and I'm sorry that I didn't.' He broke eye contact and looked towards the ground again, as though gathering his thoughts or finding the words to articulate them. 'I've been a failure as a husband, I'm well aware of that. I've not given you or our marriage the time or attention I should have, but I want . . . I want things to be different.'

She was shocked at his open admission of his failure, but not enough to not respond to him. She couldn't let his contrition in that moment cover up the chasm that had always been there and he'd never tried to bridge, despite her efforts on that front.

Reshma clicked her fingers. 'Just like that? And I should just fall into line with that new-found wish of yours? You know, Zafar, it's not just about you being here or the fact that your dad told you to come. It's more than that. I'm not blind or deaf or slow on the uptake. Our relationship has never really taken off, so I can't even say that it's deteriorated. You've never been interested in me or being with me or getting to know me. I'm wondering why you ever agreed to marry me in the first place.'

His mouth parted as he stared at her, unblinking, for a moment. 'I wasn't forced, if that's what you're insinuating. I had the freedom to accept or not accept the match with you and I chose to accept it. I *chose* to marry you.'

'And is this what you envisaged married life to be?' Because she certainly hadn't. 'I don't expect declarations of undying love from you. I don't expect you to devote yourself to me and forget everything and everyone around you, but I do expect some semblance of a relationship beyond material comforts, Zafar. I expected a connection. Honesty. I don't put a great deal of stock in love from others. God knows, it's not come my way from the people who you'd expect to offer it unconditionally.' Reshma ignored the shaft of pain she felt in the region of her heart at her own words. She wasn't unfamiliar with love and affection, she'd received it in abundance from her uncles, aunts and cousins. But the kind of love one got from parents or grandparents was something she'd never had.

And then she'd seen Zafar, and while she wouldn't go as far as saying it was love at first sight for her, she had developed strong feelings towards him and what he represented. What they could become to each other. She'd been a fool. Her mother had gone down that destructive path and where had that led her?

Maybe this was a blessing. A way for her to stop and realise where she was headed before it was too late.

There was confusion on Zafar's face, along with a spark of interest lighting his eyes. She didn't want to go into her family history, so she steered the conversation back to the point it had started at while she still had the wherewithal to do so. 'The fact of the matter is that we don't have a relationship, Zafar. We've been married for thirteen months and in all that time, we've barely spent a weekend in just each other's company. You're a devoted grandson, son and brother and that's praiseworthy. Your work ethic is admirable. But that's all there is to your life. There's no place for a wife, let alone more of a family. I don't even know what sort of future you see for yourself and, if I'm honest, I'm beginning to lose sight of my own.'

Zafar hadn't taken his eyes off her while she'd been talking as they now stood there silently, regarding each other.

She knew that he wasn't a bad person. In fact, he was a wonderful man. He just wasn't the husband she had thought he would be. She had thought – hoped – that they would have a connection which finally made her feel like she had found where she truly belonged. A man who, like he did with everyone else around him, would make her feel special and treasured. Like she mattered to him. But that hadn't happened.

'Are you telling me that you don't want to give us a chance then?' He sounded uncharacteristically uncertain.

'I don't know what I'm telling you. But I know that I'm tired, Zafar.' She took a shuddering breath as she felt all the suppressed emotions in her chest rise. 'I'm fed up of being the only one trying in our relationship. All my life, it's been me trying, wondering what the hell it is I do wrong that drives people away or makes them decide that I'm not worth the effort. I'm done with that. I'd rather have no expectations of people than be let down repeatedly because, believe it or not . . .' Reshma closed her eyes as she sucked in another shaky breath, willing the tears threatening the corners of her eyes not to fall. 'It hurts. A lot.' Her voice broke at the last bit. She felt emotion well up from deep inside her and took three wobbly steps to the armchair beside the sofa and lowered herself into it.

Despite her effort to stop herself, a tear rolled down her cheek as all her pent-up pain, frustration and unfulfilled desires threatened to pour out through her eyes, leaving her with nowhere to hide except behind her hands.

With no strength left in her to hold it back, she allowed it all to come out. She didn't know how long she sat there before she sensed Zafar come and kneel down in front of her.

She hated this feeling. This helplessness. The sense of weakness and neediness that she was sure made her look pathetic in front of him.

'Reshma?' His voice was low as he gingerly touched her hands, keeping his fingertips there for a moment. He slowly eased her hands away from her face and she let him, having zero energy to do anything else. Her tears, it seemed, hadn't quite finished as her eyes filled with them once more, barely holding back before they made their inevitable descent.

He squeezed her hands and then let go, surprising her by gently swiping his thumbs across her cheeks as he cupped them in his palms. 'Don't cry, Reshma, please. I know I've upset you, hurt you, but I swear to God, I have never, ever meant to. Please believe me, hurting you is something I'd never want or do deliberately. But I accept that that is what I've done. I've been so focused on other aspects of my life that I didn't stop to embrace or even appreciate the change you had brought into it.'

She dropped her gaze but didn't push him away and after a moment, he got up and moved away, only to come back, holding a bottle of water out to her. She took the bottle from him and after a few small sips, she reached forward and put it on the low table. She ran the back of her hand across her mouth and, after taking a trembling breath, she got up. 'I'm going to sleep. I'm tired and . . . Good night.'

She didn't look at him, speaking to his shoulder instead, and moved towards the bed, getting in and enveloping herself in the duvet. She didn't bother switching her bedside lamp off, needing the oblivion of sleep more than anything. Anything to stop the torrent of emotions battering her right now.

7

Zafar

Zafar felt like someone had cleaved his heart in two and the pain of it was enough to make every breath he took difficult. A sense of guilt crushed him worse than any he'd experienced before – and he was well familiar with guilt, this wasn't the first time he was facing it – because this was all his fault.

The sight of Reshma crying, sobbing her heart out was something he never wanted to see again. Her spiky eye lashes, shiny trails down her cheeks, it had made his heart squeeze painfully, knowing he was the cause of her anguish. Her distress had been palpable and he'd felt helpless in the face of it. He hadn't known what to do or say to make it stop, to make her feel better. He'd felt more useless then than he ever had before. Each sob had felt like he was being flogged – and flogged he should be for this.

He was grateful that she hadn't pushed him away when he'd gone to her, but then she seemed just about able to sit upright and the fact that she'd got up and gone straight to bed, curling into herself under the duvet despite it being as warm as it was told him how exhausted she was. Of their situation. Of him.

Never in a million years would he want to be the cause of distress to Reshma, one of the gentlest souls he'd ever met. The whole idea behind not telling her the truth straight up was because he hadn't wanted to hurt her. Of course, in hindsight he could see that perhaps that might have been the lesser of the two causes of pain to her. She wouldn't have broken down like this if he'd come clean in the first place.

Zafar padded towards her bedside and switched the lamp off, looking down at the bundle that was his wife.

His wife.

The woman he'd promised to care for. To cherish. To be with through thick and thin.

He'd done none of those things. He cared for her materially, ensuring she lacked for nothing, but that didn't make him a good husband. Reshma was an independent woman, more than capable of taking care of herself, she didn't need him for that. She'd never expected or asked it of him either. He'd done it because he had thought it was the right thing to do. But what about the rest of it?

Zafar moved away from the bed and, opening the patio door, he stepped outside.

He had to acknowledge that he hadn't been there for Reshma.

So, their marriage had been arranged and they weren't in love with each other. That didn't mean he had to distance himself from her altogether. Being arranged didn't doom a marriage or the people involved in it. Arranged or not, it was still a marriage and it required the same level of effort and commitment and the fact of the matter was that Zafar hadn't given it enough. Any really.

It was a hard truth to acknowledge and accept, but if he couldn't be honest with himself right now, then when else would he be?

Heaving a beleaguered sigh, he sat on the balcony chair, which during the day would have a splendid view of the ocean. Right now, he could only hear it, catching the briefest shimmer of the water if he kept his eyes on the horizon.

His mind went back to Reshma's statement about wondering why he'd agreed to marry her in the first place. His life had gone through a series of twists and turns leading up to that point. Twists and turns he'd never envisaged before but which had gone on to shape his thinking into what it had become now.

He hadn't had any plans to get married at the time, he hadn't even had a serious girlfriend since he'd come back home after three years away. He'd been focused on doing what he needed to do to take the place his grandfather had wanted him to take. The place he was supposed to have taken, until he had decided he wanted no part of his grandfather's archaic empire and had tried to forge his own path away from it all, only to come back and agree to take the helm at his grandfather's and father's behest.

His match with Reshma had been arranged around that time and with everything looking in favour of the match, persuasive advice from his grandfather and with a lack of prospects of his own to put forward, Zafar had seen no reason to refuse and more reasons to agree to the marriage. Not least because aside from the fact that most of his family had been in agreement and approved wholeheartedly of Reshma, he had too.

She had appealed to him in ways he had never stopped to analyse and using his family's approval as a springboard, he'd gone ahead with the match. But the truth was, he had liked her and chosen to marry her of his own free will. Had his family's approval contributed to his decision? Yes, it had, but the final decision had been his. At least he'd had more of a say in the matter than his cousin Safiya had when it had been her turn.

But here they were.

In the last year, he'd made no effort to take their relationship forward. He'd given nothing of himself to her and he'd not bothered to get to know her any better either. His mind went to her statement about love.

I don't put a great deal of stock in love from others. God knows, it's not come my way from the people who you'd expect to offer it unconditionally.

There was so much to unpack there and the stuff she'd said about not knowing what it was she did that drove people away. It alluded to so much more, deeper issues about things that went beyond him and their relationship, and he felt more guilt at not knowing what those issues were. He wanted to know what she meant.

His phone buzzed and he pulled it out of his pocket.

Murad: Awake?

Murad and his uncanny ability to get in touch in such moments. Zafar shook his head in some awe as he messaged him back.

Zafar: What's up?

Murad: You didn't send me an update so I thought I'd ask for one myself.

Zafar: I spoke to you this morning. What did you think I'd accomplish in ten hours?

Murad: Obviously not as much as I would have 😊

Zafar debated telling Murad about what had happened just now and decided against it. He needed to get his own head around it and figure out a way forward for himself on this one, for now at least.

Zafar: 😳

Murad: Keep in touch, mate. And remember what I said.

Zafar: What bit? You talk a lot.

Murad: Lol. Simple gestures.

Zafar put his phone down, shaking his head at Murad's idea of *simple gestures*. It was easier said than done, especially after the way this evening had turned out. At this point, Zafar felt that anything he did had the potential to blow up in his face no matter how small or *simple* it was, but he couldn't let that deter him.

He needed to do *something*, there was no doubt about it. Something to show Reshma that she and their relationship were important to him. He didn't want to be another person who let her down and caused her hurt and disappointment as she'd alluded to.

Heaving a tired sigh, Zafar made his way inside to sleep. He slept on and off and when he did manage to fall asleep, he was restless. He was wide awake at six the next morning, watching the morning light filter in through the gaps he'd left in the curtains when he'd drawn them haphazardly last night.

Last night.

Memories and feelings from the night before assailed him, but rather than let them anchor him down like they had last night, Zafar decided that with the new day, he'd start afresh.

He peered in Reshma's direction. She was deep asleep, her cheeks lightly flushed and her lips slightly parted. One arm was tucked under the duvet and the other was thrown over her head. Her nose stud sparkled as the soft morning light reflected off it. The skin under her eyes was puffy from all the tears she'd shed, making his heart squeeze painfully at the reminder. Loose strands of hair that had escaped her plait framed her face, and as tempted as he was to push them back, he didn't. He didn't want to risk waking her and it was probably a good idea to keep his hands to himself. He needed to remember that they weren't in a place where he had the freedom to do that.

He carefully scooted out of bed and fifteen minutes later was swimming lengths in the pool again, remembering how much he enjoyed this particular form of exercise. Work commitments and family responsibilities had slowly curtailed the time he spent on working out and he limited it to runs, going to the gym or occasionally going to the boxing ring with Ash. It would be ideal if he had a pool at home, but he wasn't that big money – not yet at least. He couldn't justify such an expense. But once their hotel deal was a go, maybe he'd be able to do that.

With his mind on work, he powered through the water, swimming length after length. The hotel deal was at a crucial phase for them and it was essential that all their T's were crossed and their I's were dotted. It was a long-held dream of his grandfather's that he'd never been able to realise in his lifetime and if Zafar could see this deal completed and announce his first step in that direction in time for the date that would have been his grandfather's birthday – 10 December – he'd be content that he was on the right path to making his grandfather proud.

Feeling the build-up of lactic acid in his thighs, he slowed his pace down and reached the end of the pool, leaning against the edge to catch his breath. He faced the beach, seeing it just above some artfully arranged flower boxes, and he realised that in no time, he had fallen back into work mode. Less than an hour ago, he had woken up and seen the after-effects of tears on Reshma's face and instead of thinking about what he was going to do to bring them to a better place – to do better himself – he was thinking about work.

Zafar shook his head, running a hand through his hair. This was wrong. He was wrong. He needed to push thoughts about work to the back of his mind – unless some shit hit the fan back home, in which case Ibrahim or Murad would let him know – and concentrate on being present in the moment. It was difficult but not impossible. And it was important.

He hauled himself out of the pool, and after a quick shower, he was in the kitchen, deciding that he'd get a head start on making breakfast.

He was cracking eggs in a bowl when Daadi came through the corridor and into the living area.

'Well, would you look at that.'

He looked up as she came towards him, her walking stick nowhere in sight.

'Where's your walking stick?'

'I don't need it.'

'Yes, you do.'

'My knees are feeling good. The heat here has warmed my joints and bones. I feel like I could be doing cartwheels in a few days.'

Zafar's heart lurched at the idea and he was about to read his grandmother the riot act when he saw her grinning at him.

'Gotcha!'

He shook his head as he whisked the eggs after seasoning them. 'Imagine what Daada would have said if he'd heard you?'

'Ha. Your grandfather needed to look away from his work for that to happen, sweetheart. May God rest his soul.' Daadi shook her head this time before slowly settling herself in a seat at the island, watching him work.

Zafar frowned at her words as he dropped a knob of butter into the frying pan. 'What do you mean? He doted on you.'

She laughed softly. 'If only life was as rosy as the eyes of youth found it to be. Oh, my darling boy. You saw your grandfather and grandmother; you didn't see a husband and a wife. They are two completely different things. Especially someone with your grandfather's way of thinking.' Her tone sounded less fond and more . . . disenchanted and Zafar was shocked into freezing for a moment, until the butter started sizzling and he remembered what he was supposed to be doing. 'Anyway, let's not dwell on days long gone. Where's that precious girl of mine? Still sleeping?'

Zafar flicked a glance upwards. 'I think she's awake, I heard her moving about in the room.'

'And so you thought you'd make breakfast.'

'Something like that.' He moved the eggs in the frying pan, avoiding his grandmother's eyes as she stared at him.

'I'm happy to hear that, sweetheart. Sometime I worry you're trying too hard to be like your grandfather, and while he had some admirable qualities, emulating him in every aspect of life isn't something I think is a good idea. In fact, I know it's not a good idea. You need to be *you*. You need to make an effort to be more present. More romantic. All it takes is a simple gesture.'

'Morning.' Reshma came down the stairs and paused momentarily when she saw him standing there with a whisk in his hand.

He smiled and she dipped her chin, moving her fingers over her ear as she came towards Daadi, kissing her on the cheek when she presented it to her.

Zafar hadn't missed the echo of Murad's words in his grandmother's. He just hoped that whatever he did helped bridge the distance between them.

Reshma moved around the island and pulled a glass out of the cupboard. She filled it with juice and then came to where he had made a mess on the worktop. She reached for the loaf of bread, but he put his hand over hers, feeling hers stiffen the instant he made contact.

'I'll do it. Go and sit with Daadi and I'll bring the eggs and toast. Would you like any of the pastries?'

She pulled her hand back and shook her head, not making eye contact with him.

'Yes, come and sit here, Reshma. Let Zafar take care of breakfast today,' Daadi said jovially, though her eyes were on the pair of them like a hawk's, probably sensing the frostiness between them. Thankfully, she didn't say anything about it if she did notice it and Reshma smiled at her and went and sat beside her with her glass of juice.

As much as Daadi and Murad emphasised *simple gestures*, Zafar wasn't sure they would cut it. The issues that had come to the surface last night – and, more importantly, the ones that had been alluded to – needed more than an offering of breakfast to be resolved.

He just hoped that while they were here, he could figure out what it would take and be able to successfully deliver it.

8

Reshma

Reshma took a small mouthful of scrambled eggs with an equally small bite of toast. It was the first time Zafar had made them breakfast since they'd been married and instead of enjoying the moment, she felt suffocated. It was ironic really that after yesterday, instead of taking her up on the offer of leaving, he made breakfast for them all, making it clear that he had decided to stay.

Well, it was up to him. She'd told him he didn't have to, so if he was staying, then it was his choice.

Last night had been . . . She didn't even have the words. She hadn't wanted to break down like that in front of him, but having said that, she wasn't embarrassed or ashamed at having done so either. She'd been bottling up her feelings for long enough, so it was only a matter of time before all those feelings found their way out of her.

She'd thought she might lie awake for hours after that, going through every thought and word in detail, but she'd slept like a baby, not hearing Zafar come to bed or leave it. She'd felt momentarily awkward this morning, wondering how she would face him after last night, but the feeling hadn't lasted for more than a handful of seconds before her resolve had kicked in, and with her shoulders pushed back and her head held high, she'd come downstairs. Only, the sight of Zafar holding a whisk had stunned her, until she'd spotted Daadi and carried on.

Daadi was sitting with them at the dining table now, happily chatting to fill the silence. She knew that if Daadi got the slightest inkling that anything was amiss, not only would it upset her a great deal, she'd make it a point of trying to fix things for them and Reshma didn't want either of those things to happen. It was best to try to act normal in front of her, for the time being at least.

To be fair, it wouldn't be all that difficult because she and Zafar didn't share an openly affectionate relationship anyway. The most they did was talk in front of others and never more than a handful of sentences. Gestures like hand holding, kissing, small affectionate touches here and there weren't for them and if the thought brought with it a fresh pang of pain, then she resolutely ignored it, shovelling another forkful of eggs into her mouth instead.

She wasn't going to sit there and wallow over what she didn't have . . . had never had. She was here to celebrate her cousin finding and marrying the love of her life and Reshma was happy for her. Just because she didn't believe she would ever find that for herself – especially after yesterday – it didn't mean she didn't believe in it for others or wasn't happy for them. She was going to celebrate every single moment she could with Saleema because she wanted the best for her. She had a chance to spend time with her family and she was going to make the most of it, starting now.

'I'm going to get changed and head to Auntie Bilqis' villa and see what they're all up to. Would you like to come, Daadi?'

'No, thank you, sweetheart. I think I'm going to rest this morning.' Daadi cast a concerned glance between her and Zafar but carried on speaking. 'I'm catching up with a few of my friends later for tea, but you carry on. Have fun.'

'Which friends are you meeting up with?' Zafar asked his grandmother over the rim of his coffee cup.

'Well, *Dad*, I'm meeting Imtiaz's mother and her cousin may be joining us. There might be some boys there too.' Daadi winked at her and Reshma couldn't help but laugh at her antics. She knew exactly how to push her grandsons' buttons and sometimes she showed them no mercy. She took it in turns to tease all of them.

Zafar rolled his eyes, but she saw him smiling behind his coffee cup.

Reshma got up and after clearing away the debris from breakfast – because apparently Zafar needed double the utensils anyone else did to make breakfast for half the number of people – she made her way to her aunt's villa.

Uncle Jawad opened the door to her and beamed when he saw her. 'My morning just got better. How are you, pet? Slept well?'

Reshma nodded as she hugged him, circling her arms around his barrel-like torso and resting her head against his shoulder. She took a deep breath of his shower gel and the residue of engine oil which never seemed to leave him. Either that or she could conjure up the comforting scent from her childhood and his days spent in his garage, feeling a sense of peace fill her like nothing else could.

Uncle Jawad squeezed her back before bellowing loud enough that Reshma felt her eardrums vibrate. 'Bilqis. Reshma's here.'

Reshma eased away from her uncle and went towards the sofa, slipping her sandals off and easing onto it, pulling her legs up under her.

Her aunt came along the corridor that presumably led to her bedroom. 'It's lucky your voice is as loud as it is, Jawad. At least now the rest of Mombasa knows that Reshma is here and that someone by the name of Bilqis needed that information.'

Reshma laughed at her aunt's words as her uncle scowled at them playfully, mumbling under his breath.

Auntie Bilqis smirked at her before bending towards her and kissing the top of Reshma's head. 'I'm glad you're here, darling. Come to my room with me. I'm sorting through some clothes and you and Niya need to choose which suits you want. Since you're up and here first, you get first pick. It'll teach Niya for sleeping in so late.'

'Yay.' Reshma felt some of the gloom lift off her by just being around her uncle and aunt. She followed Bilqis into the room and saw that she had indeed laid out a huge selection of clothes on the bed, along with boxes of what Reshma knew were sets of jewellery, some of which were heirlooms and had belonged to previous generations on both sides of the family.

She went straight for a midnight-blue outfit with rich gold and pops of pink embroidery on it. The design was simple but the colour was statement enough.

'Perfect. I was hoping you'd choose that one. It'll look marvellous on you, especially with this jewellery set.' Auntie Bilqis opened a box to reveal a gold and sapphire set. There was a necklace, studded with sapphires and diamonds, and matching earrings. There was a ring with some adjusters attached to it and a maang tikka – a large pendant on a single chain which sat in the centre parting of the hair attached with plenty of hairpins so the pendant rested on the forehead. A magnificent and regal-looking piece of jewellery. 'This was my grandmother's. My mother wore it and when I married Jawad, she gave it to me. I want you to wear it when you wear this suit.'

Astonished, Reshma looked at her aunt. Surely, as Auntie Bilqis' daughter, Haniya should rightfully get that set? It had belonged to her great-grandmother and had been passed down through the generations. Reshma wasn't a part of that lineage.

'I know exactly what's going through your head, young lady, and if you utter a single word of refusal, I'll have to think up an adult equivalent of the naughty corner for you.'

Reshma smiled and unable to stop tears from filling her eyes and spilling over, she crossed over to her aunt and held her close, allowing Auntie Bilqis to smooth her hand across her back, the action soothing away some of the edginess she'd woken up feeling. She took comfort in the arms of the woman who had stepped in and mothered her like Reshma was her own.

Uncle Jawad and Auntie Bilqis had more generosity in them than Reshma could ever fathom and whenever she was on the receiving end of it, she felt both loved and humbled by it.

Auntie Bilqis eased away and brushed her hands across Reshma's cheeks. 'Just because I didn't give birth to you, it doesn't mean that you're not my daughter. You are, in every other sense of the word. Don't ever think you're not, no matter what anyone else says. In fact, you're lucky in that you've had two mums. Hafsa, may God bless her soul, and me. Though I'm sure Ruqayyah will try to wriggle her way into the count too.' She wrinkled her nose and Reshma gave a watery laugh on cue.

She really was lucky and that's what she needed to focus on and remember. There were all these people around her who loved her without any reservations or expectations. They loved her unconditionally. After her mother's death – and some shunting around thanks to her feckless father – her uncle and aunt had stepped up and Auntie Bilqis had taken over her care just as a mother would. While raising Reshma along with her own children, she had never – ever – differentiated between them and if anyone had tried to, she'd been ferocious in her defence of Reshma, including against Reshma's own paternal grandmother, who would often say it wasn't Bilqis' job to raise Reshma, it was her father's job, but for Auntie Bilqis, many a time, it was a case of in through one ear and out through the other.

Reshma had so much to be grateful for. She didn't need to dwell on what she didn't have with Zafar when she could be around all this love. *This* brand of love she could trust. It wouldn't let her down. It was time to focus on this and take that other type of love and lock it away in the deep recesses of her heart, never to be visited again.

She stayed with her aunt, going through more suits, putting aside what Auntie Bilqis was considering wearing herself for the various upcoming events and some she wanted to give as gifts to Auntie Ruqayyah, Saleema and a few others. She had another outfit each for her and Haniya, who joined them half an hour later, still in her pyjamas, clutching a big mug of tea.

When the three of them finally left the room and went to the living area, Reshma stopped in her tracks. Zafar was sitting there with Uncle Jawad and Shoaib.

Shoaib had his attention half on his phone and half on the TV, while Zafar was sitting opposite Uncle Jawad playing some card game. He looked up as she followed after Auntie Bilqis and Haniya and as she lowered her eyebrows in confusion, he winked at her.

Reshma's eyes widened and she blinked them, probably looking like someone who'd just had their photograph taken with the world's strongest flash.

Zafar grinned at her before turning his attention back to his hand while Uncle Jawad scratched his head. 'I think I've got you again, son. Good thing we're not playing for money. Bilqis would have my hide for cleaning you out. You're married to our girl after all, need to think of her. Though she's more than capable of taking care of you.' His chuckle reverberated throughout the villa.

'Ahem. I'm right here, Jawad Mir.' Both men put their cards face down as her aunt made her presence known. 'Hello, Zafar dear. When did you come?'

'Not all that long ago. Hello, Niya. Reshma.' He said it as though they hadn't seen each other less than a couple of hours ago.

'Long enough that he's lost the last three hands,' Uncle Jawad said with a great deal of delight in his voice as he gathered all the cards. 'Oh, Bills, I forgot to mention, Imtiaz popped over and said that they want to have a small prayer gathering this evening. Start everything off with blessings for the couple and then have all the events. You'll need to go and check on Ruqayyah. If I know my sister, she's probably flapping about as we speak.'

'Hmm. She did mention as much yesterday. That's fine, I'll go and see her after lunch. Reshma, Niya, I think you can both wear the suits I gave you this evening, the plainer ones of the two, they'll work perfectly for the prayer gathering.'

Reshma took the things her aunt had given her and after bidding everyone a brief goodbye with a promise to see them all later, she left the villa. She hadn't taken more than half a dozen steps when she felt a tug on the bag holding her new clothes and jewellery.

'Here, let me take that for you.' Zafar had his hand around the handle, just under hers.

Reshma gave it a gentle tug. 'It's fine. I can carry it myself.' She turned to carry on walking, but the bag didn't move. Zafar was still standing there, holding the handle, a small smile teasing the corners of his lips.

She pulled at the bag, but rather than let go, she saw his fingers tighten around the handle and the smile on his face broadened.

'Come on, Reshma.' He shook the bag, but Reshma tightened her hold on it.

She didn't know what it was about the moment, but it felt like something more than just about the bag. She shook her head and pulled the bag towards herself, though, of course, with Zafar on the other side of it, it was impossible that it would come her way. Instead, she found herself shuffling towards him as he slowly pulled the bag closer towards himself, standing there rock solid.

'There is no way' – his voice was soft but deep as he said the words, enunciating each syllable as though he had all the time in the world – 'you can take this bag off me unless I let you, and I don't plan on doing that.'

She took another half a step towards him as he pulled it again, a playful expression on his face. What was he doing? And how did he think she'd be up for this? Was she supposed to forget yesterday had happened? He certainly seemed to have, coming and playing cards with Uncle Jawad and now acting as though all was well with the world.

Well, she wasn't going to go along with it. 'Fine.' She let go of the bag, turned and walked off without a single glance back in his direction.

'Reshma? Hold on.' Her legs weren't as long as his, so it took him no time to catch up with her. He held the bag in one hand and, with the other, he gently cupped her elbow. Reshma looked down at where he held her and then up at him and he promptly let go of her.

'You wanted to hold the bag and I gave it to you. So, now what?'

'I . . . I wanted . . . I was hoping . . .' He rubbed his hand across the back of his neck and Reshma suppressed her look of surprise at seeing him lost for words. Not only did he sound lost, he actually looked lost as well, but it wasn't for her to help him.

'Let me know when you've figured it out.' With that, she tried to move past him, but he sidestepped and stopped her.

'I wanted to thank you.'

That made her stop. He wanted to *thank* her? That was the last thing she'd expected him to say. 'Thank me? For what?'

'For keeping things between us. For not sharing what happened with Daadi or with Uncle Jawad and the rest of the family.'

'Is that what you came to check?' She felt disappointment war with anger within her. She had wondered what he was doing at her uncle's villa, but she hadn't for a moment thought that he was coming to test the water, as it were. To see if her uncle was ready to blow a hole in the villa's roof because someone had upset his niece.

'No. That's not why I came. I came because of you.' He rushed to answer, but she'd heard enough.

'Leave it, Zafar. I don't need to hear any explanation. You can go wherever you want, whenever you want and do whatever it is you want to do. I don't want any part of it.' She'd been there, done that, got the T-shirt and decided she didn't want it anymore. In fact, she was ready to dump it.

She moved past him and marched towards the villa. She let herself in, not bothering to see where Zafar was. She just left the door open for him.

Daadi was sitting on the sofa, her phone held at arm's length. 'Here they are. Reshma, come and say hello to this troublemaker.'

Taking a deep breath to try to steady her fraught nerves, she made her way to Daadi and sat down beside her just as Zafar came through the front door and closed it behind him, his expression giving nothing of his thoughts away.

'Reshmaaa! How's it going?'

'Fine, thanks. How are you?'

Harry beamed at her, ignored her question and asked her one instead. 'Did you like Daadi and Zaf's surprise? I saw the video. You looked too cute.' He opened and closed his mouth, mimicking her just like Saleema had, and Reshma rolled her eyes at him.

'Very funny. Why didn't you come along too?

Reshma smiled at him, but before he could respond, Daadi handed her the phone. 'Here. You talk to him while I go and get some water. Talking to him is so exhausting.'

'She knows I can hear her, right?' he asked Reshma, one eyebrow quirked.

'Of course, I know that. Why do you think I said it out loud?' Daadi scoffed.

Reshma shook her head at their banter and caught sight of Zafar as he looked her way. He put her bag on the table and then slowly rounded it before coming and sitting next to her. His thigh brushed against hers as he sat down and rested his arm behind her on the sofa. He was so close, his warmth immediately surrounded her.

She faced him and realised that his face was particularly close to hers. Close enough that as he looked her way, she saw the lighter flecks of rich honey in the dark brown of his eyes, surrounding his pupil. The combined scent of his shower gel and aftershave went straight to her nose and reached her senses before she could move an inch and she gritted her teeth both at him and herself for reacting to his proximity.

'Zaf! How are you?'

'I'm all right, mate. How are things with you? Are you keeping out of mischief?'

'It's so boring here without you two.'

'I heard that,' Daadi said from across the room, where she stood as she took a sip of her drink. 'I take it I'm not being missed then.'

Reshma tried to shift a bit to the side, but the armrest only allowed her to shift about three inches. Not enough to put a decent amount of distance between her and Zafar. 'I'm sure you're keeping yourself entertained at everyone else's expense,' Zafar said knowingly.

'Hmm. How are you finding it, Reshma? Missing me yet?'

'I am. There's no one here who's as fun as you. Though, I have to say, it's lovely catching up with all my relatives. They've got lots of things planned in the coming days. It's a shame you're missing out. Weren't you going away somewhere with your friends though? When is that again?' She was finding it difficult to focus on the conversation with Harry with Zafar sitting so close to her. Why not just wait his turn to speak to Haroon? Or, better yet, call him himself later.

'Tonight. That's why I thought I'd call and see how you guys are doing. I'll be away for five days. Not sure how often I'll be able to get in touch.'

'OK. Well, stay safe and don't forget to send me lots of pictures of where you are.'

'Yeah, I will. Where's Daadi gone? I hadn't finished filling her in on what happened when Dad was looking for his phone after I messaged him to say he'd left it behind. It was hilarious. You guys have to hear the story.'

'How is him forgetting his phone funny?' Zafar asked.

Harry rolled his eyes. 'I *messaged* him to say he's forgotten his phone. On his phone, slowcoach. He came back home and started looking for it. I was taking the pi— mickey.' He corrected himself before foul-mouthing within earshot of their grandmother.

'Didn't he lose his stack with you?' Zafar asked, his voice laced with humour.

Harry looked mortally offended. 'Of course not. I didn't use *my* phone. I'm not an idiot. I used Ash's.' He looked supremely pleased with himself.

'How do you know his passcode? And which other pass-codes do you know?' Zafar sounded alarmed and Reshma bit the inside of her cheek at Harry's expression. He really was the sweetest.

'Time to go. Love you all. Have fun. Byeee.'

Before anyone could say anything more, he ended the call.

'Doughnut.' Reshma heard the affection for his youngest brother in Zafar's voice.

She locked the screen and shifted forward to try to get up, but as she did, she felt herself being pulled back. The momentum had her dropping back down and she turned to look at Zafar in annoyance, only to find him looking at her in confusion.

Mindful of Daadi being in the same room, Reshma widened her eyes at him and dipped her chin, trying to indicate the lack of sufficient distance between them. 'I need to go.' She said the words through gritted teeth and his eyebrows lowered even further.

Ignoring her whisper, he spoke at a normal volume, which was loud enough for Daadi to hear. 'Yeah, sure. Go.'

Reshma surreptitiously looked towards Daadi, who was doing a terrible job of pretending to look at some brochure lying on the island, while Reshma knew her attention was on them.

Reshma tried to get up but felt pulled back again. She looked at the tiny gap between her and Zafar.

'You're sitting on my dress.'

He looked down to where the skirt of her dress was caught under him and then lifted his face to look at her, the frown on it slowly clearing. 'Oh. Sorry.'

He stared at her for a moment and she stared back, waiting for him to move. He didn't.

What on earth was he playing at?

'Kids, I'm going to my room. Ruqayyah told me that she's arranged for prayer recitals this evening, so we need to be ready for that.' Daadi broke through the moment, addressing them as she left to go to her room, a sly smile on her face.

Reshma found her voice once more. 'Can you please move?' She ground the words out but kept her voice low.

'Oh, yeah.' Zafar stood up and she pulled her dress towards herself before standing up.

Too late, she realised that they were standing very close to one another. So close that if either of them moved just a few inches forward, they would touch. Zafar was looking at her closely, his face a slideshow of various expressions as he regarded her.

He wasn't an overtly expressive man and she knew that helped him a great deal in his work negotiations. Between them, though, they'd never been in a situation where she'd had to, or felt the need to, read his expressions. One needed a certain level of communication for that, she supposed.

Reshma raised her chin and took a step back, away from him, and then, grabbing the bag with her things in it, she made her way upstairs, deciding to get a head start on getting ready for the gathering later rather than stay downstairs and flog a dead horse with Zafar. She was feeling unsettled enough without trying to figure out what was going on with him.

9

Zafar

Zafar lifted his cupped hands to his face and then moved them down the sides of it as Saleema's grandmother finished reciting the final prayer, concluding the recital with good wishes and blessings for the couple, their future and everyone else in attendance.

Everyone was congregated in the main villa, with the women on one side of the room and the men on the other side, as was customary for such gatherings. Zafar was sitting beside Shoaib and Khalil, and from where he was sat, he could see Reshma sitting next to Daadi, with Haniya on her other side.

She had her dupatta covering her head as a sign of respect when praying and her head was slightly bowed. Her lips were moving as she prayed and then she lifted her hands to her face like he had. When she moved them away and opened her eyes, they met his.

He watched as her expression, which started off as neutral, slowly changed. Her jaw firmed and her eyes hardened. The corners of her lips turned down a fraction as her chin went up and then she looked away.

Zafar felt his heart sink. He was in deeper shit than he had realised, but as the day had progressed, the extent of the damage was dawning on him. This wasn't just a run-of-the-mill argument. Nor was it a domestic disagreement or misunderstanding which they'd get over before long. She was upset to the point where she had actually just switched off with him.

It wasn't anything she'd said or done as such, but he could tell. Though it had only been a day and she'd spent much of it away from him, in the moments they had been together, there was none of the sweetness or warmth from her he had always been on the receiving end of.

After they'd got back from her uncle and aunt's villa earlier that day, she'd spent her time getting ready for the prayer recital and when he'd gone upstairs and tried talking to her, she'd responded with monosyllabic answers, and after getting ready, she'd gone downstairs, leaving him staring after her. He figured it would be wise to give her some space.

His grandmother had immediately picked up that there was tension between them and when Reshma had left that morning after breakfast, she'd turned to him instantly and demanded he tell her what had happened to upset Reshma.

He hadn't spilt all the beans, giving her just the bare bones. 'She's a bit upset with me because she thinks I don't want to be here.' He didn't tell her that she'd overheard his conversation with his mother or what had happened after that.

'Oh, Zafar. I hope you reassured her that that wasn't the case.'

'I tried.'

'Sweetheart, you need to give your marriage and her a lot more than you have so far. I can see why she might lose confidence in it.'

His grandmother had gone on to advise him not to model himself on his grandfather as a husband and to make his relationship a priority. And she wasn't wrong.

For the first time in a long time, Zafar felt like he might be a little lost. As though he had come onto stage with a certain script rehearsed, but it turned out that the play being enacted was a different one. Would he be able to improvise his way through it or would the audience see through him?

He'd mulled over his grandmother's words, allowing them to percolate in his head before he'd decided to venture out for a walk. He'd needed to be outside and let his mind have free rein.

It wasn't that he needed his hand held by his father or grandmother or even his best friend when it came to his marriage. He didn't. He knew things weren't ideal, but he'd always thought they'd find their way organically. His work had been a priority for the last four years and the intensity of it had consumed him to the point that he hadn't made the shift he should have when Reshma had become a part of his life.

Was it an excuse? No, it was a statement of fact, but he needed to do something about it. He just needed to figure out what that something was.

Both Murad and Daadi had mentioned simple gestures and Daadi had spoken about forging a connection. How was he supposed to go about those things? Simple gestures were . . . well, simple enough, but Zafar knew deep down that those alone wouldn't suddenly get Reshma and him back to where they'd been before she'd overheard that bloody phone call. Before she'd questioned their relationship and before she'd shut down on him.

What would he have suggested to Murad or one of his brothers if they had been in his shoes? Well, he'd suggest they go back to basics. Go out on dates, get to know her, see what makes her tick and take it from there. But he couldn't do that himself. He was already married to Reshma.

But why not? Maybe he could do that. Maybe that's what Daadi and Murad had been alluding to.

He hadn't done any of that before, but he could do it now. Go back to basics and give Reshma and their marriage the time they both deserved. Maybe then she'd be able to see past this blunder of his so they could find a sense of harmony with each other. Strengthen their bond, as Daadi had said. As for love . . . well. They'd cross that bridge when − and if − they ever got to it. Many a relationship stood the test of time on the basis of mutual respect and affection. Love wasn't an essential ingredient for a successful marriage. It wasn't a need or necessity, more a nice-to-have kind of thing.

As Fate would have it, on his walk, Zafar had found himself at Uncle Jawad's villa, where the man himself had been standing outside, tapping away on his phone.

If he was a believer of signs, then this would have been a big fat one. Reshma was right there and that's where he'd ended up as well.

Uncle Jawad had flipped closed the cover on his phone, offered Zafar a cup of coffee and led him into the villa. He'd then pulled out a deck of cards while he suggested they wait for the ladies to finish with their business and had proceeded to wipe the floor with him, though Zafar reckoned that if his brain had been firing on all cylinders and not distracted by his opponent's niece, the result wouldn't have been so one-sided.

'Woah, earth to Zaf. You there, mate?'

'Huh?' He turned to look at Shoaib, who had a puzzled look on his face.

'I've called your name twice now. The prayers are done, dude. Everyone is heading outside. You coming?'

Zafar looked around the room, tuning back into the present. Almost everyone had got up and moved around while he'd been in his own head. How long had he zoned out for? He got up and tried to cover his embarrassment at being caught by Shoaib by clapping the other man on the shoulder as he turned towards the patio. 'Yeah, yeah, let's go out.' Even his voice sounded croaky, like he'd just woken from the kind of nap that left you questioning what day of the week it was.

The atmosphere outside was as vibrant as it had been the day before. The catering team stationed just beside the patio door had fired up the barbecue and Zafar could hear faint music in the background. There seemed to be more people present than there had been the previous day. He'd heard from Khalil that guests would start trickling in on a daily basis now, some to stay and some who would come for the day and go back either to their own accommodation arrangements or their own homes.

Uncle Jawad introduced him to people he wasn't familiar with, some of whom knew his father and some who had known his grandfather as a young man. It was strange hearing stories about him from people he didn't know and while some sounded true to the man he knew, others made him wonder if they were talking about the same person.

'It is odd, isn't it?' Uncle Jawad said when Zafar told him as much. 'Everybody sees the same person in a different way. We all see different facets of each other and sometimes some people's accounts of someone we're familiar with sound alien to us. I mean, take my younger brother, for instance.' He shook his head as he spoke. 'Everyone sees a dynamic, life-of-the-party type who comes into a room and lights it up, making me look like dead wood in comparison. The most boring man in the world. But ask Reshma. She sees someone completely different in him, and in me for that matter.'

Zafar followed Uncle Jawad's line of sight and found Reshma sitting with a group of people. She was talking to a woman with a small child in her lap, while a few kids ran around them, looking relaxed and at ease, though he knew that wasn't how she was feeling deep down, adding further credence to what her uncle had just said.

'Uncle Jawad? Zafar? Come on, the first round of meats and veg are coming off the barbecue.' Khalil started making his way around the gathering, telling people to help themselves to the feast.

Zafar excused himself to check on his grandmother and found that she had moved to the dining table inside with a few others and was already eating. He went back outside and decided to look for Reshma. She was sitting in the same place she had been before, a plate of food now in her hand. She caught sight of him looking at her and she pressed her lips together before looking away.

Not letting that small rebuff put him off, he loaded a plate with food and picked his way across the space towards her, pleased to see a few empty chairs around the area. He pulled one up right beside her and sat down.

'Hello, ladies.' He smiled at Haniya and the other woman sitting with them and then he looked at Reshma, whose eyes were firmly on her plate.

'Hey, Zaf. How are you finding being surrounded by your in-laws? You ready to run for the hills yet?' Haniya grinned at him.

'Actually, it's anything but. I'm having a great time, they all seem to think of me as royalty. All because of your cousin here.' He bumped his shoulder against Reshma's and was rewarded with a flaring of her nostrils. 'She's their golden child, so I automatically get to pass go and collect two hundred.'

Haniya laughed, as did the other woman beside her, who was breaking off small pieces of chicken and putting them into her baby's mouth. Said baby was more interested in playing with the bangles on the mother's wrists. Reshma stretched her lips but refrained from reacting or saying anything.

'Oh, this is Uncle Imtiaz's niece, Fatima, by the way. Fatima, in case it wasn't obvious, this is Reshma's husband, Zafar Saeed. That firecracker of a lady you met earlier? She is his grandmother.'

'Oh God. Please tell me she didn't say anything outrageous. I apologise on her behalf if she did.' Zafar hung his head jokingly.

Fatima laughed. 'Nothing of the sort. She's amazing. She was talking to my four-year-old son, Haroon, telling him that she has a grandson with the same name and that he's an absolute menace, though he can't use age as his excuse anymore.'

'I can attest to that.'

They spoke about inconsequential things while they all ate, Reshma *hmming* non-committally here and there. When they had finished, Fatima left to clean her baby up, Haniya offering her the use of one of the rooms and leading her to it.

A waiter came around with a tray bearing tea and coffee and they each grabbed a hot drink, as he took the empty plates away on the same tray. As soon as the waiter moved away and before Zafar had the chance to utter a single syllable, a little boy raced towards them, a piece of paper held in one hand and a few crayons clutched in the other.

'Reshma! Reshma!' He came full pelt towards her and landed against her knees as she moved her cup of tea to the side to avoid spilling it. 'Look. I drew a picture.' He pushed the heavily crinkled piece of paper towards her and, smiling down at the child, she took it in her other hand.

'Let's see what you've drawn.' She held the paper in front of her and Zafar saw nothing more than colourful streaks and odd shapes, certainly nothing he could make out.

'That's lovely, Haroon. Who is it for?'

So, this was Haroon. Zafar watched their interaction with amusement, as he took a sip of his coffee.

The boy smiled at her shyly. 'You.' He pointed at the big blue blob on the page. 'That's me. And this is you.' He pointed to a slimmer and longer yellow blob. 'When I grow up, I'm going to marry you.'

Zafar spluttered his mouthful of coffee out and both Reshma and her barely-two-feet-tall Romeo looked at him in alarm. He cleared his throat and wiped the back of his hand across his mouth. Eyes wide, Reshma handed him a napkin from her lap and, after nodding in thanks, he took it and dabbed his mouth before blurting out, 'Sorry, mate. She's already married. To me. You'll have to find someone else. Reshma's *my* wife.' He winked at the child, unable to keep the playful note out of his voice.

Reshma's eyes were as wide as saucers, but Haroon 2.0 looked ready for a fight. His legs were apart as he stood there, positioning himself closer to Reshma as he faced Zafar and there was a fierce scowl on his face. 'No, she's not. Reshma's going to marry me because I love her and I drew her a picture with her favourite colour.'

Zafar bit the inside of his cheek, not wanting to laugh but finding the child's argument about why he was the better prospect endearing. If he'd been old enough, Zafar might have had some serious competition. He raised his eyebrow as he regarded his adversary, but before he could say anything, Reshma intervened.

'Did you have your dinner, Haroon?'

He turned to face Reshma and his expression switched from serious to smitten in a heartbeat as he nodded.

'Would you like to have some pudding? Let's go and find your mummy and see if we can get you some pudding. Let's get you away from the crazy man while we're at it.' She mumbled the last bit under her breath, but Zafar caught it as she got up, and after giving Zafar a killer glare, she turned to leave, as her admirer pressed his hand into Reshma's. He narrowed his eyes at Zafar just before he turned away.

Fatima was making her way back towards them and spotting her son with Reshma, she smiled at him. 'There you are. I've been looking for you. I hope you're being good and not giving Reshma and Zafar any trouble.' She gave her son a look that suggested that she knew that the chances of that were fifty-fifty.

'He's been the sweetest.' Reshma gave Zafar a side eye before looking back towards Fatima. 'Very charming and loving. He's stolen my heart.' He was sure that last bit was for his benefit.

'That's kind of you to say, Reshma, but I know this rascal well. Come on you. Let's get you some ice cream so you can really bounce off the walls while I have your father watch over you later.'

She took charge of her son and, after blowing Reshma a kiss, her not-so-secret-admirer left to go and have his ice cream, the lure of the frozen dessert obviously greater than wanting to stay next to the woman he'd professed his love for.

Reshma blew him a kiss back and then turned to face Zafar. He looked up at her innocently, ignoring the feeling that had hit him when she'd kissed her palm and then blown it towards Romeo.

'All that was missing was for you to beat your chest and roar in his face, though why, I have no idea. He's four, Zafar. Four.' Her tone held a mixture of annoyance and confusion.

He ignored the first part of what she'd said, latching onto the last. 'I know, and check his audacity. Four years old and declaring that he'll marry you like that. He didn't even have the decency to go down on one knee, propose and wait for an answer.' Zafar knew he was being ridiculous, but he couldn't help it.

He stood up, not wanting to be at a disadvantage as Reshma stayed standing. He took half a step towards her and had to dip his head to maintain eye contact. When Reshma wore flats, like she was today, she only reached his shoulder. He took a more well-mannered sip of his coffee this time and she mimicked him with her tea, not once breaking eye contact.

His eyes were drawn to hers, where she'd flicked her eye liner at the ends and her eyelids sparkled. She'd lined her eyes heavily and they looked bigger and brighter than usual. Her nose stud twinkled as she lifted her chin, making him smile. Throughout the day, she'd maintained a fine balance between showing defiance and indifference towards him and he was intrigued at the fiery spirit she was giving him a glimpse of.

'That's rich coming from you. From what I remember, you didn't propose either, forget going down on one knee. Your father finalised everything with my uncle. You didn't even bother to do it ceremonially. At least Haroon was sweet enough to declare his love and draw me a picture of us. He made the effort to try to write my name on the picture too. No one forced him to.'

'Touché, Mrs Saeed. Touché.' She had him there. Romeo had one . . . no, three up on him. A declaration of love, a picture and her name on the picture. But it was his name attached to hers and suddenly he felt a need to assert it. The reason for which he would sit and ponder on later, because he damned well needed to figure out what was going through his head with regards to Reshma right now. Getting to know her or even romancing her was one thing. Being affected by her so viscerally and feeling possessive was another.

'It's Ms Mir actually.'

'I beg your pardon?'

'My name is still Reshma Mir. I never changed it to Saeed. And you know what? I'm glad I didn't. Why take the name of a man who doesn't even want to be with me?' She stretched her lips as though forcing a smile, but he could hear the hurt she was trying to cover up in her voice.

Maybe it was because he had witnessed her distress last night, but he suddenly felt attuned to the underlying pain in her voice. Surely, it hadn't always been there, had it?

Zafar cleared his throat. 'I'm not one of those men who needs or expects his wife to change her name and take his unless it's something she chooses to do and it makes her happy. I'm quite happy for you to call yourself Reshma Mir or Reshma Saeed. It doesn't change the reality that we are both linked to each other. And as for proposing to you . . . you're right. I didn't. There's lots I haven't done and, believe it or not, I acknowledge and accept it. As I said to you last night, I've failed you as a husband. But that's not a trend I intend to keep up. We might not know each other as well as we should, but I reckon you know me well enough to know that I put a lot of effort into succeeding. And when I identify any failures or weaknesses, even my own, I make it my mission to turn them around until they're a resounding success, whatever the obstacles. Including four-year-olds who try to win over *my* wife.' As he said the words, he felt a strong sense of awareness of how much he meant them.

10

Reshma

Unbidden, a shiver went through Reshma at Zafar's words. Which was utter craziness. He was just having a Neanderthal moment and she'd do well to remember that.

It had all been bluster because his ego had taken a hit from a little boy who barely reached his knees. A boy who had charmed Reshma from the moment she'd met him. She'd seen it happen before, when a child took to an adult that wasn't related to them for no explicable reason. It was the first time it had happened to her and she'd found it endearing, sweet. Little Haroon had been nothing but entertaining, giving her unconditional affection at a time when Reshma had desperately needed a distraction.

And she'd needed that distraction because of the man now standing in front of her, looking for all the world as though he had meant every single word he'd just said. And the way he'd just referred to her as his wife – her heart had swooped behind her ribcage like a butterfly suddenly free of its cocoon, the stupid organ that it was. As though the previous forty-eight hours, the past thirteen months, had been completely different and not how she remembered them.

It was all fanciful thinking on her part and just words on his and she'd do well to remember that fact too.

Thankfully, the rest of the evening passed enjoyably, with Reshma moving away from a cockily confident Zafar and spending her time with her cousins. She also managed to get into bed before him, feigning sleep as he noisily pottered about in their room and tried calling out to her. He probably knew she was pretending, but she didn't care.

The following day, Reshma managed to take time out to focus on her work for a few hours. The website she was working on was coming along nicely and she was on the cusp of securing a new client for a big website upgrade, which had her feeling excited. A feeling she relished after the exhaustion of the last few days. Work was a blessing right now, enabling her to lose herself and forget what was happening around her. She let her creativity take the lead.

Daadi was relaxing, watching TV in between making phone calls and Uncle Imtiaz had roped in Zafar, Shoaib and Khalil to help him with some wedding-related errands that required brawn. Uncle Jawad had gone with them too.

When Uncle Imtiaz had come to make his request, Zafar had flexed his biceps and waggled his eyebrows at her and she'd been momentarily stunned, before giving him a withering look and then turning the other way.

It was strange how the events of the last couple of days had them both acting completely differently. There was an ease about Zafar she'd not seen before, whereas she felt more highly strung than she'd ever been, especially among her own relatives.

Zafar was showing glimpses of being carefree and playful and Reshma wasn't sure what to make of it. Was it an act he was putting on for the benefit of their audience or was it genuinely how he was and she'd just not seen it before? Whatever it was, she needed to remain on guard. The last thing she needed was to be lulled by his charming ways and then be back where she had been a few days ago. Living in a bubble, or worse, facing more pain and heartache.

She'd come to the conclusion that she hadn't been so much in love with Zafar as she had been in love with the idea of him. She'd allowed herself to blur the lines between the two, when there was a distinct difference. Now that she'd identified that difference, she could put her feelings into a box at the back of her mind and focus her attention on other things with little to zero potential of causing her any more hurt than she'd already suffered.

Finishing her work for the day and with her renewed resolve, she made her way towards Auntie Bilqis' villa to see what she and Haniya were up to. Daadi decided to accompany her and the two of them headed over there, taking in the beautifully landscaped gardens around them. When they got closer to the villa, it was to find that the guys were back and almost everyone was congregated near the main entrance.

'What's happening here?' Daadi paused as she took the sight in, one hand holding her walking stick and her other arm linked with Reshma's. Haniya spotted them and she got Zafar's attention and the pair of them made their way towards her and Daadi.

'What's going on, Niya? I leave you for one morning and suddenly . . .' Her sentence trailed off as she saw the solemn look on her cousin's face. 'What is it? Is everything OK?'

Haniya nodded as Zafar came and stood next to her, a somewhat serious expression on his face too.

It didn't take long for Reshma's confusion to clear. Haniya spoke to her in hushed tones as Reshma watched Auntie Ruqayyah and Uncle Jawad talking to each other in the distance. 'Uncle Ahsan has just arrived with his family.' Reshma jerked her face from her aunt and uncle to her cousin, finding her looking back at her with a sympathetic expression on her face, while Reshma stared with her mouth hanging open until she snapped it shut. *Her father was here?* 'As far as I'm aware, no one knew he was coming until earlier today. Apparently, it was supposed to be a surprise, until he got to the airport and called and asked to be picked up. They've got so much stuff, they had to arrange two cars and Auntie Ruqayyah's been busy trying to sort out a villa for them. Classic Uncle Ahsan, eh?'

Reshma swallowed the sudden dryness in her throat and felt a hollow pit open up behind her sternum. It was always difficult coming face to face with her father. There was a tremendous amount of unease all around and it left her feeling completely depleted of energy. In addition to the usual awkwardness of the situation was the fact that this was the first time Reshma was going to see her father after her own wedding, at which she'd asked Uncle Jawad to walk her to the ceremony rather than her father, much to his shock.

'Niya?' Someone called for Haniya, and after promising that she'd be back in a moment, she moved away, leaving Reshma standing there feeling a tightness in her gut and instinctively taking a step back, only to feel a warm hand cup her elbow with firm support, steadying her.

She looked behind her to find Zafar looking down at her. She'd never shared details of her childhood or her relationship – or lack thereof – with her father with Zafar. She didn't even know how much he knew or how much was common knowledge in their social circles. She supposed she would find out, and if he didn't know, he would shortly.

'Are you all right?' There was comfort imbued in his voice and a steadiness in his grasp around her elbow.

She jerked her head in a nod and then focused her eyes on the scene not too far away, where her father was greeting Auntie Ruqayyah.

Neither Zafar nor Daadi moved forward to greet the newcomers and with her feet stuck to the ground, she couldn't – didn't – move either.

Her father moved back from meeting his sister and brother-in-law so his wife could do the same. He called his two sons and daughter forward and introduced them to the people immediately surrounding them. One by one, everyone hugged or shook hands with the new arrivals.

Moments later, her father came upon them.

'Auntie Mumtaz. It's lovely to see you.'

'How are you, Ahsan?' While Daadi didn't sound her usual warm and cheery self, she wasn't outright cold.

'Good, good. This is my wife, Huriya, my two sons, Anwar and Habib, and my baby girl, Sakina.'

Said *baby girl* – who was around fifteen years old, Reshma knew – didn't look too pleased with her father's description of her.

Daadi looked over everyone, bestowing a smile on her father's family after she greeted them individually. 'It's nice to meet you all.'

Reshma wanted to move further back and not have to do this, especially with everyone watching, but she knew she didn't have a choice. It had only ever been a matter of time before she would come face to face with her father and his family. They did share an extended family after all.

She'd met his wife before – who had made it clear that she'd rather she wasn't referred to as the stepmother – and seen his sons and daughter too. But this was the first time they were meeting each other in such close quarters and after a considerable period of time. When Uncle Jawad had invited them all to Reshma's wedding, only her father had turned up, saying that the others were away visiting his wife's family and so they couldn't come, something Reshma had been somewhat relieved by.

She swallowed to ease the dryness in her throat as her father stepped forward. She felt Zafar's hand move away from her elbow and her traitorous body instantly mourned the loss of contact. Even if it was Zafar, and with all the problems they had between them, at least she hadn't felt completely alone in the moment. She curled her fingers in on themselves, but in the next moment she felt them being prised apart as Zafar intertwined his fingers with hers, linking their hands together.

She chanced a quick glance his way and he gave her a reassuring smile, a corner of his mouth lifting as his eyes softened, their focus solely on her. He squeezed her hand at the same time and Reshma felt a warmth imbue her as she turned to face her father once more.

'Reshma, my dear, how are you?' Her father had one hand in his pocket as he rocked on his heels.

She caught sight of Uncle Jawad and Auntie Bilqis over her father's shoulder and her aunt smiled at her reassuringly while her uncle winked at her. The unease in her gut settled some more and she looked at the man standing in front of her again. He looked the same as he always did, smartly dressed with not a hair out of place. His closely trimmed beard had a bit more grey in it, but aside from that, she couldn't see any major difference from the last time she'd seen him.

He held an arm out and Reshma stepped forward for a side hug, her father patting her shoulder twice before easing back. 'Hello, Daddy.'

With a nod and nothing more to stay to her, he moved along and his children filed past her with short nods of acknowledgement and then his wife was standing in front of her. The same woman who had said that she couldn't raise a twelve-year-old while trying to settle in with her new husband. She had needed time and then, of course, she couldn't help a teenager adjust to a new family with a newborn baby to take care of, and so on and so forth until Reshma had realised that there would never really be any place for her in Huriya's family. Her father had never fought to have her with him either, using the excuse that she was too old to be displaced from her uncle's care by then.

'Hello, Reshma. You look well.'

'Thank you.' Reshma wasn't sure what more she could, or was supposed to, say to a comment like that, so she didn't say anything. One never knew if it was a genuine comment or a sarcastic one. Well, at least when it came to Huriya, Reshma could never be sure.

'And here's my favourite son-in-law.' Her father's laugh had a nervous edge to it as he hugged Zafar and thumped him on the back. Zafar eased back, a bland smile on his face. 'You've not met my family, have you?' He introduced Zafar to his wife and children.

'Ahsan often tells me about times he's spent with your father in their youth,' Huriya said, holding onto Zafar's hand after shaking it.

Reshma heard Daadi scoff beside her before she covered it up with an elegant cough. She leaned close to Reshma and whispered, 'Rich, don't you think? They talk about that, but not about what's really important.'

Huriya looked towards them sharply, but didn't say anything before moving away, her daughter's hand firmly in hers. Daadi's voice had been too soft for her to have heard anything, but she might have heard her scoff.

Reshma let out her breath in a soft whoosh, refraining from falling to the floor in a heap as her father and his family moved away. She felt her right hand being squeezed and realised that Zafar still held it in his. 'Shall we head back to the villa?'

She nodded.

Daadi slid her arm through Reshma's left arm once more and leaned across her slightly, talking to both her and Zafar. 'I think that's a fantastic idea. I could do with a sit-down and a cup of tea. In that order.'

11

Zafar

Zafar watched as Daadi tried to engage with Reshma, and while she was responding, he could tell that her mind kept drifting off and he didn't blame her. Her father's arrival was even more surprising than his had been. No one had known about it, and given that he wasn't very involved in the extended family, according to the snippet he'd heard Uncle Jawad exchanging with Auntie Ruqayyah, his arrival had shocked everyone. From the little Zafar knew, Ahsan Mir's contact with his family was occasional and often came as a surprise, much like it had today. Pleasant or not was yet to be seen, though he had a feeling he knew the answer to that already.

'Should we call that scamp Haroon and see what he's been up to?' Daadi asked Reshma, knowing how she doted on her youngest brother-in-law and if anyone could bring a smile to her face – from his family, that was – it was Haroon Saeed. Which, when put like that, didn't reflect very well on Zafar.

'I messaged him earlier, Daadi, while I was working, and he said that they had planned a day of exploring today. I don't want to disturb him. In fact, I think I might pop down to the beach for a walk and some fresh air. I could do with the movement.' There was an air of fragility about Reshma and Zafar felt like he needed to do something, anything, to bring her back to how she'd been before her father had arrived, even if she had been pissed at him.

But he felt ill-equipped to do anything. Who was he to offer Reshma any comfort or support when he was one of the people who had disappointed her too? What could he say or do to make Reshma feel better given where *they* were?

He didn't want her feeling any more hurt or disappointed than she already was and he could see that the arrival of her father had bothered her. He'd been there for Ahsan Mir's lukewarm greeting for his eldest daughter.

Zafar felt a flare of anger, towards Reshma's father and towards himself, because if they had been in a better place, he would know what to do. He was in this position of his own making.

Reshma made her way upstairs.

'Zafar, sweetheart, go with her, please. I'm worried about her. She's putting on a brave front, but I'm sure the arrival of her father with his family has affected her. Did you see their lacklustre acknowledgement of her?'

He nodded. 'Will you be OK?'

'I'll be fine, sweetheart. Don't worry about me. Reshma needs all of your attention right now.'

He wasn't sure Reshma would agree with his grandmother. He didn't know what he would say or do, but he wasn't going to let Reshma deal with this by herself, of that he was certain. Now wasn't the time to leave her alone. Even if they were silent throughout, he wanted to be there for her, even from a distance.

She came down five minutes later and Zafar got up. 'I'll come with you.'

She shook her head. 'You don't have to. I'll be fine by myself.' She didn't wait for any response and opened the door and walked out.

Zafar gave it twenty seconds before he left himself, spotting her a short distance ahead of him. Her head was bowed and her shoulders were hunched as she hurried down the path towards the beach.

Heavy grey clouds had rolled in since that morning and though rain hadn't been forecast, the sky looked somewhat ominous to him.

Zafar followed Reshma onto the beach and after she'd speed-walked several metres, her pace slowed down a bit until she came to a stop and turned to face the ocean. The tide was quite far out, which meant that it would soon start coming in. He could see her side profile and as he watched her, she lifted her hand and swiped it across her face, wiping away tears, and Zafar felt his heart sink.

He slowly made his way towards her and when he was a handful of steps away, she turned her face and looked at him for a moment, before turning to face the ocean once more. She didn't bother hiding the fact that she was crying, her tears falling unchecked down her face.

He wasn't sure whether she would appreciate his presence or any kind of contact, but the idea of just standing there didn't sit right with him. He wanted to comfort her, so he went with his instinct. Slowly, he touched her fingers, letting his intertwine with hers, and she let him, didn't pull away. She turned her face and looked at their hands as he rubbed his thumb on the back of her hand. He watched her face as she swallowed, her chin moving with the motion, but her eyes remained glued to their hands.

Using the slightest pressure, he pulled her arm so she turned towards him a bit more and then, softly, he spoke her name. 'Reshma?'

Her eyes were downcast, looking at the damp sand between them. She rolled her lips inwards and her nostrils flared as fresh tears fell down her cheeks. She didn't say anything as she took a small step forward and rested her forehead against his chest.

The depth of her sorrow brought a lump to his throat and he gently put his arm around her shoulder, holding her close as he moved his other arm to rest against her lower back. He tightened his hold on her when she didn't push him away or pull away herself. Instead, she rested her head just under his chin.

He felt her body shudder as his T-shirt dampened, but all he did was tighten his arms around her. One arm was around his waist and the other was held against his body, fisting his T-shirt in her fingers. Zafar rubbed his hand in soothing circular motions on her back a couple of times before securing his hold on her again. He lowered his lips and kissed the top of her head before resting his cheek on the same spot, willing all her pain and sadness away, as he stood there silently.

How was it, that in all this time, he'd never stopped to actually truly connect with the woman he had married and now, in the space of a few days, he was suddenly overcome with grief at the sight of her tears and anguish? Anyone would think that after blowing cold all this time with her, he'd suddenly turned the tap to hot, and they wouldn't be wrong. That was exactly what it looked like. One minute he didn't want to come with her, and now there was nowhere else he'd rather be.

But how could he expect her to trust him when his commitment towards her was so wishy-washy? What right did he have to offer her comfort, especially given how little he'd given her so far?

She was in a vulnerable place and with only him around, it was understandable that she hadn't pushed him away and had sought comfort in his arms, but that didn't mean it was all hunky-dory between them. He had so much work to do to earn this woman's trust, if he even deserved it. But he would try. He would try his hardest to become worthy of Reshma's trust and affection, that much he was absolutely certain about.

He tightened his hold on her anew and after several minutes of silent sobbing, he heard a small hiccup and Reshma moved her face to the side, resting her cheek against him as she looked towards the water once more. He could see the glisten of tear tracks on her face and the tip of her nose was pink, wrinkling as she sniffled.

'How can you be his favourite son-in-law when he won't even say more than six words to me?' Her voice was thick with tears. 'How much of a glutton for punishment am I that in all these years, I've still not learnt my lesson that he doesn't care? I still expect something from him.' She pulled her face back and looked up at him, the heartbreak in her eyes crystal clear. 'And how ungrateful am I, that with such a loving uncle and aunt who stepped in to raise me when they didn't have to, I'm still seeking acceptance from a man who will never give it to me? In no time at all, I feel like that eight-year-old again, waiting for him to notice me.'

Zafar felt his heart clench at the sorrow reflected in Reshma's voice, which broke on every other word. He moved his arms from around her and gently cupped her face in his hands. 'First off, you are not ungrateful. You wouldn't know how to be ungrateful, Reshma. It's perfectly natural to want your only surviving parent to want you, to accept you and to love you. That doesn't make you ungrateful by any stretch of the imagination. And that leads me onto the second thing. You're not a glutton

104

for punishment either. The fault here lies squarely with Ahsan Mir, no one else. And I have no desire to be such a man's favourite anything. Especially if he can't see how wonderful you are.'

She shook her head fervently and he dropped his arms, resting them around her once more. 'No. I'm not. Do you know how many chances he had to have me be a part of his life? Twenty years' worth of chances. I think it's pretty clear what he feels and thinks about me. I just need to get my brain and my stupid heart on the same page.' She took a shuddering breath, her hands clenched into fists against his pecs. She was looking at the neckline of his T-shirt in anger. 'Every step of the way, his feelings have been clear, it's just been me who refuses to see them for what they are. And, like an idiot, I carry that with me in every relationship and then wonder why I don't get anything back.'

Was she talking about *them*? She must be, and the thought of being grouped with Ahsan Mir, even the little he knew about him, had Zafar feeling disgusted with himself. It was as clear as day that it was the people who had let Reshma down that were in the wrong, not her, and that included him, much to his shame.

Reshma dropped her hands and moved back, making Zafar loosen his hold on her. She walked towards a small cluster of palm trees and sat down on the sand under them, facing the ocean. Zafar followed her and lowered himself onto the ground beside her. He bent his legs at the knees and rested his arms on them as he too faced the ocean. Reshma took the same pose, except her arms were looped around her knees as she rested her chin on them, looking utterly exhausted. Thankfully, she wasn't crying but the waves of sadness coming off her were palpable.

The sun was playing hide-and-seek behind the heavy clouds that loomed in the distance. There was humidity in the air and the prospect of a thunderstorm seemed pretty likely.

Zafar turned Reshma's way when he heard her take a deep breath and let it out on a long sigh.

'Thank you for coming out after me. I appreciate it.'

'Please don't thank me for that, Reshma.' It was something that should have been a given between them. If she was upset, she should have had the confidence that he had her back, but that wasn't where they were, so instead she felt she had to be thankful when he did the bare minimum. Zafar shook his head, realising how much ground he had to make up.

They sat quietly for a few minutes. Reshma lowered her knees and sat cross-legged, picking up a handful of sand and then pouring it out, making a tiny mound in front of her.

'Will you be all right seeing everyone later?' They were gathering for another dinner that evening and in the coming days there were many events and gatherings where everyone would be in attendance, including the newcomers.

She nodded. 'Yeah.' Her voice was slightly hoarse as she spoke and he could see the after-effects of crying around her eyes. 'I'll be fine. It's not like they'll bother with me anyway.'

Zafar huffed. 'I can't understand how any father can be like that with his child, especially when that's the only link he has to her mother.'

'Maybe that's why.'

Zafar looked at her sharply at that. 'What do you mean?'

'Well, he's never said it outright, but I get the feeling that maybe he thinks his relationship with my mother is best forgotten. A mistake which he ended up getting tied down to because of me. I've heard that they chose to marry each other because they were in *love*. They'd only known one another for six months before they got married and it was only after getting married that their differences started coming to the surface. They started having disagreements and their relationship became quite fractious.'

'Disagreements are normal in relationships. It takes time to adjust to your partner after marriage, doesn't it? Any of that is hardly your fault.' And he hadn't missed her emphasis on the word *love*, a feeling she seemed to be deeply unhappy with.

She gave a humourless chuckle. 'It is when they decided to separate and then my mum found out that she was pregnant, forcing them to give their relationship another go. Both their parents thought it would be the perfect thing for them to have a baby because it would bring them closer together. Newsflash – it didn't. It put a further strain on their relationship. I wasn't enough to pull their relationship out of the downward spiral it was in and it took my mother down too. She was on strong medication for her multitude of issues and decided to get behind the wheel when I was six years old. Maybe my father feels that had it not been for me, he and my mum would have separated long before that and their lives would have been completely different. Mum might still be—'

'Please tell me he's not said that to you.' Zafar felt his blood bubble beneath his skin at the thought.

A corner of Reshma's mouth turned up as she looked his way briefly before turning back. 'No, he hasn't. But sometimes a person doesn't have to say something expressly, do they? Their actions do the talking. He dropped me off at my maternal grandparents' place, expecting them to take care of me. They lasted six months before telling him to come and take me back because I reminded them too much of the daughter they'd lost. I've not seen them since.'

'Jesus. That's . . . I don't even have the words.' He'd had no idea that her grandparents had done that.

'Yeah, well. He tried for about a year and a half before Uncle Jawad stepped in. Over the years, he would often say that when the time was right, he'd take me back, but . . . well, here we are.' Her matter-of-fact tone belied the depth of hurt he knew she must be feeling. Christ, the depth of hurt *he* was feeling was so intense, he couldn't even begin to imagine what hers was.

Zafar couldn't even begin to understand what Reshma would have gone through. To face that kind of loss, displacement and abandonment at the young age she had been would have had a profound effect on her. And then to have her only surviving parent not make the effort to be a part of her life was something that had the potential of causing her pain every single time she thought about it.

And what about him?

Guilt reared its head, loud and proud, as Zafar saw his own actions fall into place in Reshma's life.

No wonder she had resignedly told him to go back home. She was used to not being a priority to people. He had so much to make up for, he wondered if he'd ever manage.

Zafar turned his face from looking at her to looking at the ocean. The tide was creeping in and the sky had darkened. He heard the distant roll of thunder.

'I think we should head back. I don't want Daadi to be any more worried than she already was when I left.' Reshma got up and brushed the sand off her trousers as she spoke.

When Zafar got up, there was barely a foot between them. 'Thank you for sharing what you did with me, Reshma. I know it couldn't have been easy. It probably brings all those feelings back to the surface for you.'

She looked up at him, her eyes sad but clear. She shrugged her shoulders and lowered her gaze.

Zafar placed two fingers under her chin and with the slightest pressure, lifted her face to look at him. 'I know my opinion doesn't hold a great deal of weight right now, but for what it's worth, I think you're incredible.'

Slowly, he lowered his head, his lips hovering over her forehead. He only waited a scant few seconds before she moved forward the last centimetre and he brushed his lips on her forehead, inhaling the scent of her shampoo.

They stood there, suspended in time, as Zafar savoured the feeling of closeness to Reshma. Even though it was her who had spent the last hour going through an emotional wringer, he felt like he needed the comfort of her touch.

He eased away slowly, reluctantly, and looked down at her, her nose stud catching the dim light and twinkling. She gave him the smallest smile, slowly lifting her hand and placing the cool tips of just three fingers on his jaw.

Her eyes roved over his face, seemingly cataloguing every part of it, and Zafar did the same, moving from her eyes to her lips, where the tip of her tongue came out and ran across her lips before disappearing. He moved the hand that had been gently holding her chin further up, cupping the side of her face with a light touch, afraid that she might not welcome more from him. But she surprised him by closing her eyes and leaning into his hand.

Zafar felt a zing of energy go from his hand all the way through his body. His nerve endings tingled to life, his heart racing.

Gradually, she opened her eyes and eased away from him, putting a few steps between them. Zafar put his hands in his pockets, acknowledging that the moment was over, and they both made their way back to the villa. The silence between them simmering with tension, but less fraught than before.

12

Reshma

Two days after the arrival of Ahsan Mir and his family, the brother of the bride hosted a games night in honour of his sister and future brother-in-law. The central garden, which was surrounded on three sides by hedges and was rectangular in shape, had been set up with various games and groupings of chairs for those who wished to spectate. Through an archway on one of the sides was another smaller paved terrace, on which buffet tables had been set up with a steady supply of food and drinks for the evening.

Reshma walked through the entrance of the garden with Haniya, watching the finishing touches being added to the space. There were fairy lights and colourful lanterns lighting up the garden, with two fire pits in opposite corners.

Energetic music was already pumping through the speakers, adding to the party atmosphere, and with people spilling into the garden one after the other, it didn't take long for the party to get started.

Young children rushed for the giant snakes and ladders and connect four and Reshma saw Uncle Imtiaz make a beeline for the chess table.

'What are we playing first?' Haniya asked as she looked around with wide eyes.

Reshma spotted a mat to her left and grabbed Haniya's arm, pulling her in its direction. 'Here. Let's play noughts and crosses.'

In no time, the pair of them were in hysterics, falling over each other and pushing each other out of the way, flagrantly ignoring any rules of the game. Shoaib and Khalil came and decided to join in with a doubles game, pitting themselves against her and Haniya and they started mucking about even more.

Reshma felt a lightness that seemed to have eluded her since her meltdown in front of Zafar and then more so after her father's arrival. She hadn't spoken to her father since then, though she'd seen him around obviously, because every evening the entire wedding party gathered to have dinner together at Auntie Ruqayyah's villa.

She was also in a strange place with Zafar where she wasn't saying anything to him as such, short of what she had to say or if they had an audience, but he was being as attentive with her as she'd always seen him be with others. More than he'd ever been with her before.

When he'd followed her to the beach, after her father's shock arrival, she'd been somewhat surprised, but that was nothing compared to the surprise she'd felt when he'd held her hand and then held her after she'd given in to the torrent of emotions that had reached breaking point inside her. It wasn't just a case of using him because he'd been the only one available. She'd seen compassion in his eyes, a connection, and at that moment she'd felt a deep need to be held by him and she'd given in to it, something that had later confounded her.

Why she had sought consolation in the arms of the man who had no interest in her, she couldn't fathom, but it was as if a greater being had pushed their differences to one side and allowed her to seek comfort from him and he'd offered it to her unconditionally. And then she'd gone on and unburdened herself to him while they'd both sat there watching the waves slowly make their way towards the shoreline.

She'd felt a strange sense of peace after that, but she'd also felt a bit rattled. How was that for a confusion of feelings?

'Right, what next?' Shoaib asked of no one in particular, looking around him to see what was available. He spotted the twister mat and made his way towards it.

They followed after him and Reshma saw Saleema, her fiancé, Nomaan, and Zafar make their way towards them.

Saleema immediately put her hands on her hips. 'I'm not playing this. I can't afford to fall flat on my face and end up with a black eye.'

Saleema decided to play referee as the rest of them got stuck in, Shoaib and Khalil being their annoying selves and sticking their foot in Haniya's or Reshma's face every chance they got. Haniya flopped out thanks to Shoaib pushing her out of the way and at the next round, as Reshma placed her hand on the red dot at the same time as Zafar, their foreheads touched and, in her panic, she lost her balance and fell.

He smiled playfully while her cousins laughed raucously. Khalil – being a cheat of the highest order – won the game, while Zafar complained about needing to see a physio for his knees, making everyone laugh.

They moved around other games, each of them emerging a victor in one or another before they all decided that they needed a break to refuel.

They sat at a table together, and had finished eating when Khalil said he had an idea. 'Let's see how well Saleema and Nomaan know each other. We'll ask you questions about your other half and see if you can guess the correct answer.' He rubbed his hands gleefully as the rest of them shouted their agreement.

It was so cute to see them sneak glances at each other as they spoke about favourite colours, foods and various other questions everyone asked them off the cuff. Unsurprisingly, they both knew each other pretty well and only fluffed up a few questions.

'It's Reshma and Zafar's turn now,' Saleema said enthusiastically and Reshma felt her stomach hollow out.

'Uh, no. It's not our wedding, it's yours. You two get to do all the couple stuff.'

'Reshma's right. This is your time to shine and soak up the limelight,' Zafar agreed with her, and the others probably couldn't tell, but she could see from the set of his jaw that he didn't want to be put on the spot.

Unfortunately, her cousins decided to band together against them and she and Zafar found themselves sitting opposite each other at the table after a reshuffle and her cousins started shouting out questions for them.

'Me first.' Saleema started things off. 'I'll begin with an easy question. Reshma, when is Zaf's birthday?'

'Third of December.'

Zafar nodded, and before Saleema could ask him the same question, he spoke.

'Reshma's is the fifteenth of May.'

'What's Reshma's favourite drink?' Nomaan asked Zafar.

'A hot chocolate with all the extras.'

Reshma nodded. 'Zafar likes coffee best.'

'These are easy questions. I've got one.' Haniya leaned forward and Reshma held her breath, unsure about what her cousin might ask. 'What's Zaf's pet peeve?'

She exhaled her held breath. The question wasn't as difficult as she'd thought it might be. 'When someone calls his name but doesn't follow it up with anything, or they call after him once he's left the room. Daadi and Harry do it deliberately for giggles.'

Zafar looked her way and he gave her a small smile as he nodded. All eyes were then on him. He shifted his weight left and right before resting his arms on the table between them. 'Umm, Reshma's pet peeve . . .' His eyebrows knit together as he considered the question. 'I don't think she has one. I've never seen her get annoyed by something.'

'Uh-uh.' Haniya made a buzzer noise to tell Zafar his answer was incorrect. 'Wrong-o. Reshma?'

'When some sniffles excessively but won't blow their nose.'

'It drives her nuts.' Haniya laughed as Zafar looked at her pensively.

'My turn. Zaf, what's Reshma's favourite type of cuisine?' Shoaib asked.

Reshma watched Zafar as he swallowed, his cheeks tinged with colour as he looked at her. 'Turkish?' She wondered if he was saying that because it was the closest restaurant to where they lived and they often grabbed a last-minute takeaway from there.

'Uh, that's not what I remember, unless her preference has changed after marriage. Reshma?'

'My favourite food is Italian. Pizza is king.' She smiled but Zafar didn't. His jaw was firm and there was a tension in him that hadn't been there till now. This game wasn't helping, it was making things worse, highlighting the fact that there were simple things about her that he didn't know. And while she might not be the happiest with him, she didn't want him to feel uncomfortable like this, especially just for her cousins' entertainment.

'Reshma, what's Zaf's favourite?' She knew he liked Mexican food best and he knew that she knew that. If she gave the wrong answer, he'd guess that she'd done it deliberately.

She was saved from saying anything though, because suddenly, the music switched off and with a short sharp buzz, the lights went out too.

'Oh.' There was a collective groan from the gathering and in the next few seconds, phone lights came on, lighting up people's faces as they held them aloft.

'I had better go and see what's happened,' Khalil said as he stood up and Shoaib followed him.

'I'm going to go and check on Daadi.' Zafar moved away too, and in the faint light, Reshma watched him go, the confidence in his stride in complete contrast to how he'd been moments ago when answering questions about her.

She knew it had made him uncomfortable because he hadn't known all the correct answers. It proved her point that he had no interest in her and he hardly knew her. So why was she feeling bad for seeing him feeling so uncomfortable and dejected?

Once again, Reshma felt conflicted when it came to him. Why she couldn't emotionally detach from him, she couldn't understand and it had her feeling on edge.

The lights came on after a short while and there was an audible sigh of relief. Reshma left Haniya chatting with Saleema and Nomaan and made her way back into the garden where the games had been set up. She saw Daadi sitting with Auntie Bilqis and Auntie Ruqayyah in a grouping of chairs. After checking in with them, she looked around but saw no sign of Zafar.

'Daadi, have you seen Zafar?'

Daadi looked around just as she had. 'He was here a moment ago, checking if all my fingers and toes are where he left them, what with the power cut. I can't imagine he's gone too far.'

Reshma nodded and ambled towards the entrance to the garden, stopping every few minutes to exchange pleasantries with people she went past. At the entrance was a big floral display spelling Saleema and Nomaan's names, the S and N intertwined and a big cheesy heart behind it. It looked cute. There was a small table with a guest book and a pot of pens on it and that's where Reshma found Zafar. He wrote something and then closed the book and replaced the pen.

'What message have you written?' she asked as she approached him.

It was the first time she was initiating conversation with him with no one around them watching. He looked her way, startled, as though he hadn't heard her approach.

'Just best wishes for their future. I'm in no position to be offering any advice or giving them any tips. In fact, maybe I should take a notebook and get some tips from them about how to be a good partner.' His voice was strained and laced with weariness. He sat against the table, folding his arms across his chest.

Reshma went and stood next to him, resting her backside at the edge of the table but keeping some distance between them. 'Since when are you such a pessimist? That's not like you.'

'See? You even know that about me.' He laughed, but the sound held no humour, filled instead with sadness and frustration.

'Zafar, I—'

'It was more proof of what a failure I am. Everyone's under this illusion that I'm the perfect son, grandson, brother, et cetera, et cetera, but what they don't know is how, in every relationship, I've failed people. I'm not perfect, Reshma. Far from it.'

'Who is? People say comparison is the thief of joy, but I think perfection is just as much a thief of joy. If you set out to seek perfection, you'll forever be searching for it, Zafar. It's not about being perfect by someone else's standards. It's about being true to your own. Making an honest effort and following through with that. To me, showing up and doing that counts for more than being perfect according to artificial standards.'

He shook his head. 'I've not even done that though, have I? Not when it comes to you.'

Reshma opened her mouth to respond, but then closed it. What was she going to say to that? He wasn't wrong and to say something perfunctory to reassure him would be unfair.

'So, now what?' she asked, sotto voce.

He didn't say anything, just looked at her intently as she did the same. Those tired lines that had bracketed his mouth were present, though she could swear they hadn't been as prominent over the last couple of days as they were now. His eyes held no brightness and he looked downright exhausted. His shoulders were hunched forward slightly, as though they carried the weight of the world, and for Zafar, they did. He carried the weight of his entire family on those shoulders, every day of the week, month and year. Family traditions, his grandfather's legacy, his work and the family business, everyone's expectations. Every single person she knew in his circle had expectations of this man and, as a result, he had extremely high expectations of himself. When did a man like that ever take that burden off his shoulders and just breathe, or do something for himself? Where were his own dreams in all of this?

Reshma swallowed as that thought took root in her brain, moving her gaze from him to look at her sandals. How was this the first time she was seeing him in *this* light? She'd never really paused to see how many different directions he was being pulled in. All she had seen was that he hadn't taken any steps in her direction, and while she hadn't been wrong in that, she was big enough to acknowledge that she hadn't considered the whole picture from his perspective.

He sighed. 'It's always been the way. When I tried to be a good grandson, I failed as a son and as a brother. When I tried to be a good brother, I failed as grandson. I try to be a good businessman and thus grandson and I fail as a husband. It's almost like it's impossible for me to win in any scenario.' He turned to look at her and Reshma saw utter sadness on his face, making her heart stutter.

She swallowed the immediate lump that had come to her throat, robbing her of the ability to speak. She'd never thought of Zafar as a shallow man, but she'd also never expected such a depth of complexities in him. She'd fallen for his outward appearance of confidence and surety, just like everyone else and the realisation didn't leave her feeling great.

Her thoughts were cut short as she heard voices approach them and suddenly her father's children came around the corner and stood in front of the flower wall. Sakina went through a box of props and pulled out oversized glasses and put them on before handing one brother a Stetson and her other brother a multicoloured wig.

They were at an angle where she and Zafar weren't in their direct line of sight as they took various pictures, their excitement clear to any onlooker. Two minutes later, their parents joined them and Reshma felt her breath hitch in her chest as they all stood together and took a family shot. The symbolism of being on the outside not lost on her.

13

Zafar

Reshma's eyes were on Ahsan Mir and his family and Zafar's eyes were on Reshma. He watched her as the colour slowly leached from her face, leaving it pale.

Ahsan took pictures with his wife and kids, with just his wife, with his sons and then with his daughter. Well, his younger daughter. His elder daughter stood beside Zafar as stiff as a board, as though the slightest movement might shatter her.

Zafar slowly covered her hand that rested on the table between them with his own, squeezing it and hoping the warmth from his hand would penetrate into her cold one. It took her a few seconds to react, but she lifted her hand off the table and turned it in his, holding on tight as he strengthened his grip.

The transformation in her had been instant. Not five minutes ago, she was giving him words of reassurance no one else ever had before, aside from Murad, though Murad's angle had always been different. He thought he was a robot of his grandfather's creation, when that wasn't quite the case.

With Reshma, there had been no sarcasm or judgement – even though she was well within her rights to give him the old *I told you so* line after his poor performance in front of her cousins. Instead, she had listened to him and offered her softness in return, her compassion. She'd not offered him empty platitudes but had been gently matter-of-fact and he'd never been more enamoured.

And then Ahsan Mir's children had come around the corner, followed by his wife and then the man himself and Reshma had turned to stone.

After their rounds of photographs, they moved out of the way as other guests came to use the flower wall for the same purpose. His family were heading off when Ahsan looked Zafar and Reshma's way, his neutral expression changing to one of uneasy surprise as his eyes landed on Reshma and then pleasant surprise when they landed on him.

He said something in his wife's ear, who turned their way, gave a brief smile and then carried on after her children, while Ahsan made his way towards where he and Reshma were. He hoped the man wouldn't say or do anything to make Zafar's already stiff neck and tense shoulders any worse. He knew how to be pleasant with unpleasant people, but he had his limits.

'Fancy seeing you here?' Ahsan had a bland smile on his face as he nodded at Reshma and then his smile broadened when he looked at Zafar.

Reshma's shoulders were almost touching her ears and he could sense the tension in her body because her ice-cold hand in his was stiff, her knuckles protruding and pressing into the flesh of his fingers.

'Hey, Daddy.' Her voice was subdued and Zafar tightened his hold on her hand, willing her to relax.

A waitress holding a tray bearing tea and coffee cups moved past them towards the entrance and Ahsan stopped her to take one. He stirred in a couple of spoonfuls of sugar as he looked past Reshma and addressed him.

'Tell me, Zafar, how are you enjoying my sister's hospitality and the wonders of Mombasa? You're having a good time, I hope.'

Zafar came to a conclusion. Before, he hadn't been entirely sure, but now, he was. Absolutely certain. One hundred per cent. He didn't like Ahsan Mir. Not one bit. His initial opinion had been based on hearsay, but now it was based on primary evidence. He'd seen him in action with his own eyes and he didn't like what he'd seen.

Apart from the fact that he'd not stepped up to the plate and cared for Reshma like any loving parent would – personal issues aside – he still acted like she didn't exist, barely looking her way and giving her no attention whatsoever. How could he be more interested in knowing if *he* was having a good time rather than his own flesh and blood?

But his grandfather had taught him the importance of diplomacy, so Zafar gritted his teeth and exercised it. 'I'm having a great time, thanks. Everyone's been wonderful and Mombasa is just as magical now as I found it as a child. In fact, more so now because I have the chance to explore it and see its wonders with Reshma.' He put his arm around her shoulders and pulled her close to his side. Why he felt a need to do that he wasn't sure, but he wanted the man in front of him to acknowledge Reshma.

Ahsan looked her way and smiled, though it seemed strained, before he was looking towards him again. 'I'm glad. She's lucky to have you as a husband.'

What? Was he serious?

First off, what did he know about either of them to make such a statement? And secondly, surely he should be telling Zafar how lucky he was that Reshma was his wife? But, then again, Ahsan Mir was hardly a model parent or one to use as a yardstick. Uncle Jawad filled that role in Reshma's life and he did a spectacular job of it. In fact, Zafar thought of him as his father-in-law more than the man standing in front of him.

'You're wrong.' He felt Reshma's hand come around his back and squeeze him on the side Ahsan couldn't see, probably in warning, but in that moment, his diplomacy disappeared in a puff of smoke, leaving behind raw honesty. 'Between the two of us, I'm the lucky one. But you wouldn't understand that because you don't know how special Reshma really is. For that, you'd have to get to know her, and given that since we've been married, you've not seen her or spoken to her, I don't think you know her at all.'

'Zafar, please. Don't.' Reshma's voice was soft, barely above a whisper.

He looked her way and saw sadness in her eyes, but there was also a sense of resignation and that broke his heart. As though she didn't deserve better. As though whatever it was this man did was OK to ignore. Well, not on his watch.

This was completely out of character for him, but he felt out of character. Maybe it was his own disappointment in himself that lent itself to do the talking. He was usually the level-headed Saeed, the one who smoothed things over, while Ashar was more likely to be found calling a spade a spade in the most colourful language he could. But not now, not in this moment. He felt compelled to speak out.

'Why not, Reshma? He's categorically ignored you since he's been here and seems to believe that I'll be OK with that.' He turned to face Ahsan Mir, his cheeks now taking on a ruddy hue and his mouth pinched. 'I'm not OK with that. If you don't have time for my wife, then I have no time for you.'

Zafar pulled his arm away from Reshma's shoulders, interlinked his fingers with hers once more before turning and leading her away. She didn't pull away from him or say anything as he moved back into the garden, through the archway and into a now empty dining area.

He let go of Reshma's hand and went to the drinks table, pouring himself a glass of water and drinking it in one go, before refilling it and another one and taking them to where Reshma stood. She still looked wide-eyed, but there was a hint of colour returning to her cheeks.

'What was that?' Her voice sounded dazed, like she wanted confirmation of what had just happened.

Frustration and annoyance were still coursing through him. Some of it was at himself, but a great deal of it was at the way Ahsan had behaved – or not, depending on your point of view – with Reshma. 'That was me politely giving that man a very small piece of my mind. He deserved a lot more than what I dished out, I can tell you.'

'Why would you do that?'

Zafar looked at her, his expression now likely just as dazed as hers. 'Is that a serious question or a rhetorical one?'

She shook her head, taking a sip from the glass he'd handed her before licking her lips and speaking in a tone full of resignation. 'You shouldn't have said anything.'

'Please tell me you're not upset with me for saying what I did to him?'

She put her glass down and lowered herself onto the bench attached to the picnic table. 'I'm not upset with you. I'm not upset, angry or annoyed with him either, believe it or not. He's doing what he's always done, there's nothing new there. And while I . . .' She let loose a weary sigh, lifting her shoulders and dropping them in time with it. She looked up at him with a tired smile on her face. 'It's my cousin's wedding, Zafar. Auntie Ruqayyah and Uncle Imtiaz have gone to a lot of effort to put this wedding together and having a moment like that with a man who doesn't give two figs about the matter you brought to his attention has the potential of ruining things for the people who are very dear to me.'

He ran a hand through his hair, his frustration still at its peak, though her words had got through to him. He understood exactly where she was coming from, but his irritation at Ahsan Mir wouldn't ebb away. 'I was annoyed, Reshma. I couldn't bottle it up right then. Since he's come here, he's not exchanged more than a casual greeting with you and walks around without a care in the world and that bothers me. You being ignored by him bothers me. You being upset bothers me. Him having treated you the way he has throughout your life fucking bothers me, Reshma.' He was breathing harshly as he stood in front of her, his fists tightly clenched and his back teeth grinding together hard enough to make his jaw ache as he looked her way. He didn't make it a habit to swear in front of her, but his emotions were running so high, it had slipped out.

She looked at him intently for a loaded minute, her expression giving nothing of her thoughts away. 'Why?' She whispered the word, but he heard it clearly, despite the noise filtering through to them from the party.

If any of his family members were to hear how he'd behaved, they'd never believe the person telling them the story, it was so unlike him. He normally de-escalated situations, dealt with things logically and rationally. Smoothing things over until all parties were in agreement. His grandfather had always emphasised the importance of knowing the difference between honey and vinegar and knowing when to use one over the other. But this evening he'd been led by his emotions and lashed out at a man he barely knew but disliked intensely. And Reshma's question was perfectly valid. *Why?*

The sound of footsteps close by had both of them looking in the direction of the party and they found Uncle Jawad making his way towards them. His usual jovial smile was in place as he looked at him, but as soon as his gaze landed on his niece, Zafar saw his expression change.

He came to a stop beside Zafar, his gaze honed in on Reshma. 'Pet?' He tilted his head to the side in question.

'I'm OK.'

'Sure?'

She nodded in response, but her uncle didn't look convinced.

'Auntie Mumtaz was wondering where you two had disappeared to. She doesn't have a set of keys to your villa, so she just wanted to make sure you've not decided to duck out of here without giving her a set.'

Uncle Jawad looked his way, one eyebrow held higher than its twin.

Zafar exhaled loudly before admitting what had happened. 'I had a go at your brother for ignoring Reshma and I don't think she's best pleased with me for it.' He blurted the words out and was rewarded with wide eyes from both his wife and her uncle, though their expressions were slightly different. Reshma was wide-eyed in horror, while her uncle looked wide-eyed in surprise.

They stood in silence for a few minutes, Zafar wondering how Uncle Jawad was going to react. He might well give him an earful. It was his brother at the end of the day and Reshma's father. Maybe he should have held his tongue after all. Just answered Ahsan's superficial questions and left it at that. But the thought of doing that didn't sit right with him.

Uncle Jawad stuck his right hand out towards him and Zafar stared down at it as if it were a snake, before tentatively clasping it with his own. The older man gave it a firm shake. 'Well done, son. You've done something I've never felt in the position to be able to do.'

'What?' He and Reshma spoke at the same time, but, again, the expression behind the word was different for both of them. She sounded shocked as she stared at her uncle, while Zafar was curious.

Uncle Jawad shrugged his shoulders like a belligerent teenager, and at any other time, Zafar might have laughed. 'I know he's my younger brother, but you're his daughter. I never felt it was my place to tell him how to parent you, but maybe I should have. Maybe if I had spoken up earlier, things might not have got to where they are. Who knows? But Zafar doing it is different. He's speaking on behalf of his partner because he doesn't like how she's being treated. That's a good thing, no?' He looked Reshma's way as he asked the question.

She returned his look blankly, didn't say anything.

'Answer me this, pet. If someone mistreated him,' he pointed at Zafar, 'would you say something? Do you feel anything when you can see everyone demands a piece of Zafar and he gives it to them without batting an eye or giving any thought to himself and his own needs?'

She looked at Zafar and he in turn looked at her uncle. It was uncanny how the conversation he'd been having with Reshma before her father had turned up was linked to what Uncle Jawad was saying.

Unaware of his thoughts, her uncle carried on speaking to her. 'Do you remember when my mother was unhappy with me for bringing you home?'

Reshma nodded, her bottom lip pinched between her

teeth, making him want to run his thumb over the indents she was making on it.

'What happened that day, when without any thought to the fact that you, Niya and Sho were in the room, your grandmother was grilling me?'

'Auntie Bilqis stopped her.'

'Exactly. She could easily have let me get roasted, it was my own mother and we might have told Bills to butt out, but she didn't care. She wanted to stand by me. Is that not what Zafar has just done?'

Reshma looked at him and nodded, the emotions swirling in her eyes making him itch to take her into his arms.

'And, aside from all of that, calling BS on something that is categorically BS is not a bad thing and something perhaps we should all do more of rather than pretend it's not happening or that it's OK.' Uncle Jawad shook his head, as though coming to some conclusions of his own and in the next moment, his expression changed and he was smiling at them once more. 'Right, are you two coming back inside or calling it a night? If it's the latter, I'll need a set of keys for your grandmother, son.'

14

Reshma

'Is there a reason you're frowning and not fawning over me? We get one afternoon to ourselves amid all the pandemonium and I feel like you're not giving it the reverence it deserves.' Haniya aimed popcorn into her mouth, tossing it inelegantly and trying to catch it in her mouth. If Auntie Bilqis were to see her, she'd hit the roof.

Haniya had come over to Reshma's villa to spend some time with her, while Daadi, and Auntie Bilqis were at Auntie Ruqayyah's villa going through some more last-minute discussions about the wedding, i.e., a chinwag with tea on tap. Uncle Jawad, Zafar and Shoaib had gone somewhere together, Shoaib only saying it was a guy thing when asked where they were off to.

Reshma had been sitting at the table working when the doorbell had rung and Haniya had made her way inside, holding her laptop and a bag full of snacks. She'd harassed Reshma until she'd stopped working and now they were sitting on the sofa, trying to decide what to watch but struggling to choose. By the time they decided, the others would probably be back.

While Haniya had been flicking through the various titles on whichever streaming service she had moved on to, Reshma's mind flicked through the events of the night before. Namely, the way Zafar had sat there, calling himself a failure and then, in the next moment, not only had he physically supported her when she'd witnessed her father playing happy families in a unit she wasn't a part of, Zafar had gone further than that and actually spoken up on her behalf against her father, rendering the other man speechless. Then he'd taken her hand and walked away from him without a backward glance.

Reshma hadn't known how to react. She hadn't known what to say or do in the face of such defence on her behalf. Especially from Zafar. It had touched her, no doubt about it, but it had also added to the tumult of feelings she was going through because of him.

There were so many different emotions and resulting contradictions to try to figure out. Reshma wondered how much of what was happening she could attribute to time and place. Was it being here – somewhere different and exciting, away from normal life – and the fact that she and Zafar were spending extensive periods of time around each other? Back at home in London, that had never been the case. People saw them as a couple here, whereas at home people saw them as Zafar and Reshma.

There was also the major factor of Zafar's work to consider. At home, his work consumed him. That's what he did with over ninety per cent of his time, maybe even ninety-five. Here he didn't have that. But did that mean that when they got back, things would go back to how they were?

'Hellooo? Earth to Reshma? Do you copy?' Haniya threw popcorn at Reshma's head with each word she spoke.

Reshma stuck a cushion in front of her face to shield herself. 'Grow up, Niya! And you're going to clean this mess up yourself.'

'Well, it's good to know you're back with me and not away with the fairies. So,' she closed her laptop and turned on the sofa to face her properly, her legs folded under her and her head resting on her hand as she propped her arm against the backrest. 'Talk to Niya. What's bothering you, child?'

Reshma groaned as she pressed the cushion onto her face, making it sound like a suppressed scream. 'Am I that obvious?' She lowered the cushion and stared at Haniya the bloodhound.

'To me? Yes. To others . . .' She shrugged her shoulders and tossed more popcorn into her mouth. 'Uncle Ahsan? Or his family?'

'Partly.'

'O-K. And the rest of it . . .?'

Reshma blew out a breath through her mouth and her lips juddered with its force. 'Zafar.'

'Ah.' Haniya moved the popcorn away and made her way to the kitchen, pulling two mugs out of the cabinet and setting them in front of the coffee machine.

She brought two steaming mugs back and took some chocolate-covered biscuits from her snack bag before settling in the same position and then eyeing Reshma with interest.

'I'm ready now. Talk.'

Reshma burst out laughing. 'You're such a joker.'

'What? I'm serious.' Reshma wiped tears of laughter from her eyes. 'Well, at least you don't look as morose. Glad I could put a smile on your gorgeous face. Now, tell me what's going on in that overactive imagination of yours.'

Reshma groaned again, but softly this time as she reached for a biscuit and her coffee.

'So, you know how everyone seems to think that Zafar came here to surprise me?'

'Uh, I was there. In fact, we travelled together, so I know he came to surprise you.'

Reshma shook her head as Haniya looked at her in confusion. 'That's not what it was. He was forced to come out here by his dad.'

She went on to tell a wide-eyed Haniya what she had discovered the morning after Zafar's surprise arrival.

'I sensed that there was something up with you that morning when we were getting our nails done, but I couldn't put my finger on it. I put it down to my own jet lag.'

'Yeah, not quite.'

'He didn't want to come. Huh. But why?'

'Because he wasn't interested. His work and his commitments back home were more important to him than coming out here for a wedding with me.' She experienced a wave of the old feelings of disappointment, though this time, in contrast, she also thought about his behaviour with her over the last few days.

Haniya frowned at that. 'That's not the impression I get.'

'You asked why he didn't want to come and that *is* the reason he didn't want to come. Except now, it's different.'

'How so?'

'I don't know.' Reshma wasn't sure how to articulate her thoughts and tell Haniya what was going through her head. She could barely make sense of it herself. 'Since we've been married, I've got the bare minimum from Zafar. He's never been unkind or uncivil, but then he's not like that with anyone. But we've never established the connection I wanted with him. The connection I've seen between Uncle Jawad and Auntie Bilqis, or now between Saleema and Nomaan.'

'I have to say, I was surprised he didn't know you liked Italian food. I let the sniffling thing slide because I thought maybe he's never sniffled in front of you.'

Reshma grinned at that. 'Zafar's not a sniffler, and thank God for that. I'd have gone batshit crazy.'

'Grounds for divorce if you ask me. *Sorry, Judge, he sniffled too much and wouldn't blow his nose.*'

They both giggled before Haniya sobered and looked at Reshma closely.

'He seems different out here, though. And maybe this was exactly what your relationship needed. Time and space. Don't forget, you two hardly had a chance to get to know each other and forge a connection before you got married. Things like that don't happen overnight, or even over a year. And, to be fair to him, anyone can see that despite Uncle Nasir being there, it seems like the entire weight of the Saeed family sits on Zaf's shoulders, and that includes their family business.'

Reshma rested her head back against the cushions, her mind going over what Zafar had said to her last night. She'd come to that conclusion herself too. There was a great deal of pressure on Zafar, and no matter how capable he was, he was a human at the end of the day and with all those balls he was juggling, it was inevitable that he'd struggle to keep each and every one in the air.

It was just her luck that the ball he had dropped was their relationship.

But he'd picked it up and was now giving it the attention he hadn't so far and he'd proved how much he cared when he'd stood up for her to her father. The man who was the poster boy for uninterested.

'He's different now without any of those responsibilities demanding his immediate attention, but what about when we go back home? What if it's the time and place that's making him say he wants things to be different between us? What if when we go back and all those responsibilities are there, we fall back into the same groove? I can't carry on like that, Niya.'

'Reshma, darling, no one can offer you a guarantee on that front. That being said, I think you're being a tad unfair on him and you're jumping way ahead. Rewind a bit. You said he apologised to you and he wants things to be different. Surely that's a great starting place? If he really wasn't interested, or if his work was really that much more important, wouldn't he have left when you told him he could go back?'

Reshma plucked another biscuit out of the packet and nibbled on it. She ate in silent contemplation, letting all the thoughts bounce around in her head, along with her inner demons and insecurities. She wanted to believe positive things, but her experience had set her default at negative, making her doubt herself before she did anything else.

'I don't know. I honestly don't know what to think or believe anymore. My brain is going through phases of going blank and then remembering everything but seeing it through a distorted lens in which everything looks negative, except when it comes to *our* family. You know Auntie Bilqis gave me your grandmother's jewellery?' she said, going off on a tangent and making Haniya blink owlishly for a moment before she smiled at her, as though she'd known the plan all along.

'You know *our* Naano thought of you as her grand-daughter just as much as she did me. She'd be happy for you to wear her jewellery and I'm more than happy for you to have it. Mum is over the moon about passing it down to you, what with you being her favourite.' There was no censure in her voice or resentment. Just affection.

She shuffled closer to Reshma, clasping her hand with hers. Reshma rested her head against her cousin's shoulder, who was more like a sister to her, and Haniya rested her head against Reshma's.

Reshma swallowed the lump in her throat at Haniya's words, determined not to cry. 'I can't help it, Niya. I want to believe that I deserve love and attention and someone who cares as much as anyone else, but I can't help but feel that it won't happen, or that there are strings attached, or that it'll be short-lived. The only people I don't feel that with are Uncle Jawad and Auntie Bilqis.'

'Uh, rude.'

Reshma tutted as Haniya sniggered. 'You know that includes you. And even though Auntie Ruqayyah has been amazing, the fact that she lives here and we live in London puts a natural distance between us, though I feel the same way about her when we're together too.'

They sat in silence for a few minutes, Reshma soaking in the comfort of nearness from the cousin who'd accepted her with open arms when Uncle Jawad had taken her home to stay with them permanently. Not once had she resented Reshma's presence in their lives and neither had her brother Shoaib, treating both Haniya and Reshma with a little bit of love and a great deal of tolerance, as brothers were wont to do.

'Permission to call a spade a spade, please?' Haniya said cheerily and Reshma laughed at her question.

'Like you need my permission. And that phrase has always confused me. Why a spade? Why not . . . I don't know' – she grabbed the bottle that had been on the side table next to the sofa – 'a bottle. Let's call a bottle a bottle.'

'O-K. I think you really might be losing it, so I'll say what I want to say while there's still an active brain cell between those ears. What happened between your parents isn't on you.' She untangled herself from Reshma's side and turned to face her. 'I'll repeat that for the brain cells at the back. What happened between your parents isn't on you. And after Auntie Hafsa passed away, whatever Uncle Ahsan did isn't on you either. All the crap you've seen as a child is something no adult should have to deal with, so the fact that you went through all that as a kid sucks, but none of those things were because of you, Reshma. You are amazing and more deserving of love than anyone I know. But you need to stop considering it a favour when you are on the receiving end of it. You act like someone's attention is a great favour they're bestowing upon you.'

Reshma wrinkled her nose, but she couldn't refute what Haniya had said. She knew that deep down that was how she behaved in most of her relationships.

'I'm both surprised and glad that you said what you did to Zaf. He should definitely have made a better effort over the past year and it's kind of disappointing that he hasn't, but that doesn't mean you should ignore any effort he makes hereafter. Sure, don't go all in, but don't keep him all the way out either. Not unless that's what you want deep down.'

Reshma groaned. 'I don't know what I want deep down. And can you stop being so mature and wise right now.'

'Is that what you really want?'

Reshma dropped her head on the cushion in her lap so her answer came out muffled against it. 'No.'

'Yeah, I thought as much.' Haniya went quiet for a couple of minutes before speaking again, her voice gentle. 'Deep down, you want to believe in love. You want to be that special person for Zafar and you want him to be that special person for you, but you're too scared to say it out loud and commit to it fully because you're afraid you'll be rejected by him like you have been by various other people in your life before.' Reshma sucked in a breath as Haniya really called a spade a spade. 'And wanting that doesn't mean that what you have with us isn't enough for you. Wanting something with Zafar doesn't negate what you have with us, it's different. You need to allow yourself to go all in, Reshma darling. But if you want to make Zaf work for it, then there's no harm in that,' she said with a cheeky grin and a wink.

'What if I go all in but he—'

'Don't think like that, Reshma. Give the guy a chance. I accept that you two didn't conventionally choose each other, but Mum and Dad saw something in him, which is why they introduced him to you, otherwise they wouldn't have. I reckon you both liked something about each other to go ahead and get married, so trust that.'

Reshma wanted Haniya's words to be true, she really did, but she couldn't help that sense of fear from making its presence felt. That inner gremlin that told her that when it came to the crunch, Zafar wouldn't choose her. He wouldn't be there for her like she wanted or needed him to be. She couldn't help the voice coming from deep inside her that told her that she hadn't been good enough to heal the rift between her parents. The rift that had ultimately led to her mother's demise. She hadn't been important enough for her father or her mother's parents. In times of weakness, the inner voice also told her that she'd been a necessary burden on Uncle Jawad and Auntie Bilqis, they'd had no choice but to take her in.

It stood to reason, then, that Zafar might also consider her an obligation, or a responsibility he had to bear but didn't want to. Who was there in her life that had chosen to be with her with no responsibility, no obligation, no promise? All she had ever wanted in her life was for that sense of belonging, that sense of being a part of something that would be incomplete if she wasn't there, and she didn't feel that way about any relationship in her life. As much as she loved her uncle and aunt, she wasn't supposed to be with them. It was their kindness that had led to them making her a part of their family.

'Be honest, Niya, do you think I'm ungrateful? For wanting to belong to a dynamic organically?' Haniya's face reflected the seriousness Reshma was feeling. 'Uncle Jawad and Auntie Bilqis took me in and treated me no different to you and Shoaib, but I wasn't supposed to be with them, was I?' She laughed, but the sound held no mirth. 'God, if they ever heard me, they'd be devastated, wouldn't they? They'd hate me.' She covered her face with her hands as her thoughts spiralled.

Haniya grabbed both of Reshma's hands in hers. 'You are not ungrateful, Reshma. I understand what you mean, though I'll never truly appreciate it because only someone in your position would understand exactly what's going through your mind. It doesn't make you ungrateful and my parents could never hate you. Believe it or not, I think they'd understand what you're saying as much as, if not more than, I do.

'All these thoughts are going through your head because the last few days have had you questioning everything since you found out about Zafar and because Uncle Ahsan has turned up with his family. And I don't think it's a bad thing to allow these questions to crop up. What's not great is if you let them consume you or answer them with that negative narrative of yours. Dust the negativity off, be bold and be brave. Give this a go. Besides, technically speaking, he's on your turf. Make him work for your affection.'

Reshma looked at the glint in her cousin's eye and felt

a flicker of confidence. Haniya was right. She needed to be bold and brave and let Zafar do what he had assured her he wanted to do. If he wanted to right his wrongs, then she would let him and, in the meantime, she would guard her heart from any further risk by keeping it locked away. She didn't have to put it on the line. She didn't have to fully invest in anything until and unless she wanted to.

She allowed a corner of her lips to lift. 'You're devious, Niya, but I happen to like your brand of deviousness. Let's see what he does over the coming weeks. Not that I'm going to say anything to him. If I see a genuine effort, then I might give it a chance.'

'Otherwise?' Haniya lowered her eyebrows in consternation.

After a loaded moment of silence, Reshma shrugged her shoulders, leaving the question unanswered.

15

Zafar

It had been just over a week since Zafar had been in Mombasa and at times it felt like he'd been there for ages and at others it felt like he'd just got there. It was strange, to say the least. He couldn't remember when he'd last had this much free time and while he felt more relaxed than he had in a long time, he felt guilty for sitting there and not doing anything productive.

His grandfather had always loathed idleness, and instilled those sentiments in Zafar, pushing him to use his time wisely because only a fool squandered such a valuable commodity. Zafar had never stopped to think on those words or challenged them, but now, as he gave them thought, he could see that it was a very harsh way of thinking, that put no stock in pausing, or resting the mind and body. Or sharing the smaller moments with loved ones or pursuing hobbies and pleasures a busy schedule didn't allow for.

With that thought in mind and no wedding-related plans for the day, Zafar decided to do something different with his day. His grandmother thought his idea was perfect, though she wasn't up for joining him, saying she was going out for lunch with her friends. He just had to see if Reshma was up for it.

He found her in their bedroom, folding a basket of her clothes.

'What's the plan for today?'

She looked his way as she folded a T-shirt. 'Laundry first and then I'll see if Niya or Saleema want to do face masks.'

'The mask that makes you look like something out of a horror film? It's just got eyes and a slit for your mouth and nose.' Zafar shuddered.

Reshma stared at him open-mouthed, the kameez in her hand forgotten. 'I do not look like that. So rude!'

He grinned at her. 'You don't see yourself with it, sweetheart. You struggle to talk properly with it as well, adding to the weird factor.' He bit the inside of his cheek as he saw Reshma pause, her cheeks tinged pink.

She finally came out with, 'It makes my skin glow.'

'You're already beautiful. If you look any prettier than you do, Romeos like your little friend Haroon will be harder for me to fight off.'

Reshma looked at him with wide eyes. He had no idea where that had come from, it had been completely off the cuff and he could feel his own cheeks going warm.

He cleared his throat and rushed through what he had initially come up to ask her. 'Would it be possible to postpone any plans? I thought we could do something today.'

Her eyebrows knit together as she resumed folding her kameez, her hands not as steady as they had been moments earlier. 'Such as?'

'It's a surprise.'

'I'm not sure how I feel about surprises anymore, Zafar.' She was very matter-of-fact and he didn't blame her.

'It's a good surprise, I think. And if you don't agree, I'll . . . I'll do one of those scary masks with you. But I'm counting on you to be honest and tell me if you genuinely like the surprise.'

'You'll do a face mask?'

He nodded and though she looked sceptical, she agreed. 'OK, fine. Do I need to do anything?'

'Just get into comfortable clothing to go out in. Jeans and a T-shirt will do. And boots or trainers. I'll see you downstairs when you're ready.'

She joined him half an hour later, dressed appropriately for what he had planned. He led the way towards the car and, once they were both settled, the driver silently put the car in drive and moved off, Zafar having already told her where they were supposed to go.

'Can I have a clue? Please?' Reshma turned in her seat, as much as her seat belt would allow, and gave him a pleading look before looking around her to see if she could figure out where they were going.

'Hmm, a clue.' Zafar folded his arms and lifted a finger to tap his chin as though he was giving it a great deal of thought. He was happy for them to be on neutral ground where there was none of their usual baggage and they could be a more relaxed version of themselves. 'Ah, I know. There will be sand and I think there might also be a body of water, but it's not the beach.'

She scowled at him before turning to look out of the window on her side again and Zafar laughed. She could be really cute when she wasn't conscious of what she was doing. In fact, she could be downright grumpy sometimes but he found it endearing. It made him want to be even more cheerful around her.

'It's a surprise, Reshma. I want you to enjoy it.'

It didn't take long for the driver to pull into the car park of their destination, and after Zafar had confirmed their pick-up time and place, she left.

Reshma was reading the board welcoming visitors.

'An animal sanctuary?' She turned to look at him, her eyes wide and excited.

'You can't really come to Kenya and not experience some of their wildlife, right?'

Her smile was bright and beautiful as she nodded in agreement and closed the distance between them, though there was enough of a gap that they weren't touching. 'This is amazing. A wonderful surprise. Thank you.'

Zafar felt his stomach somersault as Reshma directed her smile fully at him. He'd put that pleasure on her face and he felt ten feet tall for it. He also felt a sense of peace lodge itself in the vicinity of his heart at putting a smile on her face, where a handful of days ago it was he who had caused the tears in her eyes. That wasn't to say that all his crimes were atoned for, but it was a start.

'Don't thank me just yet. You might not enjoy it.'

She shook her head. 'Even if I don't enjoy it, thank you for thinking about doing this. I appreciate it.'

God, why was she letting him off so easily? This was nothing compared to the fact that he'd practically ignored her for as long as he had. She should put a bulk order of humble pie in for him, but instead, she was showing him open appreciation and gratitude for the simplest gesture. She really was something.

'OK, which way?'

Zafar smiled as he spread his hand out for her to precede him, where, hopefully, her second surprise was waiting for her.

They turned the corner to the main reception area of the animal sanctuary and there stood Haniya, Shoaib, Khalil and Saleema.

Haniya and Saleema shrieked, 'Surprise!' when they saw Reshma and she joined in with their hollering as she ran the short distance towards them.

'No way! What are you guys doing here?'

'It was Zaf's idea.' Shoaib gave him a high five which became a back thump as he spoke and Khalil did the same. 'He suggested we all come out here today, but he sent us ten minutes before to surprise you. Said you could do with a pleasant surprise, whatever that means.'

He saw Haniya waggle her eyebrows at Reshma and she rolled her eyes in return. Zafar had no idea what that meant, but she looked happy and that's all that mattered. Initially, he had thought just he and Reshma could go out. The two of them could spend the day together. But then he realised that involving her cousins would make the trip a lot more special for her, so he'd run his idea past them and they'd happily agreed. He wanted it to be just the two of them, but more important than that was the need to earn Reshma's trust and do what would make *her* happy. He was glad he'd made the right call.

'Right. I've got all the details. I think the nature walk will be best because we can take it at our own pace. There are rangers throughout the sanctuary to help and they said walking the trail is a great experience, though it can be done in a car too.' Saleema handed maps out as she spoke. 'Let's start together and then see how we go. Just make sure no one is left behind.'

She turned and led the way, Haniya's arm linked through hers, and Khalil and Shoaib followed them. Surprisingly, Reshma didn't join the girls and kept pace with him.

'Thanks. Again.'

Zafar shook his head. Again. But responded with a soft, 'You're welcome.'

The smile on her face stayed very much in place as they followed behind Khalil and Shoaib while Saleema and Haniya led the way.

The sanctuary homed a variety of wild animals and visitors were able to walk through their natural habitat. The team leader of the sanctuary had assured him when he'd spoken to her to make the booking that it was perfectly safe to walk around the animals because they had staff members dotted around the sanctuary who were trained in handling them and the animals were used to being around people. None of the animals were carnivorous, so they needn't feel like they were in a *Jurassic Park* film – the safari edition.

They'd barely gone twenty metres when Shoaib paused to take some photographs, and seeing him do that, his sister came and decided to take centre stage just to wind him up. Khalil and Saleema moved ahead, looking at the map in Saleema's hand, and they began pointing in opposite directions.

Zafar grinned as he moved past them. Sibling language was universal throughout the world. If it annoyed your sibling, you did it, it was that simple. He looked back to see where Reshma was and found her crouched beside a tree as she observed the foliage growing at the foot of it, interspersed with what he presumed to be wild flowers.

He made his way back towards her, standing a few feet behind her and letting her take her time as she took pictures of the flowers on her phone. He knew she enjoyed gardening and took an interest in plants and flowers, though aside from some domestic gardening, he'd never seen her take her interest any further.

After a few minutes she got up and turned towards the trail, finding only him standing there.

'The others have moved further up the trail after a bit of obligatory monkeying around,' he explained.

She grinned. 'Harry would have fit in perfectly with this lot. It's a shame he couldn't come too. I'm sure he would have loved being here.'

'That he would have. He's a king mischief-maker but great fun to be around. Everyone loves him.' Zafar couldn't stop the pride he felt when he spoke about his youngest brother. Harry was nine years younger and at times Zafar felt more like an indulgent parent than older brother. Maybe because Harry had tended to come to him with anything and everything when he'd been a little boy and the others had no patience with him, while he had all the time Harry needed, much to his grandfather's displeasure.

Let the boy go to his mother. You must stop babying him, Junior, and concentrate on your own responsibilities. Funnily enough, that was one of the areas in which Zafar had always gone with his instinct and taken care of his brother.

'Not as much as you do though. Anyone can see how much you dote on him and he on you.' He turned and looked at Reshma, her voice pulling him away from his thoughts, which had been swinging more and more towards the nuggets of *advice* his grandfather had given him, seeing some of them in a new light.

'I do. But so do you.'

She agreed readily. 'Absolutely. He's the little brother I never had. He welcomed me into your family with open arms and zero judgement or expectations.'

Zafar's smile slipped as her words hit him. His baby brother seemed to have more wisdom and maturity when it came to Reshma than he did. And yet most people thought he was the smarter Saeed. Just went to show.

'I didn't mean anything by that, I just—'

'It's OK, Reshma. You don't have to justify anything.' He tried to smile reassuringly, even though he felt dreadful. But if he wanted to make his way towards a better place for them, then he had to face his failures and shortcomings head on. It was all part of the process, was it not?

Movement beyond her shoulder caught his attention and he alerted her to it.

'Turn and look behind you. I think those are waterbucks.' He looked at the leaflet Saleema had given him, which had a map and descriptions and pictures of the different animals at the sanctuary. Sure enough, up ahead was a small herd of waterbucks, and not too far beyond that, he could see oryx, their long horns looking like majestic crowns.

It was a unique experience and something completely out of the ordinary for him, if a little daunting, given that these weren't exactly domestic animals one was used to walking around.

Reshma took her phone out and took pictures, as did he, both of them momentarily forgetting their conversation and soaking in the atmosphere and beauty around them.

The animals, as they'd been told, didn't mind humans in their space and calmly moved around, some stopping to have water or munch on the grass. It was both awe-inspiring and humbling, being around such animals in their habitat.

They moved along the trail taking pictures when Zafar's gaze landed on Reshma's side profile just ahead of him as she avidly watched animals walking in the distance. The sun shone on her hair, making it shimmer like a dark jewel. Her cheeks were flushed and loose tendrils of hair that had fallen out of her ponytail framed her face. He trained his camera on her and took a few snaps and then sent her one. He heard her notification chime and when she looked at the message, she turned to look at him, her nose slightly wrinkled but the beginning of a smile on her lips.

He closed the distance between them, slowly walking towards her, her phone gripped in her hand. Her lips were parted. Her tongue poked out and ran along her lower lip before coating her top lip with a sheen of moisture, making

147

his spine and fingers tingle. He wanted to touch her, see for himself if she felt as soft and warm as she looked.

Bizarre really, because he knew what she felt like, but he'd not felt such a deep-rooted need to just touch her before, with nothing else to it. It had always been a functional element of their relationship. But the need, the desire he felt coursing through him now felt different.

Her gaze moved from left to right across his face before slowly lowering to his mouth, her lashes fanning out across her cheeks, their darkness in sharp contrast to her skin. She slowly lifted her eyes to his again and Zafar raised his right hand, his fingers hovering around the left side of her jaw, where tendrils of hair danced in the soft breeze. His eyes were lasered in on Reshma's, looking for the smallest sign for him to close the gap between his hand and her face. Or, better yet, for her to close the distance between her lips and his.

And then she gasped, 'Oh my God! Zafar, look!' Her loud exclamation had him jerking back to attention, finding her gaze fixed over his shoulder. He turned his head, trying to bring all his faculties to order while his brain tried to comprehend the sight in the distance.

A tower of giraffes was gathered not too far away from them and there was a pair of uniformed staff members emptying bags of something into large buckets.

Reshma put her hand on his forearm and moved in that direction and Zafar let her lead him. They made their way closer to the giraffes, watching as one of the team members placed the empty sack to the side under a small boulder, and then hefting the bucket, he held it out. One of the giraffes slowly ambled over – said amble covering a few metres in one step. It looked absolutely magnificent as it covered the distance between itself and the bucket of feed, gently lowering its head and taking a mouthful before rising once more to chew it.

Zafar paused a few metres away from where the feeding was taking place and watched as another giraffe made its way towards the second team member and did the same. Although she'd led them closer, Reshma now stood just behind him, as though she were wary of getting any nearer. She had a hand on his right shoulder as she peered at the giraffes over it.

'How beautiful are they?' She whispered the words in his ear and all his nerve endings went on high alert, his hair standing on end. Warmth emanated from her, permeating through the fabric of his T-shirt and making him feel like the right side of his body was glowing red. He couldn't do more than nod in agreement as he swallowed to ease the dryness in his throat. 'Oh, Zafar, look. There's a baby giraffe. Aww.' Her delight was palpable as she stepped out from behind him slightly to take a closer look and Zafar couldn't help the genuine smile that took over his face.

The calf stayed close to the mother as staff members continued to hold out buckets of feed for the giraffes. One of the staff members spotted Zafar and Reshma watching from a distance and beckoned them over. 'Come. Come and try. They will eat with you holding the bucket if you would like to feed them. They are very friendly animals.'

They moved closer, towards the feeding area, but as they neared, Reshma moved behind him again. He felt her hands hovering around his biceps, as though ready to grab it. As Zafar took another step closer, a giraffe loomed over them, making Reshma squeak and circle his arm with her hands, ready to pull him back.

He placed his hand over hers and looked over his shoulder at her, smiling in reassurance. 'It's fine. I think it's just being friendly. Wants to say hello to the lady and her handsome husband.'

She scoffed and Zafar was reassured that she wasn't terrified, just nervous.

Zafar stepped forward and took the proffered bucket of feed from the staff member and held it out to the giraffe like he was instructed to, Reshma staying behind him, her hands now firmly grasping the fabric of his T-shirt at his waist as she peeked around him at the giraffe.

'It's actually eating.' She whispered the words in wonder, the warmth of her breath tickling his ear as the giraffe lowered its head and took a mouthful of feed.

One couldn't appreciate how large an animal it was until you were standing at a mere six feet and four inches beside its impressive height of almost eighteen feet. Zafar felt a sense of reverence at the wonder that was nature and their place as humans in it.

'Why don't you try it? They're really gentle and happy,' the staff member addressed Reshma, who was still ducked behind him and observing proceedings over his shoulder. Her grip had moved to his shoulder and was tight, making him aware of their positions. She had bunched his T-shirt under her fingers and now that he was focusing on her touch, he felt her other hand around his arm as though it were a source of heat, slowly warming him, one degree at a time. Her touch elicited an awareness in him and he nearly lost his hold on the bucket. He adjusted his grip just as the giraffe lowered its head for more.

Another giraffe ambled towards them and the staff member beside them held out a bucket for Reshma. 'Let me hold it with you. You'll see how friendly they are. They love all this attention.'

She came and stood beside him, still tucked away a bit, and held the bucket with assistance as the second giraffe lowered its head and took a mouthful of feed.

'That's it. See?'

Reshma turned and looked at Zafar, her eyes wide and her smile the broadest he'd ever seen, before she mouthed an 'oh my God' to him.

The experience was truly mesmerising and Zafar couldn't think of another time when he'd felt this relaxed in the last seven years at least. His life had been a series of twists and turns, and while he had some major regrets, coming out here wasn't one of them, even if the lead-up to it and how it had happened was. He was glad that he'd come, he just wished he had done so of his own accord.

The buckets emptied and the giraffes ambled away when there was no more food to be had, losing interest in hanging around. Zafar watched them with Reshma as they regally made their way across the wilderness. He turned and found her staring at the giraffes with a serene smile on her face before she turned that smile on him.

16

Reshma

Reshma placed her napkin on her empty plate and let out a soft sigh of contentment. If a week ago, someone had told her that she'd be looking over the beach with her husband, as the sun set while they had dinner at an Italian restaurant because he'd discovered that Italian food was her favourite, she'd have checked their temperature and asked them if they needed a doctor.

Yet, here she was.

With each inhale and exhale of ocean-scented air, Reshma felt another small piece of her tension from the past ten days wash away and a sense of peace take its place. She couldn't remember the last time she'd felt so . . . relaxed and at ease. That wasn't to say that every aspect of her life had fallen into perfect place. It hadn't, but things were certainly looking up and she felt happier than she had in a while.

Unfortunately, the situation with her father was more fraught than ever after Zafar's confrontation with him, though she'd been on the receiving end of a few acknowledging nods from him whenever she'd seen him. She didn't have a great deal of hope that things would miraculously be perfect between them, she wasn't that naive. But she would have liked . . . Her sigh this time was tinged with sadness, some of her earlier happiness dimming. Maybe she was naive after all. She didn't expect him to start treating her like he did his other children, but some connection would have been nice, she supposed.

On the upside, however, things with Zafar were looking . . . well, up. Reshma smiled at her own thoughts. She felt giddy thinking about it even now, but today had been incredible. It had been one surprise after another and she had loved each and every one of them. Firstly, his idea to go to the animal sanctuary and then to include her cousins when he could have easily let it be just the two of them. It would have given them a chance to spend some time with each other without anyone else around, but he'd involved her cousins knowing it would make her happy, and it had. Very much so.

Spending time with him, talking to him as though they were a regular married couple having a chat had been such a novel experience for her, too. And to top it off, he'd booked a table at a nearby restaurant and this time, it *was* just the two of them. The restaurant was on the beach and with their table on a deck under an awning, the soothing sound of the waves in the background, and sumptuous Italian food, Reshma had felt like she was dreaming.

Because that was what the day had felt like, something out of a dream. They'd watched the sunset as they ate, conversation flowing easily from one topic to another. They spoke about his work, her work, the trip so far and then the conversation moved onto family, except this time rather than discuss her family dynamics, they'd spoken of his.

They'd finished their meal and the waiter cleared their plates and took their order for tiramisu and coffee.

Zafar leaned back in his chair, looking relaxed and handsome as he watched the waves. The setting sun cast a

153

golden glow over him and he looked like he belonged on a magazine cover sitting there. His hair looked lighter, as did his eyes. The stark white of his linen shirt contrasted against his sun-kissed skin and Reshma watched him intently as he swallowed, his Adam's apple moving with the motion, drawing her attention to it and the exposed skin beneath it at the top of his chest.

The waiter snapped her out of her intense focus on him as he placed their items on the table and left. Zafar leaned forward, adding sugar to his coffee and stirring it gently. She zeroed in on the movement, his wrist rotating the spoon rhythmically, almost hypnotically. He pulled the spoon out of the coffee, set it in the saucer and then lifted the cup to his lips, Reshma following each and every movement of his as though she was under a spell.

The cup paused in its tilt as Zafar rested it against his lips and when she looked at his face, he was staring back at her, one eyebrow raised a fraction.

She immediately looked down and loaded her fork with a huge bite of tiramisu and put it into her mouth, eliciting a rumbling laugh from Zafar which warmed her in ways that were completely new to her and making her smile. Well, as much as she could with her mouth full.

'I meant to ask you.' She swallowed her mouthful and tried to get conversation back on track after her *little moment*. 'When was the last time you were here in Mombasa? Or Kenya for that matter? Daadi said you holidayed here often as a child.'

'We did. We used to come out here every couple of years, but once we were mostly teenagers, the frequency reduced. And the last time I was here was six years ago for my cousin Safiya's wedding, though, sadly, it wasn't a happy time for us, because soon after that, our family fell apart.'

Reshma knew of Zafar's cousin Safiya, but no one ever spoke about her and she'd never braved asking anyone about her either. She could hear the sorrow and pain in Zafar's voice crystal clear.

He stared at his cup, his mind seeming miles away, and Reshma placed her hand on his arm and gently squeezed it. 'You don't have to talk about it if it upsets you, Zafar. I wouldn't want that.'

He smiled as he moved his arm and held her hand in his own, squeezing it before letting go. 'I'd like to, if you're up for it? I have to warn you though, it's a long story and doesn't make for pleasant listening.'

She answered his smile with one of her own. 'I'm listening.'

He took a deep breath and then told her about their family dynamic when he'd been younger.

'My grandfather was a traditionalist and had very firm ideas about what he considered to be right and wrong. The margin of grey between the two was very small. My mum was his choice of daughter-in-law so he considered her "right". My aunt – his younger son's wife, that is – was my uncle's choice and so my grandfather never made a secret of his disapproval, though Daadi was more accepting. Personally, I could never understand why he was against the match. They seemed happy with each other. Anyway, my uncle's son, Qais, was born a year before I was and while everyone was happy at his birth, it was nothing compared to the celebration when I was born. In my grandfather's eyes, his true heir had been born. Not only was I a son, I was his eldest son and chosen daughter-in-law's child. And when my aunt then had a daughter while my mother gave birth to another four sons, you can imagine my grand-father's different responses to them.'

Reshma could imagine all too well, sadly. It didn't seem to matter what century they lived in, some people would always celebrate the birth of a son more than that of a daughter and Zafar's grandfather had been of that ilk.

'Anyway, when we were kids, we didn't realise anything was different as such. We all got on with playing and going to school and just being children, but my grandfather always treated us differently. He treated me really well, while he treated the others, especially Qais and Safiya, with less affection. In his eyes, I was the heir, I could do no wrong and anyone who tried to say anything to me would face his wrath, which meant I got off scot-free on many an occasion. Everyone was scared of him.'

'That's dreadful.' Her mind went to her own father and the difference in his approach to her and his other children. 'I can't understand how people can treat children so differently. I know people have favourites, but to treat children like that is so . . . unpleasant.' She would have used stronger language, but she was mindful that they were speaking about his grandfather. The word *abhorrent* felt more apt.

'You can say that again. To be fair, it was only him that did that. No one else was as divisive. As for me, I made sure I always did what he would want or expect me to do. Any praise from him made my day and when it came to him, I didn't even listen to my parents. For me, my grandfather's word was the law. I chose my subjects at school with him, any extra-curricular activities had his approval and if I wasn't at school or with my brothers, I could be found with him.

'As I got older though, I saw his divisive behaviour for what it was. I couldn't understand why he didn't give Qais the time of day as his eldest grandson and treated me as though I was the eldest. There was no question that I was his favourite. Big clue in the name.' He laughed, but the sound held no mirth.

Of course. He was named after his grandfather – Zafar Saeed II. The things he was telling her had Reshma gaping in disbelief. If someone else had told her this story about Zafar's family, she wouldn't have believed them in a million years. Even now, she found it hard to believe. The fact that a man could behave like that and then actually get away with that behaviour. But then she thought of her own father and the way he had behaved and decided that it was entirely possible.

As he spoke, Zafar sounded bitter and resentful, two emotions she would never have associated with him. There was a coldness about him which she hadn't encountered before and it was unsettling. But she wouldn't stop him, she could sense there was more he had to say. Reshma wondered if Zafar had ever said these words out loud. Probably not. Who would he have shared them with? Later, she would wonder at the fact that he felt able to tell her.

'As I got older and started seeing the world through the lens of Zafar Saeed II rather than Zafar Saeed I, I started seeing the reality of what my grandfather had set up, the order he had put in place. But rather than cause any conflict, in my own way I tried to involve those my grandfather neglected – mainly Qais, Saf and Ash. Ibrahim, Rayyan and Haroon didn't really feature because they were that much younger at the time. He treated them like the children they were.

'Even though I was "The Chosen One", I tried not to let it become a thing between me and the others and, to be fair, it didn't. No one knew any better to begin with and when we did, we just went along with the status quo because no one ever went against my grandfather's decree. But once Safiya had graduated my grandfather arranged her marriage with a guy who lives here in Kenya. She told him she wasn't in agreement, but he didn't listen. Daadi and my uncle also tried to get him to change his mind, but he didn't listen to them either. He laughed Qais and Ash out of the room when they tried and so I went to him.'

Reshma swallowed the dryness in her throat, the tension in her gut tightening with each sentence Zafar spoke in the retelling of this part of his family history. She sensed he was getting to a part of this whole tale which had had a deep impact on him.

'Can I get you anything else? Sir? Madam?' The waiter had silently approached the table and Reshma realised that they'd finished their food and it was time to leave.

Zafar paid the bill, thanking the waiter, and they both made their way down to the beach from the restaurant deck, deciding to take a walk back to the villa the scenic way.

The churning in her gut had abated a bit with the enforced break in Zafar's story and with the moonlight glinting off the water and the waves splashing against the sand, Reshma felt some ease work its way into her muscles. She hadn't appreciated how tense she had become sitting there listening to what he had to say. Zafar presented such a perfect front to the world and yet there was a great degree of sorrow hidden within him that he kept tucked away from everyone.

She glanced his way. He was looking down at the sand as they strolled along the beach, his hands tucked into his trouser pockets, the sleeves of his shirt rolled up to his elbows. Going with her gut, Reshma linked her arm through his and, aside from pausing momentarily at the initial shock of it, Zafar kept going, squeezing her arm against his side and holding her close.

It was amazing how in just one day, she felt as comfortable as she did with him. Enough that she was initiating contact. She needed to be careful though, otherwise she'd fall back into old feelings in a heartbeat and that was exactly what she'd promised herself she wouldn't do.

Except, for some reason, she felt completely detached from everything in that moment. From their history, their personal issues and the lead-up to both of them being in Mombasa. It all felt like something that she ought to remember to take into account tomorrow, but for just that evening she could put it to one side and concentrate on them.

There was something about the openness and vulnerability Zafar had shown her that had melted some of her reservations. She wanted to hold on to that for a bit longer and see where it took them.

'You said Safiya's marriage was arranged here in Kenya. Does she live here? Are you going to try to see her while we're here?'

In the silence surrounding them – save for the sound of the water – she heard him take a deep breath and let it out slowly. 'Yeah, she lives in Nairobi. Daadi told me that Safiya might be coming to Saleema's wedding. It turns out that Uncle Imtiaz's mother has some distant connection with Saf's in-laws and they've been invited. There's a chance we might see her. To be honest, that's the only way we'd get to see her. Since her wedding, she's not spoken to any of us.'

'That's such a shame, given how close you guys were.'

'Maybe that's why. I let her down, Reshma. I failed her. Qais, Ash and I fought on her behalf with our grandfather and while he didn't give them any airtime, he tried to reason with me about how it was the best decision for Safiya. In the end, his decision prevailed and it's been six years since we've seen or spoken to Safiya. She refused to have anything to do with the family. After her wedding, when the rest of us went back to London, nothing was the same. Our family broke down and it was . . . it was all my grandfather's fault.'

The words came out in a rush, but Reshma could tell the depth of emotion Zafar felt as he tried to drill it down to basics. His body language told a story of its own. He looked so tightly wound up, she feared he might well snap.

She hadn't paid attention to when her other hand had clasped around his arm so she was holding onto him, their steps slow and measured as they followed the route through the beach back to the villa.

After a few moments of tense silence in which she could hear Zafar's harsh breathing and the drumbeat of her own pulse in her ears, Reshma sucked in a deep breath to try to calm the tension she felt in her chest at what she'd heard. It was in complete contrast to what she had believed about the dynamic of the family she was married into. It was like seeing a hidden dark part of a sunny picture. Something which couldn't be unseen after that.

'If the decision was your grandfather's, why did Safiya stop speaking to everyone else?' she asked gently.

He looked her way, lines bracketed his mouth and his eyes appeared dull and tired in the faint moonlight. He'd run his fingers through his hair and half of it stood up at odd angles, while the other half was still neatly styled as it fell back into its layers.

'Safiya's marriage shattered our family in more ways than one, Reshma.' He huffed out a laugh and its chill made a shiver skate down her spine. 'It shattered lives. Mine included.'

If she could, Reshma would have lowered her eyebrows further, but she couldn't. Her jaw ached from the tension she was holding in it.

'Before that dark time, I used to be the apple of my grandfather's eye. I could do no wrong and I *didn't* do anything wrong.'

Zafar bowed his head as he shook it and then lifted it to look at the sky. The delineation of his jaw showed the tension he was holding in it and Reshma felt her fingers tingle with the need to ease his pain. To put a reassuring hand on that granite-hard jaw and help him find a sense of peace, but she held back, keeping her hands around his arm and willing some warmth into him as he took a deep breath.

He had said it wouldn't be easy listening. She'd just not appreciated how hard it would be for him to say it.

'I tried to reason with him, told him that it was unfair and unreasonable to force Safiya to do something she didn't want to do. She wanted to travel, work, experience life. She certainly didn't want to emigrate, leaving behind everything that was familiar to her for a complete stranger and his family in a country which she didn't think of as home like our grandparents did.

'For the first time in my life, I stood toe to toe with my grandfather. I argued with him. Not just for Safiya but for the others too. I challenged him and, in the end, I lost. I failed my cousins, my brothers and, ultimately, I failed myself. We came here for Safiya's wedding and that was the last time we saw her. When we got back to London, Qais left home and my uncle and aunt moved away too. And on the back of all of that, I walked out of the family business and home and told my grandfather that he could take care of it all himself how he saw fit. I wanted no part of it.'

'You left home too?' Reshma didn't know how, but every new facet of this story was shocking her afresh. It sounded unlike anything she could have imagined, and she'd thought *her* life story had been complicated. 'What did you do? Where did you go?'

For the first time since he'd started telling her about this part of his history, she saw the beginning of a genuine smile on his face as he glanced at her. 'Murad Aziz came to my rescue.' He laughed and this time there was honest humour in the sound. 'I stayed with him for a bit until I found myself a job and then, when I could afford it, I rented a place. Murad and his parents helped me a lot at the time. Of course, I was in touch with my brothers and Mum and Daadi, but my dad didn't want to upset his own dad so we didn't really keep in touch. Though my mum used to tell me that he always asked after me. I lost contact with Qais and I felt too guilty to keep in touch with my uncle and aunt.'

'But you eventually went back home, obviously.'

'I did.' His smile dimmed. 'Three years later. My grand-father's health had declined a great deal in that time and he suffered two heart attacks back to back. Thankfully, he survived, but they weakened him a great deal. He saw his end in sight and wanted to reconcile with his estranged grandchildren. Only one of us responded.'

'You.'

He nodded. 'Me.' He blew out a breath, fatigue evident on his face. Reshma herself felt pretty exhausted. It felt like they'd had a thirty-six-hour day rather than twenty-four. 'He called me and I came back, taking my place as his right-hand man for the rest of his life and doing what he'd always wanted me to do. The crazy thing is, when I saw him, I felt guilty for having done what I did. I saw another person I'd failed.'

Zafar's previous words flashed in her mind like lightning. *I've been a failure as a husband, I'm well aware of that.*

And he hadn't just said it once. He'd repeated himself.

This man, who she thought was infallible, had such a deep insecurity and she'd had no idea. In the past year, she'd not seen a single sign to suggest he felt insecure about anything, let alone being a failure. She'd been pretty quick to point out his lack of interest in her, but how much effort had she made to get to know Zafar on a deeper level? To know what his past was made up of. She'd always assumed he'd had a glorious life, filled with an abundance of all the good things that were on offer to a privileged young man who was loved by all. Not in her wildest dreams would she have imagined the things he'd spoken about this evening. She heard him take an audible breath before he spoke again.

'He passed away a year before we got married. In fact, our marriage was one of the last things he arranged. He'd learnt his lesson with Safiya and didn't force the matter, but I knew it was what he wanted and . . .' He went quiet.

'You didn't want to say no to him. I get it.' She didn't have to like it, but she got it.

Reshma watched him as his cheeks took on a peachy hue. This bit didn't really come as a surprise to her. She knew he hadn't agreed to marry her because he was in love with her or she was his choice of partner. She knew their match had been arranged. She was very much his grandfather's choice – dying wish even – and so here they were. Except for her, it was more than the fact that Zafar

163

was someone her uncle and aunt had chosen for her. She had chosen him too.

All the people in her life that had shown her affection, acceptance and love had been people who didn't have a close bond with her. People like her aunts and uncles, her cousins and Daadi. Those who actually had a closer connection with her were the ones who she was least close to. Where she got the least attention. The least love. Her parents – though her mother had never really got the chance to forge a relationship with her before she'd lost her. But her father had had a chance and had chosen not to take it. None of her grandparents had bothered either.

And then there was Zafar.

Her husband.

The man she'd thought would prove to her that she was worthy of a close relationship, cherish her in a way she had always desired deep down. But that hadn't happened. He had broken her heart and her dreams, and even though she felt the tentative flicker of a connection right now, she couldn't let herself be in the position of opening herself up to more heartbreak. She couldn't and wouldn't let it happen again.

17

Zafar

Zafar pushed himself harder, kicking his legs every other stroke for momentum. He could feel the strain in his muscles as he pushed, but he welcomed the burn because it gave him something else to focus on instead of taking turns in thinking about his turbulent family history or the feel of Reshma pressed against him.

To be fair, between the two, he would prefer to fixate on thoughts of Reshma, but he knew that way lay trouble of a different kind than ruminating on his family history and the pain that struck him anew whenever he thought about it.

The funny thing was, whenever he let his mind wander free with thoughts of Reshma, his thoughts would circle back to his grandfather anyway because he was the one who had chosen her for him. He'd also been the same person to strictly warn him against letting someone become so important to him that she consumed his thoughts. Because if she was consuming his thoughts, then who was taking responsibility for the family or the business? Another one of his grandfather's great life tips.

When his arms began feeling like they were made of lead, Zafar moved to tread water, allowing himself to bob in the Indian Ocean. He'd forgone a swim in the pool today because Daadi had company at their villa. Reshma had come with him and decided to walk while he swam. He saw her now, moving through the shallow waves, their things piled on the blanket they'd spread further up the beach.

He slowly swam towards her and when he was close enough, he began wading through the water, his legs still burning. He got to her and she gave him a shy smile which made his heart skip a beat. Zafar remembered her giving him smiles like that after they'd got married, shy and tentative but hopeful. But then they'd stopped and, the fool he was, he hadn't even realised when that had happened. He'd been too busy focusing on those responsibilities of his instead of on her.

His grandfather had always drummed the importance of focus into him and he'd said that distraction of any kind should be eliminated before it became a liability and Zafar had taken most of his lessons to heart. Except he was now coming to the realisation that not all of those lessons were correct but it was hard work breaking a lifetime of teachings.

They made their way to the blanket and picked up towels to dry themselves off. After positioning the parasol near them over the blanket, Zafar sat down, watching as Reshma patted the towel on her face and then began brushing sand off her bare feet.

The time she had spent in the sun had lent her cheeks a warm glow and he could see faint streaks of light brown in her dark hair. She had a soft kind of beauty that had him wanting to keep looking at her, taking in one feature at a time, like her rosy lips. They were slightly parted as she slowly pressed her lower lip between her teeth, concentrating on the task at hand.

The sensation he'd felt at the animal sanctuary yesterday, when she'd been close to him when they'd fed the giraffes, snaked through him now. He'd felt the same feeling last night when she'd linked her arm with his on the walk home, except last night, along with desire, he'd felt a connection. Unwavering warmth and support. Right now, his desire for her felt stronger. He wanted to replace her teeth with his thumb, press down on the pillowy softness of her lips to see how they felt. His feelings towards her had many facets and he wanted to explore each and every one of them.

She looked up at him, as though he had voiced his thoughts, and stopped biting down on her lip. The way Reshma was looking at him made him feel like she could see inside his head. He hoped not, because he'd hate to scare her off and, right now, his thoughts were unclear to him, so God only knew what she'd think of them.

This reaction he was having towards Reshma was something he didn't know how to deal with. It seemed like more than he'd hoped for, but it also felt like more than he could manage. He had wanted mutual respect, affection. A connection which would mean they'd be together in harmony. This didn't feel as straightforward as any of those things, even if it beat the look of hurt and disapproval she'd had on her face when she'd found out the truth about his arrival and everything had come to a head.

The closest he could come to describe what he was feeling was to call it a strange sort of sensitivity which made him feel like his skin was too tight. He wasn't sure how to handle it, especially when he'd only ever seen feelings like this through the negative lens his grandfather had always used, branding desire and love towards a partner as nothing but a severe distraction and a sign towards the road to ruin.

His grandfather's words swept through his mind. He would often tell him that while it was important to keep your wife happy and make sure she lacked for nothing, it shouldn't ever lead him to forgetting his duties and responsibilities towards everything else. The relationship between a husband and his wife should be one of respect and some level of affection – which was what he thought he was striving for – but feelings like attraction, desire and love were destructive and led to nothing positive.

He'd often give Zafar the example of his uncle, who had married for love but then faced nothing but a lifetime of disappointment and that's what he'd caused others. Now, with the benefit of hindsight and his own experiences, Zafar wasn't sure he could see his grandfather's perspective on the matter.

As time went on, there were more and more things he found his opinions differing on from those of his grandfather, both in his personal life and professional life. And he was finding himself able to acknowledge those differences more vocally, though at times it was with a heavy side of guilt.

But the strange thing was that despite acknowledging these differences, he still found himself missing the man. He still loved him as much now as he did when he was a child, and there were times when he wished he could go to him and simply have a chat, as opinionated as those chats could be.

He could imagine his grandfather telling him to steer clear of the feelings he was beginning to develop for his wife. That they would lead to nowhere good.

Would he ignore such an edict or accept it?

He had rejected his grandfather's way of thinking once. Was it wise to make the same mistake again? Should he ignore his grandfather's teachings that came from his own experiences, which were a lot more than Zafar had? Was it a risk worth taking? What about the cost? Was it unwise to nurture desire towards Reshma like this? He hadn't really thought about the risks. Was he courting danger and potential ruin?

'Zafar?' Reshma squeezed his arm and jolted him out of his thoughts. 'You were miles away. Did you hear me? Look, Niya and Sho are coming.'

He turned to look in the direction she was pointing in and, sure enough, Reshma's cousins were making their way towards them, Shoaib lugging a picnic hamper.

'Surprise! Ha. Seems like a running theme, doesn't it?!' Haniya said as she flopped down beside Reshma. 'One surprise after another.'

'Not really. You messaged to say you're on your way. I told you where to meet us.' Reshma shook her head as Shoaib laid down another blanket and began unloading the contents of the hamper.

Zafar was glad for the distraction after the track his thoughts had taken. His feelings towards Reshma were something he needed to consider with a clear head and with a better handle on exactly what these feelings were.

They spent the next half-hour eating and chatting about the upcoming henna ceremony.

'I'm looking forward to it. Henna ceremonies can be so much fun,' Reshma said as she bit into a large strawberry. Zafar watched as she licked droplets of juice from her lips, leaving them glossy and very much kissable.

The thought had him shifting on the blanket, pulling his gaze away from the sight before him. He'd heard that the eating of a strawberry could be deemed seductive and could send a bolt of desire through the person seeing it and today he could say he'd experienced it.

Completely oblivious of the impact it was having on him, Reshma reached for another strawberry. Zafar suppressed a groan and contemplated going for another swim, even though he was knackered.

'How much time do we have before we have to get back?' Reshma asked as she licked juice off her fingers. Zafar swallowed hard a couple of times, resisting the urge to close his eyes and give his frustration away. In his head, he focused on trying to count back from one hundred.

'We've got at least another two hours before we seriously need to start getting ready. If we go back now, we'll either be roped in to run errands or just get bored. I've got an idea, let's play truth or dare,' Haniya said cheerily.

'What? No!' Reshma didn't even entertain the idea.

'No, Niya.' Shoaib was succinct in his refusal as he lay down on the blanket.

'There aren't enough of us for it to be interesting.' Zafar tried to be diplomatic, but Haniya wasn't having any of it.

'Bock, bock. Bock, bock. Bock, bock.'

'Urgh, someone deal with this woman-child. You need to grow up, Niya.' Reshma rolled her eyes as she took a breadstick through a tub of hummus. The resounding crunch of it punctuating her words.

'BOCK!'

'For God's sake, Niya,' Shoaib groaned.

Zafar kept quiet this time.

'We've got time to kill. Just one round.' She ignored the protests and grabbed an empty fizzy drink bottle and putting it in the middle of the blanket, she spun it with a flourish. It landed on Shoaib, who shook his head, resigned that his sister would get her way, as he sat up. 'Truth or dare, Sho?'

'Argh, she's relentless.' Reshma groaned as she started putting lids back on containers and clearing up the food debris around them. Zafar helped her. He needed more of a distraction from the thoughts that had plagued his mind moments ago and knowing Haniya, they weren't likely to get up until she had extracted her pound of flesh from them.

'The words dog and bone come to mind,' Shoaib griped. 'Dare.'

'Fab. Sing us a song.'

What ensued was one hundred and twenty seconds of hilarity as Shoaib sang a song dreadfully off-key.

It took them a few minutes to recover from that, Zafar feeling his abdominal muscles protesting as he tried to stop laughing. The girls were wiping tears from their cheeks and they only managed half a dozen seconds of silence before bursting into fits of laughter again – Shoaib included.

'Right, my turn.' He spun the bottle and it landed on Reshma.

'I'm not playing.'

'If you co-operate, it'll be over quicker.' Zafar tried to reason with her. 'Trust me, I've suffered at the hands of siblings. They're unrelenting in the extreme.'

'Argh! Fine. Dare.'

Shoaib grinned at her maniacally. 'I dare you to sit in Zaf's lap.'

'Yesss! That's brilliant.' Haniya high-fived her brother like they were both six years old.

The pair of them were beside themselves with excitement while Zafar's entire body went on high alert. He tried to get his tongue to dislodge from the roof of his mouth to intervene before things became super awkward, but the stupid thing wouldn't budge.

Reshma narrowed her eyes at her cousins, enunciating her words slowly as though she were speaking to idiots. 'That has got to be the silliest of dares ever and I refuse to do it.'

'Are you forfeiting then?' Shoaib asked her mischievously.

'Yes.' Zafar felt immensely grateful at her refusal and overwhelmingly disappointed at the same time, the conflict making him grit his teeth in frustration.

'No. You're not allowed to forfeit,' Haniya protested. 'It's truth or dare, so if you won't carry out the dare, then you can tell us a truth.'

Zafar watched the silent exchange between the two women for a moment and then he saw Reshma's shoulders slump as she looked in his direction and he froze in a bid to stop himself from fidgeting, keeping his expression as neutral as he could.

Reshma got up and circled a finger towards his legs. 'Stretch them out, please.'

'No, cross them,' Haniya shouted from where she sat.

Reshma turned, pointing her finger in Haniya's face. 'The dare is to sit in his lap, so I'll choose how. I'm not a child, so I'll be doing it in as ladylike a fashion as I can. Any of our relatives could happen upon us.'

Wordlessly, Zafar stretched his legs out and with her back to him, Reshma sat on one knee, keeping her feet on the ground. He could tell she hadn't put all her weight on him properly and the way she was sitting had her bones digging into him.

She nearly lost her balance as Zafar moved his knees to get more comfortable, until he moved his arm around her waist to steady her as he grunted under his breath. 'It'll be more comfortable for both of us if you sit on both of my thighs. You need to move back a bit. Please.'

From her side profile, he saw her close her eyes, her cheeks going pink.

She got up and Zafar moved so his legs pointed towards the ocean rather than the blanket. He held his hand out to her and gave her what he hoped was a comforting smile.

She placed her hand in his and he closed his fingers over hers, swallowing her petite hand with his much larger one. As she lowered herself onto his legs, he swapped her hand into his other one and his now free hand landed on the small of her back, steadying her as she finally sat back. She was as stiff as a board and that made him tense, though his nerve endings were currently singing songs of praise in chorus at their closeness.

She shifted and he bit back a groan as his thigh muscles twitched. This seemed to be more a test of endurance for him than anything else. Her warm and woody perfume mingled with the scent of the ocean and bombarded his senses as her warmth seeped into his body, warming him in a way the sun had nothing on.

She shifted once more and before it got any worse for either of them, Zafar moved his hand that had been on her back towards her right hip and pulled her up his legs to sit in a more central position. 'There. That's better.'

It wasn't. Not really. Nothing would be better until she got up and he submerged himself into an ice bath to try to cool himself down enough to form a rational thought. What the hell was happening to him? It was like the doors he'd had closed this whole time on any attraction towards Reshma had been flung open and it was all pouring in faster than he could process it.

Reshma seemed to have gathered herself from the awkwardness she was feeling – *good for her* – and moved forward to spin the bottle before moving back again.

Zafar tried to focus on the scene just beyond her, hoping it would slow his breathing and heartbeat down before Reshma noticed either. Getting caught by her while he was losing it would kill him. He tried to concentrate on the waves of the water, the reflection of the sun shining on them, the clear blue sky above it all. But when Reshma flicked her hair back over her shoulder, his gaze went to her. The shell of her ear and the small studs she was wearing. Small droplets of water clinging to her hairline before s-l-o-w-l-y making their way down. The winking of her nose stud, which mesmerised him whenever he looked at it.

He must have moved or made a sound because Reshma turned her face and looked directly at him. Her face was close enough that he could see the tan line along her hairline and the lighter flecks in the dark chocolate of her eyes, fringed by dark eyelashes. There was a faint set of vertical lines between her eyebrows, which slowly deepened as she looked back at him, bringing about an equally faint horizontal line on her forehead.

His eyes went to her lips as she pressed them together and Zafar felt his mouth go dry as his lips tingled, wanting to close the distance between them. He watched her slowly release the clamp on her lips and then they lifted at the corners as she smiled at him, her hand squeezing his. He looked down and belatedly realised that they'd not let go of each other after he'd offered her his hand as she'd sat in his lap. He looked at her beautiful face again, zoning in on the feeling of her closeness and the warmth of her gaze on his, making him respond in kind.

'Ahem.'

Reshma abruptly turned her face, as did he to find her cousins staring at them with utter glee on their faces. Zafar felt her stiffen once more, but it didn't last long. She looked down at the bottle pointing at Haniya and she relaxed again, giving Haniya a sweet smile, which he was sure promised something only the other woman understood.

'Truth or dare, Niya?'

Haniya grinned and chose a dare.

Reshma scowled at her.

Zafar's mind went back to similar antics with his brothers and he had an idea. He leaned forward and whispered it into Reshma's ear, realising too late that doing that was a bad idea. Goosebumps erupted on his skin and he was sure she shivered as he spoke.

She grinned playfully at his suggestion and he felt a sense of pride bloom in his chest to have that look directed his way. He distracted himself by pulling his phone out of his pocket and cueing up a song before handing it to Reshma.

'OK, Niya. Your dare is that you have to stand over there and dance to the song that plays.'

'What? Nooo, that's sooo awkward.'

'Ha. As if I'm going to show you any mercy. Off you go.'

'I swear, Reshma, I'll get you good and proper after this. The gloves will totally come off. I'm warning you.'

'Bring it on, sister.'

The awkwardness lasted barely thirty seconds before Haniya got into what she was doing as they all clapped along, a handful of beachgoers stopping to watch her and adding their applause when she finished and curtsied.

When Zafar had suggested the dare to Reshma, he'd had no idea that Haniya was so good at dancing. He just remembered getting one of his brothers to do the same and then all of them laughing their heads off.

She came back to the blanket and after glaring at him and Reshma, she spun the bottle.

Reshma had completely relaxed now as she sat more comfortably and while he felt like he wanted to shift and get a bit more comfortable himself, he didn't want to move and break contact with her. *Crazy.*

This went way beyond his desire for mutual respect and affection to a different kind of desire and there was an acuteness to his feelings that he was certain he'd never felt before, and while a part of him thought he ought to back away from it all, he didn't.

'Zaf.'

'Huh?' He'd zoned out and hadn't realised that Haniya had spun the bottle and it had landed on him. He looked at the bottle and then at Haniya. 'Hang on a second. That's way too convenient, how can it have landed on each of us so perfectly to complete a round. No doubles at all?'

They all looked at him as though he'd lost his marbles. 'She spun the bottle and it landed on herself so she did it again and it landed on you,' Reshma said softly.

'Yeah, pay attention, mate. Last one and then we can pack up and leave,' Shoaib said as he riffled through the hamper and pulled out an apple.

Haniya smiled as she looked at him. Zafar could see the deviousness in her eyes from a mile off.

'Truth or dare, Mr Saeed?'

He cleared his throat. Dancing on the beach or moving for anything wasn't something he felt capable of doing just then. Especially if it involved Reshma, which, judging by Haniya's expression, he knew it inevitably would. And he wasn't about to be made to serenade Reshma on the beach either. 'Truth.'

That seemed to please Haniya. 'OK, then. Tell us your first memory of Reshma.'

He felt Reshma immediately tense where she sat, her back going straight. His throat went dry and he swallowed hard as he saw Shoaib give Haniya a high five and congratulate her on her choice of question.

'Um . . .' He thought back to when he'd been introduced to Reshma. Both Haniya and Shoaib had been there, but aside from the facts, they wouldn't know what his thoughts had been and that's probably what Haniya was trying to get at. And then, like an animated light bulb switching on in a character's head, his mind went to another memory.

'When Uncle Jawad and Zafar's dad introduced us. Remember? You were there, right next to me,' Reshma cut in.

Haniya merely smiled back at her sweetly, not the least bit intimidated by the scowl on Reshma's face.

'Actually, it was just before that.'

Reshma turned her face to look at him and he watched her frown slowly morph into a look of confusion.

'We were at the same event, I can't remember what it was, maybe a birthday party or something. Anyway, I was in the foyer of this venue, pacing a small section of it while I was on the phone and there was a group of children playing on the other side of it. I didn't realise that while I was walking one way, a toddler had come up behind me and as I turned, he fell back on his bottom. Of course, it was protected by his nappy, but that didn't stop him from sticking his lower lip out and looking up at me in accusation before letting out an outraged wail.'

Much like everyone else, Reshma's eyes were glued to him and he saw the moment the penny dropped with her. Her eyes didn't widen so much as they brightened with the memory and he saw a smile tease the corners of her lips. Her hand, which was still in his, gave a little squeeze and he felt it all the way to his bones.

He had pushed the memory to the recesses of his mind, not so much deliberately, but more as a moment he'd experienced but not thought anything much of until now. Until Haniya had asked him what his first memory of Reshma was. Reshma seemed to have thought it was when they'd been formally introduced to one another which meant that until now, she had perhaps forgotten about it too.

'Oh my gosh, yes, I remember. He was so annoyed with you.' She giggled and shook her head as she joined in with remembering that moment.

'You can say that again. I knew he wasn't hurt, but he bawled as though the whole venue had come crashing down around him.' He turned to face his rapt audience. 'Reshma had come through the main doors and saw what had happened. She crouched down in front of the little boy and asked him if he was all right.'

Reshma laughed. 'It was Auntie Bilqis' great-nephew. I asked him what had happened as I helped him up and he pointed at Zafar with a ferocious frown on his face and called him a bad man.'

'Reshma grabbed his hand and blew a raspberry on it when he showed her where he thought he'd been "hurt" and in no time the pint-sized fraudster was laughing with glee as she carried on blowing raspberries up his arm and then moving on to the other arm. She swung him up in her arms and spun him in a circle and that's when I saw her properly for the first time.'

He'd felt a buzz of something at the time but had dismissed it as a random reaction. He'd attributed it to the moment he'd shared with her and ruthlessly pushed it to the back of his mind, never to be visited again. Until today.

This time when Reshma looked at him, he felt the same sense of awareness, but rather than push it away, he allowed it entry, seeing where it went and how it made him feel. Maybe it was because of where they were, her close proximity, the past few days they'd had or numerous other reasons. He didn't know why and, frankly, didn't think the *why* was important. All he knew was that he was happy to stay where he was and let the feeling have free rein.

'Then what happened?' Shoaib's voice broke through the moment he was having.

Reshma looked away, her beautiful face tinged pink as she looked ahead. Zafar faced the other two.

'She pointed the toddler's finger at me as she held his hand and pretended to tell me off, asking me to say sorry for bumping into him. The little boy pointed at himself in case I was in any doubt as to who the apology was for as he told me to say sorry too. I shook the little man's hand and apologised and that was it. He gave me a toothy smile, wriggled out of Reshma's arms and darted off.'

Zafar remembered standing beside her, watching the little boy run away, then she'd turned to him, a broad smile on her face and a twinkle in her eyes, telling him that he owed her one. He'd thanked her for rescuing him and she'd thrown her head back and laughed, her nose stud sparkling in the light. He'd found her charming, he remembered that clearly now.

He even remembered that she'd said that it wasn't every day she had the pleasure of rescuing six-foot-somethings from someone who wasn't even three feet tall yet. She'd smiled and then walked into the main hall, leaving him standing there watching after her before his silent phone had sprung back to life and pulled him out of that moment.

'Oh my God, I had no idea that you two had met before. I thought your first time was that awkward moment in front of the whole family and I thought it'd be funny to hear you recount that. That's actually a really sweet story. One to tell the grandkids,' Haniya said, her chin resting on her clasped hands.

The tip of Reshma's ear which he could glimpse through the loose strands of her hair went bright red and he felt his cheeks heat at Haniya's words, which was absurd really. They were married, for God's sake, remarks like that were normal, nothing to blush about.

'Right, folks. As wonderful as this interlude has been, we definitely need to head back now. Time to pack up.' Shoaib looked at his watch and then slapped his thighs.

With the late-afternoon sun shining down on the beach, they packed everything up and made their way back to the villas, everyone sporting a smile.

Zafar felt pretty relaxed and he didn't need to question much as to why that was. Being with Reshma without any other obligations, responsibilities or strings attached was giving him a chance to allow their relationship the space to naturally develop, one day at a time. Sure, they weren't in a perfect place with each other and he still didn't have a clear sign from Reshma that she had forgiven him for what had happened, but they weren't in a terrible place either and he'd take that because it gave him hope. Hope that they could definitely have something more than they'd had up until now.

They went to their respective villas to clean up before everyone was due to meet at the garden entrance where the henna ceremony was to take place. Zafar opened the door to the villa and stepped back to allow Reshma to go in first. She placed her bag on the island and turned to face him.

'I had forgotten about that day. Neither of us brought it up after that.' Reshma smiled at him, a happy, open smile, and he felt a sense of satisfaction settle over him to have that honest smile directed his way. One he'd earned and wasn't for show or an audience.

'To be honest, I only remembered it when Niya asked me that question. But it's a good memory.' He moved closer towards her. 'I enjoyed today, even though your cousins like getting up to mischief. Although, it's nothing less than my brothers would do, but I had fun.'

Reshma scoffed. 'Calling it mischief is putting it mildly. But I agree, the past couple of days have been . . . they've been good. And while we're on the subject' – she walked around the island and pulled two glasses out of the cupboard and went to the fridge – 'I wanted to thank you, for making the effort with everyone and being a good sport, even when my cousins are being *mischievous.*'

She came back towards him and held out a glass of juice. He nodded in acknowledgement as he took it, guzzling it down in almost one go.

'You don't have to thank me, Reshma. I'm doing what I should have done all along. And, to be fair, your family make it easy to get along and join in.'

She smiled as she finished her own drink. 'I'm going to go and wash the sand and salt off me and get ready.' Her smile didn't falter and it filled Zafar with a keener sense of pleasure than he'd ever thought such a thing could as Reshma went upstairs.

He needed to clean up too, so it made sense to follow her up, but he stayed where he was, savouring the feeling of success at being in a happier place than he and Reshma had been before. There was a brightness about her that he'd not seen since the early days of their wedding and whereas back then he hadn't paid it any attention, he now felt like he wanted to see what more he could do to keep that brightness intact. He longed to see more of the joyful, playful side of her nature and if that led to more intimacy between them, then he was more than happy to pave the way for it.

The flickering of desire he'd felt today had been unexpected and perhaps unnerving in its intensity but not unwelcome. Sure, before he would have considered it to be something to push to the back of his mind and focus on other things, but that wasn't how he felt today. Today, he felt like going in the opposite direction, to see if the flickering could be fanned into something more that satisfied both of them.

It went against what his grandfather had advocated, but he'd spent the past four years following the path his grandfather had chosen for him, and for twenty-six years before that, and while he still believed in some of his grandfather's teachings, he wasn't so sure that they worked in every aspect of his life. He'd just been hardwired to believe that.

Maybe if he had allowed his own instincts to guide him, he and Reshma might have been in a different place. Maybe when it came to his marriage, following his grandfather's edicts hadn't done him any favours. The moments he'd shared with Reshma proved that, as did his own feelings of contentment and satisfaction.

Of course, he'd always battle the inevitable guilt he carried when it came to his grandfather, just as he had for those three years he'd spent away from him. Sure, he'd believed in his reasons for turning away, still did, but that didn't mean he didn't feel guilty for standing up to his hero. The man who, up until then, he'd always wanted to be exactly like.

Zafar had the feeling that even with his grandfather gone, there was a side that wanted to honour his grandfather's ideals and another that wanted to stand for his own beliefs and principles. And the thing about such a war was that either way, *he* would lose.

18

Reshma

There was a buzz in the air as the events team added finishing touches to the garden for Saleema and Nomaan's henna ceremony, which was due to start in a matter of minutes.

The space was rectangular and large, with a swinging bench in the middle surrounded by chairs so that everyone could see where the main action was to take place.

The sun was on its descent, so while it was nice and warm, there was no risk of sunburn for anyone and for those seeking shade, there was an abundance of trees around the perimeter of the garden, interspersed with small hedges and boxes and pots of colourful flowers and plants.

A small gangway had been cleared between the chairs leading to the bench where the bride and groom would sit for the ceremony, beyond which there were cushions and blankets on the floor for the more traditional folk music element of the evening.

Reshma ran a keen eye over the floral arrangements, which her aunt had delegated to her, knowing that Reshma enjoyed gardening and had a knack for flower arranging. Everything looked exactly how she wanted it to and satisfied that she'd done a good job, she told the event planner that she was heading outside to join the family.

There was no colour scheme to follow for the henna ceremony, though traditionally greens and yellows were the preferred colour combination for the occasion. Saleema hadn't wanted that and with the event being outdoors, Reshma had suggested using an array of different coloured flowers so there was a vibrancy about the place which made each and every colour pop in its own right.

Reshma had got ready for the event before coming to check over the arrangements she'd planned with the events manager beforehand. Auntie Ruqayyah had arranged for hair and make-up artists and Reshma had managed to get ready in record time in order to get to the venue earlier and check that everything was as planned. The events team had followed her plans to a T and she couldn't wait to see what Auntie Ruqayyah and Saleema thought.

'Hey.' The word was softly whispered in her ear from behind, making desire roll down her spine and leave a trail of sparks in its wake, much like it had when she'd been dared to sit on his lap.

Reshma turned and found Zafar standing to the side of her near the entrance to the garden, looking fantastic in his straight-cut trousers and long silk kurta. His hair was slightly tousled, probably due to the soft breeze, and his jaw was clean-shaven. He looked so good, Reshma was tempted to touch him, but she held back, cocking her eyebrow at him instead.

He grinned as he flicked the sides of his kurta out and put his hands into his trouser pockets. She noticed that he'd rolled his sleeves up just enough to show off his forearms. What was it about Zafar's rolled-up sleeves and forearms on display that made her want to keep looking at them?

'I thought you were going to come later with Daadi?' She looked beyond him in a bid to get her errant thoughts under control.

'She's coming with Auntie Bilqis. I was at a loose end, so I figured I'd come and join you, see if you needed a hand with anything.' He looked around at the arrangement and then at her, a big smile – dimples and all – on his face. 'This looks brilliant. You've got a magic touch, you know that? Any event you've arranged has looked spectacular. The set-up you did for Daadi's party last year was fantastic and now this.'

Reshma felt warmth blossom in her chest at the words of praise Zafar was showering her with. He'd never been this effusive before, simply giving her a 'thank you' or 'this is nice' whenever she did anything. Making arrangements for Daadi's eightieth birthday party had been a chance thing because the event planner Zafar had hired fell ill days before the event and Reshma had volunteered to step in, making changes here and there to make everything more to Daadi's taste. At the time, Zafar had given her his 'this is nice' compliment and left it at that. This was the first time he was acknowledging her work with such high praise and it left her momentarily speechless, so she only said, 'Thank you.'

'But you know what?' He took a step closer and lowered his face until it was mere inches from hers, her heart suddenly racing. 'It all pales in comparison to how you look. That little Romeo, Haroon 2.0, better keep his distance today.'

Reshma felt heat suffuse her cheeks and Zafar winked as his grin widened while she blushed. She giggled like a teenager at his compliment wrapped in possessiveness. She knew he was joking, but it made her feel tingly on the inside nonetheless.

She was wearing a peach lehenga with a cream blouse. The blouse had a large bow on the back so the stylist had put her hair up so it could be seen in all its glory. The lehenga had gold print work on it, as did the matching organza dupatta. Peach and cream glass bangles jingled with the slightest movement and her gold and pearl jewellery completed her look.

Zafar took a hold of her hand and held it up as he moved the index finger of his other hand in a circular motion, asking her to twirl.

She did so, unable to stop the laugh that bubbled up her throat.

'This is so silly, Zafar.'

'No, it's not. I want to see you properly.' He twirled her three times, her lehenga flaring out with her movement and brushing against Zafar's legs. When she stopped spinning, he was standing so close that her hands landed on his shoulders, her breasts brushing against his chest. 'You look gorgeous.' His voice was deep and husky, making a pleasurable shiver go through her, which he probably felt because his hands were resting on her waist.

He lifted one hand and gently ran the tip of his index finger from her temple down her cheek, leaving a tingling trail in its wake. Reshma slowly pulled away and felt Zafar pull his hands away from her at the last moment, as if he was reluctant to let her go.

His heated gaze made her feel a resurgence of the desire she'd felt earlier on the beach but had made a conscious effort to bank. With each day, they were making progress in their relationship, but she couldn't help the slight hesitancy that always crept in, keeping her from fully committing herself to what she was feeling.

She was saved from pondering on any more thoughts because the event manager came up to her, smiling. 'I'm glad you're still here. I just wanted to confirm that the caterers are setting up on the paved terrace and we've set up table arrangements there too. We'll serve starters after the ceremony.'

'Perfect. Could you just make sure there's enough space for wheelchair users to get to the tables comfortably and that there are high chairs for the little VIPs.'

'Absolutely.' The manager left and Reshma found Zafar staring at her, a half-smile on his face.

'What?'

He shook his head. 'I just find it amazing how you think of every tiny detail. Who even remembers setting up high chairs at a henna ceremony?'

Reshma lifted her chin playfully. 'I do. It's a nice touch to think of the smaller details. Not that high chairs are a small detail to those who need them. They're a lifesaver, I'm sure.'

He nodded in acknowledgement. 'Is there anything left for you to do now?'

'Nope. We just wait for the others to arrive.'

They didn't have to wait long. Within five minutes, loud voices preceded the arrival of the bridal party. Everyone except the bride – who would make a grand entrance of her own – was there and busy marvelling at how wonderful everyone looked in their finery.

Daadi came up to her and Zafar on Uncle Jawad's arm, smiling broadly.

'Don't my children look especially lovely today, Jawad?' She pulled some currency out of her purse and ushered Reshma and Zafar forward. 'Step forward together and lower your heads. That's it.' She circled the money around their heads a few times and then put the money back in her purse. 'Remind me to give that money to charity. I'm not going to risk anyone casting an evil eye on my children.'

Uncle Jawad stepped forward, holding Reshma by her shoulders. 'My girl looks like an absolute angel today.'

In no time, Daadi pulled her phone out of her bag and demanded selfies with all of them and then had Uncle Jawad taking pictures of just Reshma and Zafar.

He pulled her close to his side in front of everyone and she gasped. They'd never even held hands in front of their families. 'What are you doing?' She spoke through her smile.

'Taking pictures with my wife.' He winked at her.

The comment was simple enough, but the resulting flutter she felt had her thinking that her heart might fly right out of her chest. There was a tenderness in his eyes and smile, his touch and his words, and Reshma wanted to bask in it, but the moment was soon over. Auntie Ruqayyah was ushering everyone inside because Nomaan and his family had arrived and she wanted everyone in place to greet them.

There was much fanfare as the groom arrived and took his place, followed by the bride. Family members surrounded them as they sat on the bench together and Auntie Ruqayyah and Nomaan's mother took no time in getting the ceremony started.

They invited Saleema and Nomaan's grandmothers to participate and then Auntie Bilqis took Daadi up with her. Daadi greeted both Saleema and Nomaan and then put a piece of sweetmeat in each of their mouths. She took a small amount of henna and brushed it on the henna leaf Saleema had rested on her palm and then she did the same with Nomaan. She then smeared a few drops of oil on their hairlines and, lastly, she circled money around their heads and placed it in a platter. All the money collected would be donated to charity.

Auntie Ruqayyah, Nomaan's mum and then various aunties stepped forward to take part in the ceremony and then her aunt called to her and all of Saleema and Nomaan's cousin sisters to come and perform the same ritual, followed by any other guests who wished to join in.

It was a predominantly female-led tradition but lately there had been a shift, which saw some male relatives of the bride and groom join in, which is how Khalil and Shoaib were found in the mix, smearing henna on Saleema's arm instead of her hand and pouring a generous amount of oil over Nomaan's hair after stuffing their faces with enough sweetmeat that they couldn't open their mouths without it falling out, much to some of the crowd's amusement. Auntie Ruqayyah wasn't best pleased.

Once the ceremony had wrapped up with a great deal of laughter and pictures, the guests moved as one towards the dining area, where the catering team were waiting to begin serving the food, while Nomaan and Saleema went back to the villa to get cleaned up to re-join the celebration afterwards.

After dinner, some of the chairs were moved to create a makeshift dance floor and Khalil and Haniya wasted no time in making use of it. The DJ played upbeat music which had people making their way to the dance floor and it wasn't long before Haniya dragged Reshma and Zafar onto the dance floor.

They stood beside each other awkwardly, Zafar scrubbing his hand along the back of his neck, while Reshma pretended to adjust her dupatta, which was exactly where she'd pinned it earlier. Aside from dancing with each other at their own wedding reception, Reshma hadn't danced with Zafar since, and the idea of doing it now had her feeling as though her feet had been encased in ice blocks.

She couldn't move. He appeared to be equally frozen in place and she knew they probably looked incredibly silly, but she still didn't move.

Reshma felt an arm drop across her shoulder and turned to find Khalil standing next to her, though he kept his body moving in time with the music as he bellowed in her ear. 'Allow me to introduce you. This is your husband, Zafar Saeed. You're supposed to be dancing with him.' He pushed her forward, and in her ridiculous high heels, Reshma tottered across the short distance until she felt Zafar's arms close around her waist. Her hands landed on his chest and she felt it rumble as he spoke to Khalil.

'Easy, mate. She could have fallen.' There was a terseness in his voice.

'Nah. You'd never let that happen.'

Reshma looked over her shoulder as Khalil winked and then danced away from them. When she turned her head back, it was to find Zafar looking down at her, his arms still around her.

Gradually, she felt his body relax under her touch and then he began swaying in time with the music. He moved his hands from her waist to her elbows before running his fingers from there to her wrists and then her hands. He held them in his and raised them above her shoulders, bringing her body closer to his as he started moving his feet, making her move with the momentum.

It didn't take Reshma long to start moving her own body in time with the music and before she knew it, they were dancing along to the fast-paced music which was energising everyone on the dance floor.

Her cousins took it in turns to join in before drifting away. Reshma let the music take over her movements, her body undulating with the beat. Zafar was in front of her once more and the smile he sent her way had heat going through her body. As one, they took a step towards each other, coming close enough for her to put her hands on his shoulders and for him to place his at her hips as they moved in sync.

She moved her hands down and up his shoulders, feeling the muscles under his kurta twitch, and when she looked up at him, his eyes were zeroing in on her lips. Instinctively, Reshma ran her tongue across her lips and Zafar's nostrils flared as his gaze darkened. She swallowed the dryness in her throat, rolling her lips in on themselves, and she was sure she heard a growl at the same time as she felt a rumble in his chest under her hands.

The volume of the music faded out and everyone around them gradually stopped moving. She and Zafar did too, but they didn't step away from each other immediately. Reshma felt the tips of his fingers digging into her hips and she could hear that his breathing was ragged. Her pulse seemed to be matching the pace and cadence of galloping horses and she felt warmth pool low in her belly as he continued to look at her.

The DJ announced that the henna artists had arrived and that dessert and drinks were available for whoever wished to partake.

The crowd slowly dissipated, and Reshma took a much-needed step away from Zafar to try to get her senses back under control. Though it had been a short period of time, the intensity she'd felt while on that dance floor with Zafar had her feeling like her adrenaline levels had probably tripled.

As she stepped away from the dance floor, Zafar followed behind her, though thankfully he maintained the gap she'd created. She needed time and space to process the sudden spike in desire she was feeling towards him, and with his closeness bombarding her senses, it was impossible to think straight.

Reshma got herself a drink while she watched Zafar make his way towards his grandmother, checking in with her and making sure she was all right. Reshma decided to take some time out and rest her feet, taking her ice-cold glass of juice with her. She'd not danced like that in so long, she'd forgotten how fun it was but also how tiring when one stopped. She flopped down into a chair and in no time was joined by Haniya, her face shining after her exertion on the dance floor.

She held a glass of her own and drank deeply before sighing. 'That was sooo good. I'm glad you dusted your dancing shoes off and joined us.'

'You hardly gave me much of a choice.' Reshma took a sip of her drink, relishing the cold sensation as it went down her throat.

'Meh. How are things with you? Looking good from where I'm watching.' Reshma knew Haniya was referring to the situation between her and Zafar.

It was looking good from Reshma's perspective too, and that was what worried her a bit. She couldn't seem to shake off the feeling that it was either too good to be true or the other shoe was yet to drop. Either way, she couldn't bring herself to commit to the sense of joy fully. A joy she'd been feeling over the past couple of days.

'Did he grovel any more? Have you kissed and made up? What's the deal? Spill.'

'Take a breath, Niya. Your brain needs oxygen more than you think.'

'Diversion tactics. You might as well tell me because I won't rest until you do. And I won't let you rest either.'

'Jesus, you sound like you belong in a gang.' She knew Haniya wouldn't give up easily. 'He didn't grovel because he doesn't need to. I don't want him to grovel. We've spoken a lot about a lot of things and that's . . . it's helped us. We have a better understanding of each other. It's like you said, we never took the time out to connect and get to know each other before, so doing some of that has helped. We're nowhere near *fixed*, but I think we're in a better place than we were.'

'You think?'

'I know.' Reshma said it with a sense of confidence she actually felt. They were definitely in a better place. She just hoped that the momentum they'd found would keep going even when they got back home and they wouldn't fall back into old patterns. It was still early days, though, and given her history, she was afraid of hoping and having those hopes dashed.

19

Zafar

Zafar thought it would be a good idea to keep some distance from Reshma for a while because he was on the cusp of combusting. It was that simple.

Dancing with her had been a test of his endurance and restraint in a way he'd never been tested. He'd had to remind himself at least a dozen times that he was in a family setting and getting any more hands-on than he had was a b-a-d idea.

He was now sitting beside his wife's uncle – who, thank God, couldn't read Zafar's thoughts, otherwise he'd probably have one meaty paw around his throat in a flash – trying to cool himself down with a third glass of some exotic fruit juice. He couldn't say which because he'd necked the first two glasses like his life had depended on it.

Waiters weaved in and out of people, carrying trays of hot drinks and plates of desserts. Uncle Jawad lifted a plate and was about to tuck into it when his son came and swiped it out of his father's hand. 'You've already had two of these, Dad. I saw you earlier. Here, have a cup of tea instead.' Shoaib pushed a cup and saucer into his father's hand and then plonked himself on his father's other side while he made quick work of the dessert as his sire grumbled. He finished it and then got up to go and get himself a drink.

The party was very much still in full flow and everyone had a smile on their face. The DJ was on a break as Zafar's grandmother and Reshma's aunts entertained everyone with the dholki and folk songs.

Auntie Bilqis used her hands on the two sides of the drum and her sister-in-law used a big metal spoon, in lieu of a drumstick, to hit the top of the wooden side to add to the rhythm. Anyone who knew the lyrics of the songs and wanted to join in did and it didn't take long for the crowd to fall silent and enjoy the performance, many clapping along with the beat.

After the first song, they handed the dholki to Daadi who demurred for a minute before she accepted it. After striking the first beat, her hands flew across the flat sides of the two-sided drum as she provided the music for the next three songs.

Reshma was sitting beside Daadi with Haniya, both of them clapping their hands and singing along. Daadi lowered her head towards Reshma and said something and Zafar saw his wife throw her head back and laugh, Haniya joining in as Daadi waggled her eyebrows at the pair of them.

She was clearly having the time of her life and it filled Zafar with a great deal of satisfaction to see his grandmother so happy. She was mingling with friends, both old and new, and was joining in with all the fun with the same exuberance as some of the younger people in the crowd. She certainly had more exuberance than him.

Reshma also seemed to be in a better place than she had been and that too buoyed his mood. Things were looking promising on that front and he was hopeful that they would carry that momentum home with them, though he was mindful that it was early days and they'd not been put to the test with the addition of his work and family responsibilities.

'Sometimes I wonder . . .' Uncle Jawad's voice broke through Zafar's thoughts and he turned to look at the older man before following his line of sight. He was looking at Reshma's father sitting with his two sons. 'Actually, more often than sometimes, I do wonder about Ahsan. I know he's my brother but . . .' Zafar faced Uncle Jawad, the older man's eyes fixed on his younger brother. He shook his head before looking at his niece and daughter where they sat with their heads together, an indulgent smile emerging on his face. 'At least Reshma doesn't look too affected by his sudden arrival. How has she been?'

He took a sip of his tea and Zafar did the same with his drink, feeling his body temperature come down significantly as he debated how much to tell Reshma's uncle about her initial reaction at seeing her father. He had no idea if Reshma wanted her uncle to know how she had broken down at the beach the day her father had arrived, so he'd have to fly by the seat of his pants on this one.

'She's been as good as can be really. Of course, she was shocked when he arrived, much like everyone else, and there's been minimal contact between them as far as I know. In fact, since my little, erm . . . conversation with him, it's been nothing but the odd hello or an acknowledging nod from him.'

Uncle Jawad shook his head. 'My heart goes out to that girl. She's never come out and said anything to me or Bills, but I know it must bother her. How Ahsan can do what he does, I have no idea. The thought of not having anything to do with Shoaib and Haniya, or even Reshma, makes my blood run cold. They're everything to me.'

Zafar could see the anguish on the older man's face at the thought of not being a part of his children's lives. Even he couldn't understand how Reshma's father did what he did. For all his faults, he couldn't imagine his own father being that way either.

'I still remember the day Ahsan first brought her round. I think she was seven or eight at the time. She was dressed in mismatched clothes and a rucksack half the size of her petite frame was on her back, telling me how involved a parent Ahsan was.' He tsked and Zafar felt a churning in his gut at the thought of a small Reshma being neglected and forgotten about by her only parent. 'He asked me to keep her at the garage while he went to work because he had forgotten that her summer holidays had started and there was no one to look after her.

'For a week, he brought her and the poor thing spent the whole day in this little office we had there, drawing pictures or quietly playing by herself. She hardly made a sound. I could see that my brother's particular brand of parenting was going to destroy her if he didn't get any help or support and when I said as much to Bilqis, she was generous enough to suggest we offer to look after Reshma for the duration of her school holidays. Of course, it ended up being longer than that, but I wouldn't change that decision for all the gold in the world. It was the best decision we've ever made and I love that girl just as much as I love Sho and Niya, as does my Bills.' He pressed his index finger and thumb into the corners of his eyes and Zafar swallowed the golf ball lodged in his throat, taking a sip of juice to try to help it down.

'For what it's worth, Uncle Jawad, I think you and Auntie Bilqis are amazing. Not many people would do what you've done for your niece.'

He waved his hand in the air, brushing the comment away, as though it were nothing. 'She's a treasure, that girl, and I feel privileged that I get to be a part of her life. Over the years, Ahsan would make promises about coming to see her or to take her out and she'd patiently wait by the front window for him, but he hardly ever delivered. Whenever he told her that he would take her back to stay with him, he'd follow it up with the latest excuse about why he couldn't. I could always tell from Reshma's expression that she was upset, but she never said a word. She just accepted whatever came her way from everyone. If someone gave her more attention than she was used to, she didn't know what to do with it. She'd come and find me or Bilqis and burrow into our laps and become as small as she could.' A tear rolled down his cheek and he wiped it away with a chuckle. 'Even now when I think about the life she's had, it can bring me to tears. That's why Bills and I wanted nothing but the best for her future.' He turned to face him, his eyes shining and a broad smile on his weathered face. 'That's why we introduced *you* to her, son. I saw the similarities between the two of you and the way you both complemented each other. I knew you'd be perfect for each other. It pleases this old man very much to see that you both seem to be in a good place.'

Zafar swallowed a lump of a different kind this time. *No pressure then*, he thought wryly.

Before he could respond or their conversation could continue any further, he heard Daadi call out his name.

While he'd been listening to Uncle Jawad, the gathering on the floor had dispersed and he caught sight of his grandmother sitting with a few of her friends and Reshma's aunts.

'Jawad, you come over too. There's something I want you boys to do.'

Boys? Him and Uncle Jawad?

What was his grandmother up to?

He saw Uncle Imtiaz already beside Auntie Ruqayyah and a few other couples were gathered too.

'Right, husbands.' Daadi clapped her hands and got everyone's attention. 'Haniya and I have decided to have an impromptu competition this evening, with Ruqayyah and Imtiaz's blessings. Nomaan, Saleema, Haniya and I will be the judges.'

Zafar looked around him in confusion and caught Uncle Jawad's eye. The older man shrugged and Zafar felt a sense of foreboding snake down his spine. He caught sight of Haniya, who grinned at him, and immediately he felt like he needed to be on high alert.

Daadi alone was a handful. As was Haniya. The two of them together? He didn't even want to contemplate what mischief they could – and were about to – get up to.

Reshma was sitting next to Auntie Bilqis and she looked at him with . . . Was that guilt on her face?

'These beautiful wives of yours have had their henna done and, upon my request, the henna artists have kindly written the names of their husbands on their hand. It's hidden among the patterns but very much there, we've double-checked. Your job is to locate your name in the henna designs, much like you would have after your wedding if you carried out this custom. The first person to locate his name in his wife's henna shall be declared the winner.'

Zafar remembered having to do this after his wedding. Everyone had gathered around him and Reshma and he'd had to look for his name among the intricate patterns drawn on her hands. It was awkward and embarrassing, he'd felt like a show monkey and he could gladly throttle his grandmother right now if he didn't love her so much. But with the gathering around them as big as it was, he couldn't refuse without creating a scene.

'And don't even think about cheating by asking your wife to help you. Those not taking part in the competition have their eyes on you and cheating will be dealt with most severely.' Haniya made eye contact with him and her father in particular. She pointed two fingers at her eyes and then at her dad and at him. 'Take your place opposite your wife and we'll start in a minute.'

'I'm pretty sure this child of mine has links with Lucifer,' Uncle Jawad said under his breath as he sat opposite Auntie Bilqis and Zafar sat down opposite Reshma.

'And I reckon they both answer to Mumtaz Saeed.' They looked at each other in male solidarity.

When Zafar looked Reshma's way, she looked both gorgeous and miserable and he bit the inside of his cheek to stop himself from laughing. 'That bad, huh?'

'You have no idea. I was ambushed. Some of the women thought it was a great idea, they wanted to see their husband under pressure, especially since the last time they did this ritual was many years ago. But I still remember us doing it like it was yesterday.'

Before Zafar could respond, Haniya was counting down with glee. 'Three. Two. One . . . and go.'

Reshma presented her hands to Zafar and he started scanning the patterns on her right hand first. The paste was dry and flaky in parts but still damp in others, so he was careful not to smudge any of it.

He found flowers, butterflies, spirals and paisleys, and plenty of lines and zigzags which made finding his name extremely difficult. He tried to look for a Z, but it seemed as though there were red herrings interspersed in the patterns with the express purpose of throwing him off.

'This is impossible. I'm going to need my reading glasses, Bills.' He heard Uncle Jawad gripe beside him and, stifling his answering chuckle, he doubled down on his own task. He held Reshma's hand carefully in his own, her perfume finding its way to his nose, mixed with the scent of henna.

He looked up at her and found her staring back at him intently, her lower lip pressed between her teeth, making him run his tongue over his own lips. That habit of hers was going to be the death of him. Her brows were furrowed and she looked down at her palms and then up at him, before glancing around them. When he looked up, he found Haniya's eyes trained on them.

'Daadi? I think you need to come here and invigilate these two, I sense some silent communication going on.' Haniya said it loud enough for everyone to hear and Zafar felt the tips of his ears burn. He would get her back for this. She seemed to have forgotten that he was the eldest of five. Competition and one-upmanship ran through his veins alongside his red blood cells.

He focused on Reshma's hands anew and as he pulled them towards himself again, he felt his knees knock against hers, the contact sending sparks shooting through him. He couldn't understand how in all the time they'd been married, he hadn't been derailed by attraction towards Reshma and she'd been right in front of him every single day, but since coming here, he seemed to find the smallest of touches and the briefest of looks enough to heat his blood.

'Come on, hurry up,' Reshma whispered through gritted teeth and pressed her knees harder against his.

'I found it!' They heard a shout from Uncle Imtiaz a few chairs down from them, but it was soon followed up with a groan. 'That's so unfair, they've written half of my name here. A blatant false trail.'

That renewed the sense of competition around the group and Zafar moved onto Reshma's left hand, using his finger to skim his way up from the tips of her fingers to her palms and then her wrist. With his finger resting lightly on her wrist where the henna was dry, he felt Reshma's pulse, racing as fast as his was. He looked at the small slivers of skin he could glimpse through the swirling patterns and he was sure he could see the jump of her pulse under her skin. And there, right on her pulse point, he saw his name written in both Urdu and English. The patterns around it stemmed from each letter and had he not paused to look at her wrist and rest his finger against it, he would have missed it for sure.

'Got you!' He said it softly and smiled triumphantly as he looked up at Reshma.

She responded in kind and then shouted out proudly, 'We won. We finished first.'

'I just found mine too.' Uncle Jawad joined in and Uncle Imtiaz also announced that he'd finally found his name.

Daadi clapped jovially as, one by one, all the couples seemed to have completed her set exercise.

Reshma beamed at him and Zafar's mind went back to the last time they'd done this. Aside from the intense discomfort back then, he couldn't remember much else. Now, with the benefit of hindsight and whatever spell had been cast over him in this exotic place, he could appreciate the romance in the customs he'd carried out with Reshma before, during and after their big wedding.

They'd had a grand engagement party, in which he had given Reshma his grandmother's ring, though Zafar hadn't proposed, as Reshma had already pointed out to him. He hadn't actually asked her if she would marry him, even though she wouldn't have said no. He'd allowed their families to take care of finalising everything.

A few months later, their wedding events had started with a big bang. They'd had a pre-wedding fancy dress party, organised by his brothers, a dholki party, a henna ceremony, their nikah and civil ceremony, and then a big reception party which had had so many guests, he was sure he hadn't spoken to well over half of them.

In all those events, there had been smaller customs that he and Reshma had carried out together, but not once had he paused to appreciate the sense of closeness it was supposed to engender in a couple. He'd just gone through the motions. Like carrying her over the threshold, finding his name in her bridal henna which had gone from the tips of her fingers all the way to just above her elbows, with his name in the crook of her elbow on one arm and in the centre of her palm on the other hand. His grand-mother had then set a bowl of watered-down milk between them and after dropping a ring with a few coins into the liquid, he had raced Reshma in finding the ring using just one hand. It had been a best out of three, with the victor supposedly getting bragging rights for the duration of the marriage, not that he'd ever bragged.

When he thought back to those times, he couldn't think of a single moment which he'd shared with Reshma that they could both look back at fondly. He'd gone through each and every tradition, ritual and custom he'd been presented with as though he were powering his way through a checklist, giving no thought to the meaning behind any of them or the fact that it was something he was supposed to bond with his new wife over.

He'd hung about for a day after their wedding – during which he and Reshma had been surrounded by family and visitors – and then he'd been back at work the next day. When his father had asked him about going on a honey-moon, he'd said he was busy and would arrange something in due course. A year on and he still hadn't gone away with his wife for even a weekend and there hadn't been a single word of censure from Reshma.

For a man who prided himself on being pretty good at his job, made an effort to be a model grandson, son and brother – despite his numerous failures – he had a lot of ground to make up to become even half as good a husband to a woman who, after everything she'd undergone in life, deserved nothing less than perfect. A woman who had awakened feelings in him that he'd been taught to believe spelt destruction.

20

Reshma

Reshma looked at the henna on her hands and then eyed the glass on the table in front of her. 'Niya? NIYA?' she called to her cousin, who took her time ambling towards her.

'What is it? I'm watching all the grannies gang up on Sho, asking him when he plans on settling down. It's so refreshing that they're ganging up on him rather than me. Makes a nice change.'

'Poor Sho. Listen, my henna's not quite dry enough for me to use my hands yet, can you hold the glass for me while I drink, please?'

Since her henna was completely dry, Haniya stepped forward and held the glass while Reshma used the straw to ease the dryness in her throat. She'd been talking and laughing so much, she finished most of the contents of the glass in one go.

Things were beginning to wind down – finally – and most of the guests had left, leaving just a few stragglers and close family members behind. Reshma felt exhausted and couldn't wait to get back to the villa. Her feet were killing her and her ears were sore with the weight of the earrings weighing them down.

She spotted Daadi sitting with her friends, still going strong, and wondered how she had the energy to keep going. Well, if

Daadi was in the mood to keep on partying, then she was free to. Reshma was ready to call it a night. She'd been up since the crack of dawn and with the nikah ceremony tomorrow, she desperately needed some shut-eye. She bid Haniya a good night, and spotting Zafar still sitting with Uncle Jawad, she made her way towards them, each step making her wince.

She reached her uncle and bumped his shoulder. 'What have you two been nattering about all evening? You've had your heads together whenever I've looked your way.'

'Didn't you feel your ears burning, pet?' Uncle Jawad chuckled as he turned to her, his jovial face a comforting sight as always. Unlike her own father. She'd caught glimpses of him, but they hadn't crossed paths all evening. He'd not sought her out and she'd not looked out for him either. She had run into his wife, however, who had offered her a tight smile when she was told by Auntie Ruqayyah that Reshma had made most of the arrangements that day after she'd complimented them, before giving her aunt a list of things her own children excelled at.

So mature.

'How is my girl doing anyway?' Uncle Jawad asked. 'Happy?'

'Yes. Look.' She held her hands out for her uncle to see, much like she used to as a child whenever she had henna done for Eid.

'It's lovely, just like you.'

She giggled. He always said the same thing, whether it was her or Haniya. Even when they wore new clothes, he'd say they were lovely, just like his girls.

He grinned at her and then cupped her cheek. 'Tired?'

Reshma nodded. 'Yeah, my feet are sore.'

'Hmm. I believe that's a summons for you, son.' He looked towards Zafar, who smiled as he stood up.

They bid everyone a good night, but Daadi said she wanted to stay a bit longer.

'Are you sure? It's been a long day for you,' Zafar said in concern.

'Don't worry about me, *Dad*. If you give me the keys, Jawad or Bilqis will bring me back. You two carry on.' She waved them off and turned back to the conversation she was having with Uncle Imtiaz's mother.

They said another round of good nights because that was how her family rolled and then she and Zafar were slowly making their way back towards the villa. Her high-heeled sandals were really causing her grief, the balls of her feet feeling like they were on fire, but the idea of walking barefoot made her squirm when Zafar suggested she take her sandals off.

'Eww. No, thanks. I'd rather deal with the after-effects of the sandals. Besides, it's not far now.' Though it was still further than she'd have liked.

Zafar stopped and faced her. She stopped as well and looked at him in confusion. He looked around them, presumably observing the silent path behind them and in front of them.

'What is it? Did you hear something?' She instinctively moved closer to him. She hardly expected a lion to leap out at them, but still, that didn't mean there wasn't some kind of rodent or reptile lurking. She'd seen a few lizards – or were they geckos? – around the area.

'Lift your arm. And be careful of your henna, don't want to ruin it.'

'Huh?' She automatically did as he asked and lifted her arm closest to him but had no idea what he meant until he swooped and in one fluid movement lifted her up in his arms. She instinctively put her arms around him, mindful of her forearms as they almost brushed against his kurta.

'What are you doing?' Of course, she knew what he was doing, but what she meant to ask him was why.

'I'm carrying you so that you don't have to walk the rest of the way to the villa and your poor feet won't be any more battered than they already are. Otherwise, you'll have to wear trainers to the nikah tomorrow.'

'Oh.' She didn't know what else to say. In some way or another, this man was surprising her every day and she was getting to a point where she had no idea what he'd do or how to respond to him at times. Like now, though she knew she felt touched by his consideration.

He started walking towards their villa, and she was about to grip his shoulder when she remembered that while the henna was mostly dry on her hands, the dry and flaky paste could still stain his kurta if it hadn't already, not that he seemed to mind. In fact he seemed completely at ease with her in his arms.

His aftershave wound its way through her nose as she took in a breath and she felt the urge to bury her nose in the crook of his neck.

She shook her head to try to dislodge the thought and Zafar looked at her in question. 'Everything OK?'

She nodded, bouncing slightly in his arms as he effortlessly covered the remaining distance to the villa, coming to a stop at the welcome mat outside the front door. She looked up at him and his eyes were focused on hers before they slowly moved down to where she had her lip clamped between her teeth. It was something she caught herself doing quite often lately and she had no idea why. Maybe it was her version of a nervous twitch.

Zafar's lips parted and Reshma's eyes zoned in on them as he snaked his tongue out and rolled it over his lips, slowly and sensually, making her back arch infinitesimally.

He began lowering her legs, bending his knees as her feet touched the ground, sending shafts of pain and a tingling sensation up her legs. His other arm was firmly clamped around her waist and held her close to him while she tried to keep her henna-covered hands off him. What she wanted to do was move closer, run her hands across his broad shoulders and chest and feel the firmness of them through the thin fabric of his kurta, like she had while they'd danced together, but she couldn't. And thank God for that. Tiredness was making her delirious.

'Keys?' His voice sounded like his throat was coated with gravel and Reshma felt a shiver of pleasure careen down her spine. She wanted to hear him say her name with that voice.

Seriously, what had got into her? Her mind was warring with her heart, which was warring with her body. She was in such an intense state of confusion, she wasn't sure which would come out on top, but what she did know with some certainty was that her body seemed to be the heavyweight in that battle this evening.

'Reshma?'

Oh God. The way he just rolled the R of her name. She wanted to close her eyes in ecstasy.

'The keys? Daadi took my set.'

'Th . . .' She cleared her throat, giving herself a moment to find her ability to speak coherently. 'They're in my bag.' She slowly eased away from him, lamenting the loss of contact, and held her arm out, from which her little pouch was dangling.

It looked so ridiculous in his hands as he untied it from around her elbow and pulled the keys out. He opened the door and then stepped back, scooping her up once more and surprising her, because he didn't have to. She only needed to take a few steps into the villa.

He stepped into the villa and, using his shoulder, he closed the front door. He walked towards the sofa and lowered her onto it, hovering over her as her back hit the cushions. The soft light from the lamps reflected in his eyes, making it look like there were small flames in them. They roved over her face and she did the same, taking in his features as though she were seeing them for the first time. Which, in some ways, she was. It was certainly the first time she was seeing this side of Zafar.

A corner of his lips curved up as he edged back and then lowered himself onto one knee beside her. 'May I?'

He pointed to her feet and she nodded – she couldn't do anything with her hands until she got the henna off them and the last thing she wanted to do was get henna onto her lehenga.

Zafar put his hand under the hem of her lehenga and clasped her ankle before she could present it to him and, with the utmost care and the gentlest of touches, he undid the delicate buckle at her ankle and pushed the strap off the heel of her foot before removing the sandal and putting it on the floor beside him.

He held her foot in both hands, resting it on his bent knee, and with firm pressure, he pushed his thumbs into the heel and then up, towards her toes, eliciting a pleasurable groan from her which nothing could have stopped from coming out. He massaged her toes and the arch of her foot for a moment more and when he lowered her foot to the floor and let go, she just about held back from whimpering in protest.

He took her other sandal off and gave her second foot the same treatment and short of flopping back on the sofa inelegantly, there was nothing more she could do. She probably looked like a puddle of peach and cream.

She moved her head to the side as she watched him, and when he lowered her second foot to the floor, he rested his arms on his bent knee and looked up at her, a sexy smile teasing his lips.

'Do you think you can make it upstairs or would you like a lift?'

'Hmm.' She felt languid, like her blood had turned to treacle as it ran through her veins, and she wanted nothing more than to either stay where she was or, even better, be in Zafar's arms again.

He laughed softly as he stood up, shaking his head as he grasped her elbow, and gently helped her up.

As she moved her head, she felt a sharp tug on her ear, making her cry out. 'Ow.'

She couldn't straighten her head, her earring caught up in something. She instinctively lifted her hands to free her earring when she felt Zafar grip her elbows tighter and stall her progress.

'Hang on, hang on. It's caught in your dupatta. Let me see.'

She lowered her arms and stood in front of him with her head cocked to one side, tilting towards him as best as she could to give him better access. She felt his hands above her shoulder, moving the earring and her dupatta. The back of his hand brushed the side of her jaw and she felt instant sparks on that very spot.

She must have made a sound because he paused what he was doing and looked at her. 'Did I hurt you?'

She made to shake her head, but the tug on her ear stopped the movement short. 'No.' She mumbled the word, feeling heat infuse her cheeks and body as Zafar went back to untangling her earring. She felt surrounded by him, inhaling his aftershave mingled with hints of his shower gel and the scent that was uniquely him. Warmth from his body was slowly heating hers. Or maybe that was her body's reaction to his nearness. Whatever it was, it made her feel on edge.

Her ear felt lighter and a second later Zafar eased back with her earring held between his finger and thumb. 'It's heavier than it looks.'

'Tell me about it,' Reshma grumbled, hoping that he wouldn't notice the rising flush on her cheeks or the fact that her body was now showing clear signs that it was feeling things.

Zafar stepped forward and gently took her second earring off, putting both of them in his pocket. Reshma stood frozen where she was as he slowly cupped her face and, even slower than that, began lowering his own, giving her enough time to call a halt if she wanted. But rather than put a stop to him lowering his head, she pushed herself up to close the rest of the distance and met Zafar halfway in a scorching kiss.

There were no tentative nibbles or delicate pecks. This was a tongues tangling, teeth clashing kind of kiss which had Zafar pushing his hands into her updo and anchoring her face in place as he plundered her mouth. Reshma rested her forearms against his chest as she met him stroke for stroke, tiny explosions taking place at her nerve endings as pleasure shot through her like wildfire.

She wanted to use her hands and the frustration of being restricted like she was had her growling and pulling back, panting as though she'd just run a four-minute mile.

'I need to wash this off.' She moved away from him and turned towards the staircase. She had reached the bedroom door when she sensed Zafar right behind her.

'I've got a better idea.' He closed the bedroom door behind them and, leaving her standing there staring after him, he went into the bathroom. She heard the sound of running water and then he was back in front of her, his chest heaving just as much as hers was. 'Come with me.' His voice was gravelly as he led her to the bathroom, where the basin was steadily filling with water. He turned the taps off and dipped a towel in the water and gently ran it from three inches up her wrist, down towards her fingers, before immersing her hand in the basin and gently massaging the dry henna off her hands, leaving the dark staining of the patterns on them.

The henna was ideally supposed to be left on for longer so the staining was as dark as possible, but Reshma had always found it impractical, usually waiting no more than a couple of hours before getting it off. The only time she'd left it longer was for her own wedding.

Zafar had moved onto her second hand, running his finger over the inside of her wrist where the henna artist had written his name, leaving a trail of sparks in its wake.

When Daadi and Haniya had concocted their plan earlier, Reshma had tried her best to dissuade them, but neither had listened to a word of her protest. Reshma had gone through waves of shyness, embarrassment, awkwardness and all sorts of uncomfortable feelings in the process – along with a healthy dose of desire towards her husband, which seemed to be outgrowing the box she'd put it in, making her feel inexplicably nervy.

She looked his way now, as he gently helped get the henna off her hands and then threw the towel in the basket in the corner of the bathroom before pulling out the plug in the basin.

'There, all done.' He looked at her hands as she held them out in front of her to see how the henna had turned out. 'It looks great.'

Reshma nodded, looking up at him.

He lifted his hands and held her face, just like he had downstairs, resting his forehead against hers. 'Tell me to stop. Tell me if you don't want this because, try as I might, I'm struggling. I don't know what's going on, but I feel like I'm on a runaway train and only you can help control it or steer it for me.'

Reshma felt her pulse pick up pace again, thundering in her ears with the force of a stampede. Her breath sawed in and out of her and her mind warred with her body. 'I don't know what's happening either. Things have never been . . .' She shook her head, trying to find the right words and coming up with nothing. '. . . Like *this* before. I don't know but . . . I don't want you to stop.' She knew that much.

With her hands now free, she moved them over his pecs and up to his shoulders, holding onto them as if her life depended on it as she slowly closed the distance between them and gently coaxed his lips apart, pushing her tongue against his. The impact was instant and electric, sending her nervous system into meltdown. Zafar's hands moved over her body, across her back, around her ribcage and then down to her bottom.

They moved back towards the bedroom and thoughts of anything else flew out of Reshma's mind as she zeroed in on the sensations running rampant through her body, making her feel like she might be glowing.

Only the back of her mind was momentarily alert to what was happening and the potential disaster it could lead to. It was easy enough to open up to Zafar's attention in this moment, but what about what came after? When they weren't in this bubble of theirs and the reality of life stormed back in. Would they still be this into each other or would their relationship fall back into the groove it had been in since they'd got married?

Reshma ignored that voice of reason which urged caution. Caution wasn't what she wanted to exercise in that moment. In fact, it was the last thing she wanted to think about. And if her mind went to the box labelled with the L word, which she'd slammed shut after it had threatened to break her in a way she'd never be able to recover from, then she ignored that too. Those were things best addressed in the light of day. Even if that box wasn't closed shut as tight as Reshma had thought it might be.

21

Zafar

Sunlight shone through the curtains they'd failed to draw the night before and streamed into the room, filling it with golden light. Zafar stretched his arms and heard his back click in at least two places. He lay against the pillow, a deep sense of contentment filling his entire being. He smiled as his thoughts went to the night before and he couldn't stop his very satisfied smile from widening.

Turning over, he looked at Reshma's beautiful face. His wife. The woman he'd spent most of the night making sweet, sweet love with. The woman he was in love with.

The thought had his mind slowly coming to a standstill as his breath lodged in his chest until he forced himself to inhale deeply. He sat up, rubbing his hand against his sternum to ease the sudden tightness there. He swallowed the dryness in his mouth as his heartbeat thundered in his chest, the sound of it reverberating through his ears until it almost drowned his thoughts out.

Almost, but not quite.

Because one thought refused to be drowned out. It went through his head like an incantation, getting louder and louder with every beat of his heart.

He felt so much more than affection for Reshma. He loved her.

He was in love with her and the thought didn't scare him nearly as much as it should have, or he *thought* it should have. In fact, it felt . . . right.

The tightness behind his sternum eased as he took another deep breath, his heartbeat slowing down gradually to its normal rhythm.

He was in love with Reshma and it felt good. In fact, he felt ecstatic about it. The world hadn't come crashing down around his ears. Everything still seemed very much in place like it had five minutes ago.

Was it because of the closeness between them last night? Perhaps, though Zafar knew it wasn't just that. This feeling hadn't come out of nowhere. It felt too familiar for that. What was new was the depth of it. It felt so much more . . . intense than anything he'd felt towards her before. It was like the seed of something that he'd given barely any thought to and now suddenly it had blossomed and the strength of its roots suggested it hadn't happened overnight.

As for last night . . . it hadn't been the first, second or even third time and yet it had felt like the first time. Not in a clumsy, awkward way, but in a magical, beautiful way. The feelings and emotions that had bombarded him from all sides had left him feeling like his entire being had fallen off its axis and then been put back again but the right way this time. The sense of closeness he'd felt to her had been unlike anything he'd experienced before and he was certain it had been different for her too.

He looked at her again, feeling himself fill with a lightness as he gazed down at her sleeping form. She lay on her side, her arm flung out of the duvet but her other hand tucked under her cheek. Stray strands of hair sat against her rosy cheek and her nose stud glimmered up at him. She looked peaceful. Content.

His eyes went to the henna patterns on her hands, the staining on them even darker than it had been last night. He could smell its pleasant fragrance and it took him back to the morning after their wedding.

It was strange how a certain smell could invoke a particular memory. For him, the scent of henna was something he'd probably always associate with the morning after his wedding because he could remember waking up to it, with Reshma's hand not far from his face, resting on the pillow. That morning too, he'd woken up and just lay there, half propped up on his elbow looking down at her and taking her features in. He remembered finding her beautiful even then, but more so now because he had got to know her more. He knew how amazing she was and how much goodness she had in her and it humbled him. She'd been nothing but giving towards him, even when he hadn't deserved it. But he wanted to. He wanted to be worthy of her and her affection. Maybe even more than that if she could bring herself to feel that way towards him. God knew he felt so much more than that for her.

Feeling a sudden burst of energy shoot through his body like a firework which wouldn't let him be still, Zafar picked up his phone and looked at the time. It was just gone ten.

He was tempted to wake Reshma and convey his feelings in some way, but she looked so peaceful and he knew they had another long day ahead of them, with Saleema and Nomaan's nikah ceremony later. There was time enough to tell her. Besides, not all feelings had to be verbally expressed. He could show her in other ways too.

He got up and put his swimming shorts on, before making his way downstairs. He noticed that Daadi's bedroom door was still closed. The party animal had got in pretty late last night and was obviously sleeping her social hangover off.

Zafar softly opened the patio door and stepped outside into the garden, going straight towards the deep end of the pool and diving in. There was no denying the daily swims had had a decent impact on his stamina and he kept going until he felt his arms and legs become heavy, though not enough that his mind had stopped going through its newfound revelation. His love for Reshma which seemed to be all-consuming.

He made his way to the edge of the pool and rested there, taking in the sight of the beach in the distance. Soft shuffling had him looking around, but he couldn't see anything. He looked up and saw Reshma leaning against the balcony, looking down at him. She smiled at him, delightfully dishevelled in an oversized T-shirt – his, if he wasn't wrong – and her pyjama bottoms. She gave him a wave.

'Care to join me?' he asked.

'No thank you. As tempting as *the pool* looks, I'll give it a miss. I've got an appointment with the hairdresser and make-up artist.'

'Pity.'

'Hmm.' She gave him another wave and went inside.

Zafar shook his head and heaved himself out of the pool, deciding to get a head start on breakfast while Reshma got ready to go out. When he went back into the villa, Daadi was already standing at the island.

'How's my favourite party animal? Ready for round two today?' He kissed her on the cheek and she scrunched her nose.

'Hmm. I needed tea five minutes ago. Once I've had a couple of cups, I'll see what I fancy committing to,' she grizzled and Zafar held back from laughing at her. He set about making breakfast, giving Daadi her tea before doing anything else.

Reshma came down twenty minutes later and they all sat down to eat, the pair of them exchanging shy, covert glances like young lovebirds.

Zafar had just put his knife and fork down when his phone rang, bursting to life with Murad's name flashing on the screen.

'Aziz! How's it going, sugar?'

There was silence on the other end.

'Hello? Murad? Can you hear me?' Zafar moved the phone from his ear, checked the screen, which showed the call was still connected and then pressed it against his ear again. 'Hello?'

'Who are you and what have you done with Zafar Saeed II? I must warn you, I'm not as rich as him and can't offer you much for his safe return, but let me see what his brothers say. Just don't break his face, he's ugly enough already.'

Zafar rolled his eyes. 'Have you tried auditioning since we last spoke? At least others might get entertained by your stupidity.'

'Oh, thank God. It's you. I got worried for a minute. You sounded so happy and energetic, I thought an imposter had taken your place.'

'Bog off, Murad.'

Reshma's eyes widened and he winked at her.

'Ah, you have company, don't you? Otherwise, you'd have used language a lot more colourful than that, I'm sure.'

'Is there a reason you called, other than needing to word vomit?'

'Tut. Yes, I did.' The cadence of his voice shifted subtly. 'Have you got five minutes to spare from your tropical retreat for me? I need to run something by you about the hotel deal.'

Zafar straightened at the mention of the deal. His dream project which he'd let slide to the back of his mind. In fact, he'd not thought about it at all in the last few days, he realised with an immediate tinge of guilt. 'Yeah, sure. Give me five and I'll call you back. OK?'

'Sure, no worries. It's not like I've got a beach to go and sun myself on. Take your time. Oh, and, Zaf?'

'What?'

'Don't panic. I just need some numbers from you. It's nothing to worry about.'

Zafar had known Murad Aziz for thirty years and knew him better than the other man realised he did. Even though he'd not said it, Zafar had picked up on his unspoken word. There was nothing to worry about.

Yet.

Zafar groaned as he undid his tie for the third time. Why couldn't he get the knot right? He'd been wearing ties since he'd been ten years old, so he'd been doing them for long enough to be able to tie one with his eyes closed. But today he was all thumbs.

He threw the tie onto the chaise and decided to find his cufflinks. He looked in his suitcase and on the dressing table but couldn't find them and his frustration began mounting.

If only Murad had allayed his concerns earlier when he'd called him back.

Zafar couldn't shake off the feeling that there was so much more Murad wasn't telling him, but he had no way to confirm that short of calling Ibrahim or his father and demanding an explanation. Or flying back and getting answers face to face. Why had Murad needed to go over the financials with him when Murad was as good with numbers as Zafar was?

He moved towards the bedside table to see if his cufflinks were there. There was no reason for them to be there because he'd not worn them yet, but his mind was racing and he was about ready to—

His thoughts stuttered to an abrupt halt as the door to the bedroom opened and Reshma walked in. She'd been gone since after breakfast, getting her hair and make-up done, and he was supposed to meet her at the main villa with Daadi.

Now here she was and she looked . . . God. She looked incredible. She was wearing a dark red outfit which he thought might look familiar, but he couldn't put his finger on why. Maybe she'd worn it before to some event they'd been to together. Her hair was half up, half down and she had heavy gold jewellery on. Her eyes looked big and smoky and her lips were an inviting shade of red.

'You look . . . wow. Mashallah.'

She smiled as she blushed, closing the distance between them. She came to a stop an arm's length away and twirled once, her skirt flaring out slightly below her knees and her bangles and anklets chiming.

'Do you recognise this?' She held her kameez out and Zafar stared at it, his mind going utterly blank.

'It looks familiar, but I can't pinpoint exactly where I've seen you wear it.' He couldn't be sure, but he thought the light in her eyes dimmed a fraction at his answer, though it could be a play of the light. It was late afternoon and the room wasn't all that bright.

'It's my wedding gharara, Zafar. I wore this at our wedding.'

Oh. That explained why he had thought he had seen it before.

'You're wearing your wedding dress to your cousin's wedding? Is that allowed?'

'Yes.' Her brow was furrowed as she responded to him. 'I'm not dressed like a bride. Saleema asked me to wear it and since hers isn't red, we won't clash. Auntie Ruqayyah, Auntie Bilqis and Daadi were all in agreement. Do you . . . do you not like it? You think I should have worn something else?'

His stomach dropped to his knees at the sudden vulnerability on Reshma's face and the nervousness that had crept into her voice instantly. He closed the distance between them in two steps, gently cupping her cheeks in his palms, mindful of her make-up. 'No, sweetheart. I'm sorry. So sorry. That all came out completely wrong, I promise. Let me start again, OK?' Her eyes were wide, but she didn't say anything or move. 'You look absolutely stunning. There's no part of you that isn't perfect, Reshma. I didn't know that it was OK to wear your wedding dress again, but now that you've explained it, I get it. I think it's actually really nice that you get to wear it again. Gives me a chance to appreciate you in it anew.'

He both felt and saw her cheeks go warm and a tentative smile came through on her face, helping restore his equilibrium.

'I'd show you how good you look, but you'd need to see the make-up artist again.'

Her smile was fuller as she pushed him away playfully and then her expression sobered again. 'Where's your tie? You're not ready yet and we need to leave in ten minutes.' She turned and made her way to the dressing room and came back with his tie, holding it out for him.

'I've tried three times, I can't get the knot right. I also can't find my bloody cufflinks.'

He took the tie from her and she went back into the dressing room, returning seconds later with his cufflinks in the centre of her palm. 'They were in my jewellery box. I saw them lying in your suitcase the other day, so I locked them with my jewellery in my case.'

'Oh.'

Silently, she put one in place and like an obedient schoolboy, Zafar presented his other cuff and she secured that one too. He held out the tie for her and she raised an eyebrow at him.

'I don't know how to knot a tie. I've never done that before. Uncle Jawad always did my school ties for me and I never untied it, I just loosened it and tightened it to put it on and take it off.'

'In that case, let me show you.'

'Zafar, we don't have time. We need to leave.'

'It won't take long.' He stood in front of her and looped the tie around his neck until the ends were exactly where he needed them. He took her through the steps, shuffling a tiny bit closer each time. Halfway through, he rested his hands on her waist but she didn't seem to realise, focusing on her task instead. 'Take the wide end and cross it over the narrow end. Just a bit higher. Perfect.'

She finishing knotting the tie and slowly tightened it, adjusting it so it sat in just the right place. Her teeth rested on her lower lip, leaving the slightest depression there as she concentrated on the job.

'You need to stop doing that.' His voice came out gravelly as he lifted his hand and rested his thumb just under her lower lip. She immediately lifted her teeth off her lip. 'You're going to ruin what the make-up artist has done and if you're going to ruin the make-up anyway, then maybe I can . . .' He lowered his head, ready to close his lips over hers, but she turned her face and his lips landed on her cheek as she giggled softly.

'We are not messing up my make-up, thank you very much. Besides, we are going to be late if you don't hurry.' She pushed at his chest gently and stepped back and he let her. Only because she was right, they were going to be late and it'd be his fault.

She picked his jacket up off the bed and helped him into it, running her hands across his shoulders from behind and making his pulse jump. He added the finishing touches to his appearance while Reshma changed her shoes into heels that brought her up to his shoulders, and then together, they made their way downstairs, thoughts of work and his phone call with Murad slipping to the back of his mind.

22

Reshma

'Aww, pet.' Uncle Jawad held her hands and took a step back, looking at her with a loving smile on his face. 'You look beautiful.'

They were standing in the foyer of the wedding venue, a plush hotel banqueting room big enough to accommodate the three hundred guests expected to celebrate Saleema and Nomaan's wedding.

'Doesn't she?' Auntie Bilqis stood beside Uncle Jawad as they both looked at her, beaming like the proud parents they were. The parents of her heart. Her chosen parents. 'She looks so much like Hafsa today, I did a double take when I first saw her.' Reshma felt warmth bubble up inside her at the comparison her aunt had drawn.

For a moment, after Zafar's initial reaction to her, she had doubted her choice to wear her wedding gharara. It wasn't poor form to wear your wedding dress at a close relative's wedding in their culture, though had Saleema been wearing any shade of red, Reshma wouldn't have out of consideration for her cousin.

She had expected Zafar to remember that it was her wedding gharara and the fact that he hadn't had bothered her, though he'd apologised to her for it. He'd been distracted since his phone call with Murad earlier that day, but when she'd asked him about it, he'd brushed her off, saying there was nothing to worry about, it was just a small work issue.

He seemed in a better mood now, so maybe it had been just that.

Reshma remembered that there was a possibility that they might see his cousin Safiya today and wondered if that could be on his mind too. Given how affected he'd been when he'd told her about their history, she was sure that the thought of seeing her would dredge up strong emotions for Zafar.

She spotted him now, standing with Shoaib and Khalil, looking devastatingly handsome in his tailored suit. She often saw him dressed like that for work and had always found him to look especially handsome, but over time she'd become immune to it. Maybe because she had become somewhat immune to him. But not today.

When she'd seen him sans tie and jacket, he'd looked mouth-wateringly good, but the whole look? Wow.

He flicked his gaze towards her and winked, as though he knew exactly what she was thinking. Reshma felt warmth bloom in her cheeks and immediately ducked her head, lest she give herself away.

Of course, her bloodhound of a cousin had witnessed the exchange and nudged her. 'Things are looking nice and toasty between you both. Anything you'd like to share with Auntie Niya?'

'Yes, actually. I think it's time Auntie Niya found me an uncle, so she can get off my back and concentrate on him.'

Haniya shuddered. 'If I wasn't dressed to the nines, I'd march you to the bathroom and wash your mouth with soap myself. This lehenga's too heavy for the effort.' Reshma laughed and Haniya grinned at her. 'Ignoring your rudeness,

I'm glad things are going well. I told you all you needed was some time and space.'

Reshma pretended to bow to Haniya and she patted the top of her head in return as they giggled.

'I'm going to grab a drink. I feel like I've not eaten or drunk anything all day and I'm starving. Come,' Haniya said as she linked arms with Reshma and they went towards the makeshift bar where welcome drinks were being served, picking up a glass each.

Reshma felt a soft tap on her shoulder and turned to find a young woman, around her own age and height, standing in front of her. She didn't recognise her, though she thought there was something familiar about her. Reshma was certain that if she'd been introduced to her, she would have remembered her because her eyes were a distinct green, like polished jade. She was wearing a gorgeous mint-green suit with golden embroidery on it and her dupatta was draped over one shoulder, gold fringing on its border. Her hair was long and loose, like a dark waterfall, ending at the small of her back.

She regarded Reshma with a tentative smile. 'Reshma?'

Reshma nodded her head and the hesitancy left the woman's expression. 'My name is Safiya, I'm . . .' she paused, her smile faltering, but she didn't need to finish her sentence. Reshma realised why she had looked familiar, yet unknown to her. She could see the resemblance with Daadi on Safiya's face, it was just the eyes that were different.

Reshma smiled back at the woman. 'I know who you are, Safiya.' She embraced her and felt Safiya's arms come around her and hold her close. They eased away and regarded each other with smiles on their faces. Reshma introduced Haniya and Safiya to each other and then looked around the gathering. 'Daadi and Zafar will be over the moon to see you. They should be around here some—'

She felt Safiya's grip on her arm. 'No. I just wanted to meet you. I'm not sure they'll want to see me, it's been too long and I don't want to cause any kind of disruption at your family's function. I just wanted to say hello to you. You're gorgeous and I hope you and . . .' She swallowed hard. 'Zaf are happy. He deserves to be happy.' She whispered Zafar's name and Reshma felt her heart break.

There was so much packed into those few sentences, a world of pain and anguish. And what Reshma knew of Safiya's story made it that much harder for her to watch her give her a sad smile and move away towards a group of people Reshma didn't recognise before she could say or do anything to stop her.

'Who is that? I know you said she's Zaf's cousin but . . . what's the deal?' Haniya asked as they both looked in Safiya's direction.

'It's a long story, which I'll explain later. I just want to make sure that before she leaves here, she gets to talk to Zafar and Daadi.'

'Girls?' Reshma heard Auntie Bilqis call them over and, casting a final glance Safiya's way, she followed after Haniya.

The pair of them went with Shoaib and Khalil to Saleema's suite, where she was with her parents. She looked radiant in dark green and gold, her eyes full of joy and hope. She hugged everyone in turn and then they all made their way to the Grand Room, where a dais had been set up in the middle for the nikah.

Nomaan was already sitting on one side of the partition, a rectangular frame with garlands of flowers wrapped around it and sheer curtains hanging from the upper part to prevent people on one side from seeing the other.

The screen would be removed after the ceremony, when Nomaan and Saleema would see each other as husband and wife for the first time.

With her parents on either side of her, Saleema made her way into the room. Khalil and Haniya walked behind them and Reshma and Shoaib followed. Behind her were some of Saleema's cousins from her father's side of the family.

Saleema took her place on the dais beside her parents and her brother, and the rest of them went to their respective seats.

A hush fell over the gathering and then the imam began reciting his sermon, talking about the institution of marriage and the responsibilities of a husband and a wife towards each other, their families and the community as a whole.

Reshma watched as the imam moved onto the cere-mony and asked Saleema if she accepted her marriage with Nomaan. He asked her the same question three times, as was customary, and then he did the same with Nomaan.

Reshma felt Zafar shift in his seat next to her and in the next moment his hand closed over hers where it rested on her leg, squeezing it gently. She looked up at him and saw him closely watching the proceedings on the dais. His expression was intent and his eyes looked bright.

This was the first time they were attending someone else's nikah ceremony after their own and, naturally, Reshma's mind went to their nikah. The set-up had been similar, in as much as they had also sat on two sides of a screen and the imam had given a similar sermon before asking them individually if they accepted each other in marriage. Reshma remembered some of those moments with clarity, while other memories were hazier.

The one thing she recalled clearly was the moment when Shoaib and Ashar had removed the screen between her and

Zafar and she'd seen him for the first time that day. She'd looked at him and he'd looked at her as soon as they'd been able to, and with everyone's eyes on them, they'd been caught and teased mercilessly. Reshma had dropped her gaze and Zafar had tried to fudge over the moment. It was a memory that brought a smile to her face.

She remembered thinking how lucky she was that the handsome man in front of her – with dimples, no less – was now *her husband*. They belonged with each other in a way they didn't belong with anyone else. And, in that moment, a small part of her had fallen in love with him.

And the truth was, she'd never fallen out of love with Zafar, not entirely at least.

Yes, he had faults and flaws, who didn't? But he'd put his hands up and owned up to them and made a conscious effort to make changes and show her a different side of himself while they'd been here and that had to count for something, didn't it? It was more than anyone else in her life who had wronged her had ever done, her father first and foremost.

OK, she'd had her complaints with Zafar and it had tainted her feelings, but that wasn't how she felt right now, in that moment. If anything, she felt closer to him than she had before, even on their wedding day.

She looked at Zafar and he turned and smiled at her, gripping her hand before nodding his head in Saleema and Nomaan's direction. She turned to watch them in time to see both of them accept their marriage with each other.

There was a thunderous round of applause and cheering at the end of the ceremony and as the cheering went on, the imam had Saleema and Nomaan sign their marriage contract, followed by their witnesses, and then their marriage was complete. Lots of hugs, happy tears and best wishes were exchanged by the whole family.

The gathering was moved into an adjacent hall where the meal was going to be served and in the midst of all of that, Reshma spotted Safiya make her way to the ladies' room and decided to follow after her, telling Zafar she'd be back shortly.

By the time she got there, Safiya was washing her hands at the basin and when she saw her, she gave her a bright smile. 'That ceremony was beautiful, wasn't it?'

'It was. Saleema – the bride that is – is my cousin and she planned the whole day down to every second. She'll be over the moon that it all went exactly how she wanted it to.' Reshma looked at Safiya as she dried her hands and then moved towards the door. Reshma sidestepped and blocked her and Safiya looked at her in confusion. 'I know we've only just met, but Zafar's told me about you. I know how important you are to Zafar and Daadi and I'm sure they're just as important to you. I know for a fact that they'd love a chance to see you and speak to you. This is your chance to do that. Please don't let that pass you by.'

Safiya stared back at her, her eyes as wide as saucers until they dimmed and almost instantly filled with tears, but she didn't let them fall, swallowing hard instead. 'It's not so simple, Reshma. It's been six years. Six. That's a long time not to speak to someone. I was angry at first, but then it just got too late. And now I don't even know what on earth I'd say if I came face to face with them. I only came to say hello to you because I couldn't stop myself. I wanted to meet the woman Zafar was married to. I shouldn't have done that.' She shook her head, talking more to herself now than to Reshma.

Reshma held her arms. 'No, Safiya. Look, I—'

Reshma was stopped from saying any more as the door to the ladies' room opened. The lady smiled at them and then moved past, but Reshma knew this wasn't the place – or time, really – to be having this conversation with Safiya.

She held the door open and Safiya preceded her out into the foyer. 'I'd love to have the chance to talk to you about this properly, Safiya. I'd hate for you, Zafar or Daadi to lose this opportunity of connecting with each other.'

Safiya looked unconvinced, but Reshma could see the longing in her eyes whenever she mentioned her grandmother or cousin. The cousin Reshma knew that Safiya had been close to during their childhood. 'We're staying until the reception and then we're headed straight back to Nairobi. If we don't get a chance to speak here, then maybe I can catch you later tonight or even tomorrow morning?'

Reshma felt relief wash through her at Safiya's agreement to at least have a chat. In a moment of clarity, she gave Safiya her phone number and took hers.

They went towards their respective tables and when Reshma sat down, she could see from the look on Zafar's face that he'd seen who she had come in with. He looked in Safiya's direction and Reshma followed his gaze, watching as Safiya sat down with her family.

Zafar's jaw looked like it had been carved out of granite and his fist was clenched where he rested it on the table. Reshma placed her hand over his, and after a moment, she felt his hand relax. He gave her a tight smile before turning to look towards Uncle Jawad, who had called out to him. Reshma turned to look at Daadi, but she was busy chatting to Auntie Bilqis.

Reshma hoped she could get Safiya reconciled with her family. She knew how much it would mean to Zafar and if she could bring him that sense of peace and the joy of connecting with his cousin once again, then she wanted to do that.

She thought back to his defence of her with her father and the way he'd been with her since he'd come here. Like Haniya said, he'd had the chance to leave, but he hadn't and he'd done nothing to make her think that he didn't want to be with her. Her feelings for him, which had simmered down to paler versions of themselves over the past year, had been renewed with a fresher and stronger sense of purpose, and on the basis of those feelings, she wanted to be there for him like he'd been there for her.

He'd given her so much more than she'd hoped for by coming here and while she was aware that they still had progress to make and obstacles to overcome, she had a feeling that they were in a better place to tackle them together.

The rest of the celebration went ahead as smoothly as the nikah had and everyone was in a happy mood. Reshma and Haniya joined Saleema's friends and cousins from her father's side of the family to collect the gift owed to them by Nomaan.

It was an old tradition, where the bride's sisters and friends would steal the groom's shoes – which were usually left outside – and only give them back to him after he'd paid the ladies for them. As time had gone on, the ritual had evolved from the taking of shoes to the taking of any other item the girls could get their hands on, with the groomsmen guarding the groom's possessions.

At such times, the bride had a front-row seat from which she observed the negotiations and blatant manipulation as families got involved, though the whole thing was great fun for everyone. Reshma remembered Haniya sitting in Zafar's seat next to her at their wedding after he'd got up to speak to a guest and then refusing to get up until he'd paid her. She'd walked away with a decent wad of cash that day.

They managed to get a healthy sum off Nomaan too, who'd then been roasted by his relatives for giving in too easily.

'I have to pay up eventually, why drag it out?'

Auntie Ruqayyah and Nomaan's mother carried out a few more traditions of giving gifts to the bride and groom and then it was time to call it a day.

An emotional farewell ensued, with tears all round as Saleema said goodbye to her family and left with Nomaan. Of course, they'd all see each other at the reception, but it wouldn't be the same.

Auntie Bilqis was consoling a sobbing Auntie Ruqayyah and Reshma noticed Daadi standing beside her, looking teary-eyed too. She made her way towards her, giving her a reassuring hug and Daadi gave her a watery smile. 'Don't mind me, sweetheart. I cried at your wedding too and you were coming back home with us. There's just something about weddings and this particular part of them that sets me off.'

Zafar appeared at her other side and folded his arms around his grandmother, tucking her head against his chest. 'Hey. Are you thinking of your time? All those hundreds of years ago when you got married.' She swatted him on his arm and he grinned down at her. 'Where's *my* grandmother who always brings *others* to tears?'

'Behave yourself.' She sniffled but smiled. 'I'm having a moment here and you're supposed to console me right now, not be mean.'

He kissed the top of her head as he swayed her gently in his arms.

Reshma let Zafar comfort Daadi and stood beside Haniya, the latter resting her head against her shoulder as they watched Saleema and Nomaan leave together.

Movement from the side of her eye caught her attention and she saw Safiya standing with a man. He was leaning close to her face and talking to her before he pointed in the direction of the crowd and then walked away, leaving Safiya standing there by herself. She shook her head and Reshma saw her rub her fingers under her eyes before looking around her surreptitiously and then moving back towards a small group of people Reshma assumed were her in-laws.

She had to try to get through to Safiya and the sooner she did it, the better.

As luck would have it, Reshma didn't have to wait long.

They'd just got back to the villa and were reflecting on how well the day had gone when her phone chimed an incoming message. It was Safiya telling her that she was free to meet if Reshma was up for it.

It turned out that Safiya and her husband and mother-in-law were staying in a villa not too far from Auntie Ruqayyah's. Safiya's husband, Ejaz, had popped out and her mother-in-law was otherwise occupied, so she was free to meet up.

Reshma agreed to meet Safiya in half an hour in the communal garden and when she got there, Safiya was already waiting for her. She hadn't said anything to Zafar, not wanting to get his hopes up if Safiya decided she wasn't ready to talk to him.

Both she and Safiya had changed out of their dressy clothes. Reshma was in jeans and a light jumper, while Safiya was in a dress and leggings.

'Thanks for agreeing to see me.'

'I'm still not sure there's any point, but I'd forever wonder if I didn't at least try while you're all here.' Safiya's tone was sombre.

'Sometimes the hardest part is just taking the first step, Safiya. I know Zafar is finding it just as difficult as you are. But once you both see each other, the rest will follow, I'm positive.'

Safiya shook her head. 'It's not that simple. I pushed them away. I was upset and angry. I felt let down. By everyone and myself. I punished everyone by shutting myself off from them, but I'd get information trickling in about them from here and there, and today when I had a chance to see them, I couldn't. I couldn't face seeing them and their disappointment in me. So I contented myself by just seeking you out. Do you know how many times I ducked away so Daadi didn't see me?' Her voice broke and Reshma watched tears pool in Safiya's eyes, but, unlike earlier, this time she let them fall, swiping them away roughly.

Reshma couldn't stop herself and gathered Safiya close, trying to comfort her, but at the same time stopping herself from pressuring her to do something she might not feel ready to do.

Safiya's breathing steadied after a couple of minutes and she pulled back.

'You said Zaf is finding it difficult. What did he say to you?'

'How about asking me that yourself, Saf?'

23

Zafar

Countless thoughts and feelings were powering through Zafar and he couldn't figure out what to focus on first. The buzzing in his ears had reached a crescendo and he felt like he was vibrating with emotion.

It wasn't like Reshma to duck out like she had with hardly a word and after seeing her with Safiya twice at the wedding, he had a feeling it might have something to do with his cousin, so he'd come after her. Even if it hadn't been about Safiya, he wanted to make sure Reshma was all right.

He'd been wanting to approach Safiya all day, but his feet had been glued to the spot whenever he'd considered making his way towards her, his old nemesis guilt holding him hostage. The fact that Safiya was so close to him and yet so far had made him want to break something. She'd looked almost the same as she always had, yet different in many ways too. She'd made her way to Reshma and spoken to her and they'd both hugged each other. Zafar had felt both pain and satisfaction at the sight and had wanted to go over there and pull his cousin – his sister – into his arms, but he hadn't. It had left him feeling incredibly frustrated.

The only time he hadn't felt like that was when he'd been entranced by Reshma. When she'd walked into the hall behind Saleema on Shoaib's arm – she'd looked stunning and his feelings for her had blossomed within him until they'd filled him completely. Her smile had been bright enough to light the entire venue.

Or during the nikah, when his mind had rewound back to when he and Reshma had been sitting on either side of a partition like that, and then the partition had been removed and he'd seen her for the first time dressed as a bride. His bride.

While Saleema and Nomaan's nikah ceremony had been going on, he'd listened to the imam's sermon and reflected on his own marriage. He no longer lamented the fact that he'd made mistakes or that his marriage hadn't had the best start, but instead he felt grateful that he'd realised his errors and had set about trying to rectify them. He was pleased that he and Reshma were in a better place than they had been when they'd both come out here separately.

The connection he'd felt towards her in that moment had been so strong, he'd felt a keen need to touch her, to know he was connected to her in every way that counted. He'd held her hand as the nikah had been concluded, feeling a sense of peace imbue his body.

And then he'd seen her with Safiya again and that restlessness had come back, except the feeling hadn't shifted. He hoped to God that whatever Reshma and Safiya had spoken about hadn't caused either of them distress.

Seeing Reshma leave the villa when they'd all been relaxing had struck him as odd and he'd been right to think something was going on.

Reshma and Safiya were standing in the communal garden hugging each other before Safiya pulled back and looked at Reshma questioningly.

'You said Zaf is finding it difficult. What did he say to you?'

'How about asking me that yourself, Saf?' He'd spoken without even realising he was about to and both women turned and looked at him in surprise.

'Zaf.' Safiya whispered the word and Zafar closed his eyes as grief overwhelmed him. Grief over the time they'd lost with each other. Grief at having failed her. Grief at not having heard her say his name in six long years and, worst of all, grief at her feeling unable to come and speak to him or Daadi. As though she had something to be ashamed about, when that was as far from the truth as it was possible to be.

Zafar opened his eyes, feeling the sting of tears in them. He didn't say anything, silently opening his arms for his cousin, and she only took a second to close the distance between them before her arms were wrapped around his middle and her face was pressed against his chest as both of them let their tears fall freely.

He saw Reshma swipe her fingers under her eyes and loosened one arm from around Safiya, holding his hand out to Reshma. She took a few steps towards him and he clasped her hand tightly in his, determined to show her how important she was to him.

He wasn't sure how long they stood there, but when Zafar felt he had a better hold over his overflowing emotions, he moved Safiya back and dried her tears with his thumbs. She hiccuped and then gave him a grin reminiscent of the kind she used to give him years before their lives had been torn asunder.

'Come and see Daadi, Saf. She'll be over the moon to see you and to be able to hold you close after so long. Give her that chance.' He watched as the brightness that had filled her eyes dimmed slightly. 'No one, and I mean *no one*, is disappointed with you. If anything, it's me who's been a disappointment. I should have done so much more for you. I should have put a stop to things more forcefully. I should have—'

Saf covered his lips with her finger and shook her head. 'You did everything you could. I know you did. So did the others. Going over that now is . . .' She shook her head, not finishing her sentence. 'I've missed you all so much. Let's not waste time by talking about the past. Let's go and see Daadi.'

Zafar turned towards the path leading back to their villa, Safiya's arm firmly linked through his, filling him with a strong sense of relief. He took one step and then turned to find Reshma walking behind them. He held his other hand out for her, waiting for her to take it before he moved. She smiled tentatively before placing her hand in his and he held it tightly as he pulled her beside him, and together, they made their way back to the villa.

Daadi became a complete watering pot at the sight of her granddaughter, only managing to stop her tears when Safiya suggested she come back later if Daadi was too upset to talk. She rallied round pretty quickly after that and sat on the sofa, holding Safiya's hand in both of hers. 'I just want to look at you, sweetheart. For six years, I've not looked upon your face and I've missed it more than I'll ever be able to express. I just want to look my fill.'

Safiya had given Daadi another quick hug before turning her smiling face towards Reshma. 'You can thank Reshma for today. I was on the fence about seeing you and Zaf, but she convinced me to. I can't thank you enough, Reshma. You're an absolute gem.' Safiya got up and went towards where Reshma was standing, enveloping her in a hug.

Zafar felt his being flood with gratitude for the fact that he'd been blessed with someone like Reshma in his life. She was so selfless in her consideration for others. In truth, without her, he didn't think he'd have been able to make the first move with Safiya. Not out of stubbornness, but more because of his guilt and a fear of Safiya rejecting him.

He moved towards her when Safiya eased back, heading over to Daadi. Reshma smiled, her cheeks filling with colour as though she were unsure about how to take the compliment.

'Saf's right. You are a gem. Thank you for making this happen.' He pointed to where Daadi was holding Safiya against her chest once more as they sat beside each other on the sofa.

Reshma smiled at him and he cupped her cheek, feeling overcome with his feelings for this woman. 'Go and sit with her. Talk to her.'

He nodded but stepped forward and gently pressed his lips against her forehead, inhaling her scent.

They all sat there chatting for a considerable period of time. Daadi asked Safiya about her life in Nairobi, but she seemed to skim over the topic, moving it back to their life in London and wanting to catch up on what she'd missed. No one broached the topic of their grandfather reaching out to her before he died and Safiya not responding. It was better to leave some topics untouched for now.

Daadi suppressed a few yawns, but when she could no longer keep her eyes open, Zafar encouraged her to get some sleep.

'No. I don't want to miss any time with Safiya.'

Safiya promised to see her again the next day and, eventually, Daadi agreed to do as her grandchildren asked, hugging and kissing them individually before giving Reshma her full attention.

'God has been very benevolent in blessing us with you. You're like a bright star, filling everyone's lives with your light. God bless you, sweetheart.' Zafar could see Reshma blink back tears as Daadi showered her with affection. Daadi then left them to go to her room and Reshma said she would go upstairs, letting him catch up with Safiya.

He was reluctant to let her go and told her as much when she got up and he followed her, but she said she was pretty tired. 'Besides, you need this time with Safiya. I know you'd be happy for me to stay, but trust me, you both deserve this moment together. Enjoy it and you can tell me all about it over breakfast.' She reached up and kissed his cheek and turned to leave. Zafar held onto her hand and turned her back, taking her face in his hands.

'You're the best, you know that, right?' He tapped her nose with his and she smiled, filling all the dark voids in him with her brightness. He pressed his lips against hers, the soft pressure of her lips fanning the dormant flames of desire within him until he heard a soft clearing of the throat behind him.

He pulled back, and after a wave at Safiya, Reshma turned and went upstairs, softly closing the door to their bedroom behind her.

Zafar turned to Safiya and watched as the smile that had been on her face the whole time slowly disappeared, her shoulders slumping and a visible fatigue taking over her frame.

There was so much unspoken between them. So much hurt, sadness, guilt. But Zafar was determined not to waste this chance.

They spoke long into the night. Safiya's husband, Ejaz, had left her for the night, as was his way, according to her, and his mother was more than happy to cover up her son's faults, no matter what their impact was on someone else.

'I can stay out and no one will care. So long as I'm there to keep up appearances when the spotlight is on them, they're not bothered.' There was resignation in her voice.

'Where the hell would he have gone?' Zafar was shocked to hear the truth of Safiya's marriage – the one their grandfather had forced and Zafar hadn't been able to prevent.

'To any number of dives in the area. I'm past caring. He stays out of my way and I stay out of his.'

'So, why the hell are you still there, Saf? Why haven't you packed your bags and come home?'

'What was I supposed to come home to, Zaf? It's been six years. I couldn't even bring myself to say hello to you or Daadi today and you think I should have packed my bags and *come home*?' She scoffed, but Zafar heard the helplessness in her voice crystal clear. She didn't think she had a home to come back to. Their grandfather had made that quite clear to her when she'd got married. Her place, as far as he was concerned, was with her husband and that was it.

Well, it was time to tell Safiya that things had changed since then. Significantly.

'That has been, and will always be, your home, Saf. You come whenever you want. And if you need me for anything – and I mean *anything* – you just say the word. It's time the wrongs of the past were righted as best as we can. There's a long way to go, I realise that, but it's not impossible.'

She nodded and smiled but didn't say anything in response to him. He knew it would take her time to process seeing them. It would also take her time to process the stuff they'd spoken about.

He filled her in about Ashar, Ibrahim, Rayyan and Haroon and then asked her about Qais. 'I've not heard from him or seen him since the day he walked out of the front door. It's like he's just disappeared. Is he in touch with you? How is he?'

'I've not spoken to him in a while myself. I spoke to him after he left home. He had no concrete plans, but I know he wasn't in a great place. Over time, I'd hear from him occasionally until he just stopped getting in touch. I think . . . it might have been around two or so years ago.'

Around the time their grandfather had passed away.

Zafar knew that now that he'd spoken to Safiya, he needed to reach out to Qais. He wanted his family whole again.

When Safiya yawned a few times, they decided to call it a night. He walked Safiya back to her villa and when he returned, Zafar felt too wired to sleep and he didn't want to disturb Reshma, knowing she'd had a long day. He decided to use the pool, hoping that the repetitive rhythm of his strokes would help him relax.

There was so much for Safiya to process, but he had a lot to think about too. He'd told Safiya that she was free to come home for a visit, or more, whenever she wanted and they'd determined to get hold of Qais too. Maybe his uncle and aunt would have some idea of their son's whereabouts, though they too kept everyone at an arm's length.

Inevitably, Zafar's thoughts went to his grandfather.

How could one man, who he'd thought of as one of the best, have got something so wrong? And the worst part was that his grandfather had had plenty of opportunities to stop matters from escalating, but he hadn't. He'd set a course and stayed true to it at a cost they, as a family, were still paying for.

But then that was the same man who had taught Zafar so much about his work and education, that had helped him reach heights he didn't think he would have without that guidance and certainly not at the young age he had. His grandfather's direction and leadership had held Zafar in good stead and that was something he couldn't ignore.

And he'd loved and respected him wholeheartedly. He had done everything in the first twenty-five years of his life to please his grandfather and make him proud. He couldn't just forget all of that.

The hotel project in London was Zafar's way of giving a tribute to that aspect of his relationship with his grandfather. It was about celebrating the best parts of him and acknowledging that he had loved and respected him. If his grandfather hadn't done some of what he had, like pursuing his dreams for the family business as ruthlessly as he had, the family wouldn't be enjoying the fruits of his labour to this day. He'd handed that responsibility to Zafar, wanting him to preserve and continue that legacy. And that's what the hotel project would be. Zafar was also keen to ensure that the family got a new start and could move away from the shadows of the mistakes and flaws of his grandfather and the past, moving forward together.

24

Reshma

When Reshma woke up, it was to find Zafar sprawled on his front, fast asleep. She had no idea when he'd come up, but she knew it must have been ridiculously late. She hoped the time he'd spent with Safiya had helped both of them heal at least a little.

She made her way downstairs and caught Daadi stepping out of her bedroom.

The pair of them had their breakfast and were sitting on the sofa relaxing when the doorbell rang. Reshma opened the door to let a cheery-looking Safiya in, who gave her the tightest hug and then made a beeline for her grandmother, who was delighted to see her. Reshma was glad that Daadi had this chance to reconnect with her granddaughter and even if nothing else came of this reunion, at least Daadi had this time with Safiya.

Reshma got on with doing some work while Daadi caught up with Safiya, having a few emails to respond to and some bits and pieces she needed to review. She had put new projects on hold till she got back to London, but she had some admin work she needed to get out of the way and it made sense to do it while she was at a loose end.

There were no formal plans today. Auntie Ruqayyah had specifically kept the day after the wedding free for people to be able to rest and relax, with the reception being held the next day. Saleema and Nomaan were flying out for their honeymoon to Sri Lanka early the day after the reception.

After the day they'd had yesterday and with the upcoming reception and then the trip home, Reshma wanted to make the most of the day they had left, so she decided to book a table at a nearby seafood restaurant for her and Zafar, which had come highly recommended. If she was feeling brave enough, she could tell him how she felt. She didn't think the L word would scare him off. They'd come a long way in a short period of time and she was confident that they were in a good place and she was sure of her feelings for him. And they only had a few days left in this glorious location. Wouldn't this be the best way to bring this trip to a close and then take that momentum back home with them?

Safiya and Daadi thought it was a wonderful idea. 'Perfect. It'll give us two a chance to catch up,' Safiya had said enthusiastically, though that's not quite how it worked out.

By the time Zafar eventually rolled out of bed, the lunchtime window had come and gone and Safiya had left. She'd had lunch with Reshma and Daadi and with promises to see them the next day, she had made her way back to her villa.

Daadi decided to go and rest after that. 'You both carry on. I'll be with Bilqis and Ruqayyah later on. Jawad said he'd come and collect me.'

Zafar looked at Reshma in confusion as Daadi went to her room. 'Aren't we going there too? Surely, everyone will still be getting together at Auntie Ruqayyah's villa.'

Reshma nodded, unable to keep the I-know-something-you-don't smile off her face. 'Everyone will be there, but that's not where *we're* going.'

He smiled at her while still frowning. 'O-K. Is it a surprise?'

'Kind of. Just get changed into something smart and comfortable.'

He did as she asked and when Reshma met him downstairs after getting ready herself, he took her breath away. He was only in a simple pair of trousers and shirt, but he looked so good, all she wanted to do was stare. Absorb the fact that this man was hers.

He made no secret of the fact that he was looking at her intently from head to toe. She was in a black and red dress which accentuated her curves and she'd left her hair in loose waves to cascade around her shoulders. Sparkly sandals and smoky eye make-up completed her look and she knew she'd nailed it because Zafar's lips were parted, before he swallowed hard, staring at her unblinking.

She closed the distance between them and pushed his chin up with her finger. He smiled at her. 'Shall we?'

'Yes.' He opened the door and let her precede him and soon they were on their way.

The restaurant wasn't far from the villas, in the opposite direction of the beach. They were led to a table by the windows with a small flower arrangement in the middle of it and a low-hanging ceiling lamp that cast a golden glow over the table. It was both cosy and romantic and filled Reshma with hope that it was the perfect place for her to say what she had to.

They settled down and ordered their starters, and as soon as the waitress left them, Zafar took her hands in his, holding them tightly. 'This is perfect. Thank you.' He smiled fully at her, showcasing his dimples in all their glory, and Reshma was sure that if she hadn't been sitting down, she would have felt her knees weaken.

'I wanted today to be special.'

'Cheesy lines incoming.' His smile turned into a playful grin as he winked at her. 'This whole trip has been special, Reshma. I know it didn't have the greatest start for us but—'

'But we've moved on from that. I'm happy with where we are, Zafar. I hope you are too.'

'I am. Without a shadow of a doubt. You're . . . you're something else, Reshma. And what you did with Safiya?' He shook his head as though lost for words, but Reshma understood his sentiments.

'You stood by me when I had to face my dad and his family. In fact, you stood up to him for me. I did what I could with Safiya. I knew how much it would mean to her, Daadi and especially you and I wanted to make that happen. It's what partners do, isn't it?'

He shook his head. 'Not all partners. Only the special ones.'

'And those who love their partners.'

He hadn't been moving before she'd said those words, but the only way Reshma could describe his reaction was to say that he stilled. He looked at her intently and with some disbelief, so she said it directly.

'I love you, Zafar. I thought I did before and, to be fair, in a way I did, but it was more with the idea of you. But being here with you and being a part of . . . *us*, I'm absolutely certain that I'm *in* love with you.'

His smile was slow in coming, but when it did, it filled his face with a luminous joy she hadn't seen before. He moved his hands so his fingers were interlinked with hers and then he closed his fingers over her knuckles. 'Reshma, I—'

His words were cut off as his phone rang, the ringtone jerking them both out of the bubble they'd been in. He shook his head and unclasped his hand from hers, turning his phone over on the table. From where she was sitting, it looked like it was Ibrahim calling.

'I need to . . .'

'Yeah, go ahead.'

'Ibs, what's up?'

The waitress came to their table with their starters and Reshma moved back as she placed the plates in front of her and Zafar, smiling as she moved away. Reshma looked towards Zafar, whose expression had morphed from relaxed to tense. Tension then escalated to shock on his face before he exhaled deeply, muttering a string of expletives.

'Why the fuck didn't you say anything before?' The anger in his voice was something she'd never heard before and it had worry unfurling within her. What on earth had happened? 'That wasn't for him to decide.' More expletives followed and after a few minutes he ended the call with, 'Fine. And, Ibrahim? Stay in touch.' His tone brooked no argument.

He put his phone down and closed his eyes, pinching the bridge of his nose, the colour high on his cheeks.

Reshma reached across the table, mindful of the plates between them, and put her hand over his clenched fist. 'Zafar? What's happened? Is everyone all right at home?'

He looked up, his jaw firm and his mind clearly in overdrive. As she watched him, his eyes slowly focused on her, and he nodded. 'Yeah, um . . . everyone's fine. It's just work.'

'Oh.'

'There've been some hiccups in the last few days with something I was dealing with before I had to come out here, but they didn't tell me.'

Reshma felt a pinch at his choice of words. *Had to come out here.* They weren't a lie, but given that he'd told her that he felt differently about coming out here, she found the words jarring.

'Things are looking dicier now, so Ibrahim decided to loop me in, but he's done it behind my dad's back because my dad didn't want him to tell me until I was back home. But it might be too bloody late by then. *Shit.*'

Reshma wasn't quite sure what to say. He looked incredibly frustrated and seemed to be half talking to her and half to himself, the food between them completely forgotten. The waitress must have noticed that because she came up to their table a moment later.

'Is everything all right? To your liking?' She had a kind smile on her face, but there was a note of worry in it.

'Yes, everything is fine. Thank you,' Reshma answered her, and after giving her a short nod, she left them alone again.

Reshma took a calamari ring and, dipping it into the small dish of sauce that had come with it, she offered it to Zafar.

'Zafar?'

'Huh?'

'The food.' She held the calamari a few inches from his lips, but he took it from her fingers and put it down on the small plate in front of him, rather than eat it. 'Did Ibrahim say what the plan was going forward?' She took a calamari ring herself, hoping that if he saw her eating, he might do so too.

'Yes, but only vaguely. I left express instructions. I was quite clear about how important this is, but Dad refused to listen to reason, thinking it's more important for me to be here. With me not there handling any crisis that comes up with this deal, there's a good chance it could slip through our fingers.' He ran his hand through his hair, completely oblivious to the impact his words had had on her.

Maybe it was just his frustration coming through. Since they'd been married – and likely before that too – he had spearheaded every crisis management situation and sitting here while others took care of *his* project in his absence was bound to make him feel irritated and wanting to be there instead.

Reshma took a calming breath and tried to reason with him. 'Have faith that Ibrahim and Murad will manage things in your absence. We're only here for a few more days and then you'll be back home and able to deal with whatever it is that's cropped up. Try to be patient.'

He finally looked at her properly and his gaze softened as a corner of his lips went up by a scant millimetre. He picked up the piece of calamari he'd put down and put it into his mouth, chewing it thoughtfully. As he took another piece, Reshma felt that she might have got through to him, and while he'd said a few things she hadn't been happy with, she knew he wasn't being personal. It was just his frustration doing the talking.

The waitress came back to their table just then, asking if they were ready for their mains just as Zafar's phone rang again. He asked the waitress for a few more minutes and answered his phone, this time excusing himself from the table and stepping outside. Reshma could see him from where she was sitting as he gesticulated with his arm, talking into his phone with a great deal of energy.

He came back ten minutes later and stood beside her. 'I'm sorry, Reshma, but can we do this another time? I need to sort this out and I can't do it sitting here in a restaurant.'

Reshma forced a smile and stood up. It wasn't ideal, but he clearly had a problem he needed to deal with and her getting upset about a thwarted date and wanting to savour the moment of telling him how she felt wasn't the way to go.

She smiled past her own hurt and frustration. 'Sure. Why don't you give the driver a call and say we're ready to be picked up and I'll settle our bill. Do you want anything for dinner to take back to the villa?'

He was already calling the driver. 'Not for me thanks. Grab whatever you'd like for yourself. I'll see you outside.' And with that, he left the restaurant with his phone against his ear again.

Reshma didn't bother getting anything. She paid for their starters and drinks and followed after Zafar, her mood drastically different from when she'd walked into the restaurant with him. She'd told him she loved him, but she never got the chance to hear what he was going to say and she couldn't help but wonder if she ever would.

25

Zafar

Zafar was buzzing, and not in a good way. It wasn't the buzz of euphoria or satisfaction. It was a build-up of restless energy and a sense of helplessness because he was thousands of miles away from where he needed to be.

Shit had well and truly hit the fan and here he was, waiting for the emails he'd asked Ibrahim to send him to load properly on Reshma's laptop. His father hadn't let him bring his own gear, insisting that he wouldn't need it while he was out there, and Zafar's irritation with the whole situation went up another notch.

He'd told Reshma he had to look into things and she'd handed him her laptop and then made her way to join Daadi at her aunt's villa for the remainder of the evening while he caught up with matters back home.

He made himself a coffee and grabbed a couple of croissants and when he sat back down in front of the laptop, his emails had finally loaded. He started making his way through them chronologically and each email upped his annoyance until he felt anger simmer through his veins.

The hotel deal was supposed to have been a straight-forward transaction, but things had started wobbling soon after he'd left London, it seemed, getting more tangled in the last few days. Ibrahim had clearly tried to manage things, as had Murad, but the seller was being difficult and throwing one obstacle after another their way, the latest being a hike in the original purchase price, with a threat of taking it to auction if they delayed in accepting his terms.

He'd seemed to be in a hurry about selling and with such a prime location and a solid building, Zafar had been keen to close the deal, having run all the necessary checks and paperwork before leaving. He couldn't understand why things hadn't progressed as smoothly as he'd anticipated.

He spent a good few hours going through what he could, getting frustrated each time he wanted a document and realised that he wasn't connected to the main server because he wasn't using his own laptop.

The seller had given them a deadline for two days' time to accept his terms before he backed out, which, according to Zafar's calculation, left him roughly thirty-six hours to get things back on track. And he couldn't do that sitting where he was. He needed to get back to London as soon as possible if he wanted to salvage this.

It was already pretty late, so it was unlikely he'd get anything today but maybe he'd be able to fly out tomorrow. He needed to get in touch with the airline. He also had to consider what arrangements to make for Daadi and Reshma. Would they stay or fly back home with him?

Frustration and the need to be doing something pounded through him. This was exactly what he'd wanted to avoid in the first place, but his father had refused to listen to him. Even now, his father had no idea that Ibrahim had looped Zafar into what was happening.

Zafar picked up his phone and called Murad.

'Hey.'

'Why didn't you say anything before? You called me, asked me a bunch of fucking questions but didn't say a thing about the shit fest we now have on our hands. I trusted you to be honest with me.'

'Slow down, mate. First things first, don't even think about offloading all your pent-up frustration my way. I'm doing the best I can, as is Ibrahim. As for trusting me to be honest, if you work your super smart brain a bit harder, you'll see that when I called you there wasn't anything concrete to say. The seller was just being annoying until then, but there was nothing substantial happening. Things escalated shortly after that, but your father gave us strict instructions not to involve you. He said he'd take care of things. I had a meeting with Ibrahim afterwards and we thought it might be a good idea for Ibrahim to fill you in so you're aware of what's happening. Your dad is still dealing with it and doesn't think there's anything to be worried about.'

Zafar heaved a frustrated sigh as he paced the space between the dining table he'd been sitting working at and the kitchen island a short distance away. 'It was supposed to be straightforward, man. If I hadn't come here because of Dad's whim, we could have sorted this out before it got to this. I want that hotel, Murad.'

'I get that, Zaf, but don't lose sight of what's commercially viable and what's not. I get there's a lot in favour of this deal for you, but the price he's now asking for is not worth it and the timeline he's proposing is also ridiculous. I've checked the numbers out and if you have too, then you'll agree with me. If anything, it's beginning to look dodgy. I know you want this to work out because it's what your granddad wanted, but come on, man. Don't let that become a set of blinkers for you. You'll end up making mistakes if you don't pause long enough to take in the full picture.'

He heard Murad's words but they did nothing to ease his worries. 'I need to come back. Let me get back and let's set up a meeting with him. I'm sure I can get this thing back on track. I'll see if I can get a flight for tomorrow.'

Zafar turned in his pacing and saw Daadi and Reshma standing just inside the front door. Daadi's mouth was hanging open, while Reshma's expression looked closed off. Her shoulders were hunched and her eyes seemed vacant before she dropped her gaze.

'I reckon you should wait, Zaf. We'll keep you looped in from here on so that you know exactly what's happening, and if we need you, we'll reach out first thing, I promise. I know you can't access documents, but if we need you for anything, I'm sure we can patch you in for a call or something. Hold your horses and let's see what we can do.'

Zafar watched as Reshma led Daadi to her room and then came out a couple of minutes later and made her way upstairs, not looking his way even once. He needed to have a chat with her at some point, but for now, he needed to concentrate on the matter at hand.

'You at home?'

'Yes. Why?'

'I'm going to video-call you. Let's go through everything with a fine-toothed comb and see where we're at. I'll feel more in control if we go through the details and then you can fill Ibrahim in with anything he needs to be filled in with and we'll take it from there.'

Murad sighed. 'OK.'

By the time Zafar ended his call with Murad and got up from his chair, it was well past two o'clock in the morning. His back and neck were stiff and achy and his eyes felt like he'd rubbed sand in them. Going through the particulars with Murad had reassured him that his groundwork was solid. He closed everything down and headed upstairs, mindful of making any noise, lest he wake Reshma up.

She had left his bedside lamp on and was turned the other way, curled up under the duvet. He knew things hadn't gone as she'd hoped this evening and, to be fair, if he could have chosen, he'd rather have been with her back at the restaurant than have to deal with what he was, but such was life.

He was feeling dog-tired, so he stripped straight out of the shirt and trousers he'd worn for their date and got into his shorts and hit the sack. He still had tonnes of work to get through tomorrow with both Murad and Ibrahim and he hoped he could resolve everything without having to cut their trip short. A small – very small – part of him was reassured that he didn't have to fly out first thing. He'd managed to go through things with Murad enough to be satisfied that it wasn't as dire an emergency as he'd believed it might have been earlier that evening, though there was still the possibility of it all falling through and him losing the hotel. Hopefully, things would work out just fine. At least, that's what he told himself before he fell asleep.

When he got up the next morning, it was to find the bedroom empty. The curtains were still drawn, but sunlight was peeking in through the gaps.

Zafar checked his phone and saw with some relief that there had been no work emergencies since last night. The second thing he noticed was that, once again, he'd slept in pretty late. When he got back to London and his usual schedule, he was going to feel it so badly, the thought made him wince. He flung the covers back and got out of bed, skipping out on having a swim and going straight in for a shower instead.

He went downstairs and found Daadi on the phone. There was no sign of Reshma and he assumed she might have gone to her aunt's villa. He kissed Daadi on the cheek before making his way to the kitchen to get some breakfast. He'd barely eaten anything last night and he was starving. He knew if he hoped to make any more progress with his work, he needed to fuel up adequately. He needed to be firing on all cylinders.

He had a small window of time before he was scheduled to e-meet Murad and Ibrahim and he was hoping to catch Reshma, so he could fill her in on what had happened. He remembered her expression from the night before and had a feeling that she might be under the impression that he planned to leave earlier than they were scheduled to and, to be fair, she wouldn't have been entirely wrong. At the point where she'd overheard his conversation with Murad, that had definitely been his plan, except the subsequent work he'd done with Murad had bought him some time.

Daadi got off the phone and made her way towards him as he finished eating. 'Morning, sweetheart. Another late night for you?'

'Yeah, just some trouble on the work front, but fingers crossed we'll get it sorted.'

'Inshallah, you will. You're not thinking of leaving today, are you?' She looked at him with concern.

'I hope not. It all depends on Murad and Ibrahim.'

She sat down in the chair adjacent to his and held her hand out for him to take. 'I love you. You're one of the most caring and considerate of boys, with a heart of gold. There's no responsibility you have that you don't fulfil with the utmost dedication. But I hope that dedication of yours doesn't come at too high a cost. It has in the past and that worries me.'

'Daadi, you have nothing to worry about. In fact, that's the last thing I want you to do.' He wasn't sure what exactly his grandmother was getting at.

'I know, my darling. But . . . do you remember me telling you about taking after your grandfather in the wrong aspects of your life?'

Zafar nodded his head as Daadi looked at him solemnly.

'I thought that since getting a break from your work and coming here, things were changing for you. You had a chance to pause and lift your head for long enough to see what you were missing and what you were letting pass you by. Reshma's such a special girl and I don't want you to focus so much on trying to make your grandfather proud and carrying his legacy forward that you lose sight of what's really important. It's better to carry no legacy forward than to carry the wrong kind of legacy forward.' Zafar watched as his grandmother shook her head. 'I speak from experience, Zafar. Your grandfather did many praiseworthy things for us, but would I say he made the effort to be a good partner to me? No, I wouldn't. He often prioritised his work over being with me or the children or even with our grandchildren. Yes, I'm grateful for the hard work he put in and the luxuries we get to enjoy as a result, but I'd trade them for him spending time with us and us sharing special moments together in a heartbeat, no questions asked.' She squeezed his hand. 'Don't make the same mistakes as him and certainly not *for* him.'

This wasn't the first time he'd heard his grandmother talk about his grandfather in less than complimentary terms, but it was the most insight she'd given him about what had made her unhappy with him. Not knowing what to say in response, he nodded. He knew what she meant. He could see her perspective and he agreed with it too. He had been about to go down a similar path but had been saved from doing so. He had no intention of doing that again, not when he could see what he would lose as a result.

'Where is she, Daadi?' His voice sounded rough.

'She's gone to Ruqayyah's place. She called her this morning to help wrap gifts to take to the reception. She's also called the hair and make-up people again for whoever wants so I think she'll be there for a bit. In fact, I'm expecting one of the boys to come and collect me, so I can join them.'

'Well, hopefully I'll get a chance to have a chat with her before the reception.'

The doorbell rang just then and Zafar let Khalil in. They exchanged greetings and Khalil asked Zafar to come with them. 'I'd love to, but I've got some work to get done and it's time-sensitive. I should see you later though.'

Daadi left with Khalil, giving Zafar's cheek a soft pat, her look communicating her feelings without any words. She'd given him plenty to think about. He just hoped that he could put into practice what his grandmother had told him, which was the hardest bit.

26

Reshma

Reshma winced as she felt the blade slice through her flesh. Blood poured out straight away and she had to run to the bathroom, still managing to get droplets of blood onto the floor and her dress. She winced as she held her hand under the cold tap until she saw someone turn it off and hold her injured hand in a towel, pressing hard on her cut.

Haniya.

Rather than look sympathetic, her cousin glared at her. 'Where on earth is your brain, woman? You actually just cut your hand with the scissors instead of the sticky tape. What's going on? You've been distracted since you got here.'

'Nothing. I'm fine.' She tried to tug her hand out of Haniya's hold, but Haniya didn't budge and Reshma rolled her eyes. 'Let me see the damage.'

'No. You need to keep pressure on it for longer. You cut the fleshy part between your fingers. I don't even know how we're going to get a plaster on that.'

'Reshma? Niya?' Uncle Jawad stood in the bathroom doorway and regarded the pair of them and Reshma felt her lower lip tremble, so she clamped it between her teeth.

She would not cry. She would not give into the emotions swamping her right now, even if it felt like they were crippling her.

Her uncle stepped forward and took over from Haniya. He pressed the towel firmly around her hand, and after a few minutes, he peeled it back to assess the wound.

She should have been paying better attention to the task at hand, but her mind had been so firmly on Zafar and what had happened since last night at the restaurant, she hadn't realised what she was doing until it had been too late.

He had mentioned going back to London while he'd been on the phone. As soon as possible. And not once had he said anything about speaking to her or about her going back with him. He'd been so focused on his work and whatever problem they were facing that it was as though anything else had ceased to exist once he had a laptop in front of him. He'd relegated her to the place where she'd been since they'd got married, resurrecting her pain and insecurities, except this time it was so much worse because it came after she'd told him she loved him.

She'd been in a dreamlike state for the last week and last night she'd woken up. Ibrahim's phone call had served as a timely alarm for her, bursting her happy little bubble. The irony wasn't lost on her. She had just told Zafar how she felt and then his phone had rung and it was as though she'd never said those words, had never opened herself up to him.

Now she could see that what she and Zafar had shared since being here had been too good to be true, because a leopard never really changed its spots, did it? Zafar was a workaholic, with nothing but the preservation of his grandfather's legacy on his mind and as soon as that came under threat, everything else fell to the wayside, including her.

His work would always be his priority, over and above her. Because if that hadn't been the case, he wouldn't have spoken about leaving, without any thought to anything

– or anyone – else. He still hadn't said anything to her. Granted, he'd been asleep when she'd woken up, but she had told Daadi where she was and he'd not come to see her or called her or even messaged her. Daadi had joined them, telling her that Zafar was up and ready to start work when Khalil had come to pick her up. It was almost like he'd forgotten about her and that hurt.

'Ow.' She winced as Uncle Jawad wiped at the gash on her hand.

'I'm sorry, pet. The cut seems to be pretty deep, but I don't think you'll need stitches. Let me bandage it up for you.'

Her uncle dressed her cut and since she was out of action with helping with gift wrapping anymore and the hair and make-up artists had arrived, Reshma got on with getting ready for the reception while her mind ran riot with thoughts of her fledgling relationship with Zafar being doomed before they'd even got back to London.

So much for her carrying their good momentum forward.

The romance of their destination, the wedding atmosphere and their close proximity had made her lower her guard while blinding her to reality. Had they been in London, things would probably have stayed as they had been. Back there, things had always been categorically clear to her, but out here she'd chosen to believe the unbelievable. Time and place had inhibited her ability to see the wood for the trees and the feelings she'd thought she'd felt had been circumstantial. Not real.

But was she jumping the gun?

Yes, she'd heard what she'd heard, but she'd not heard anything after that. Surely if Zafar had planned to leave today, Daadi would have told her that he'd been packing his bags, but she hadn't. Did that mean he hadn't left?

Her mind felt like it was on a rollercoaster which was going through one loop after another, showing no signs of slowing down.

The hair stylist and make-up artist both finished with her and Reshma got into the dark blue suit Auntie Bilqis had given her. She was adding the finishing touches when she realised that she'd left her bag of accessories at her villa.

'Niya, I've left some things back at the villa, I'm just going to see if Sho or Khalil can go and grab them for me.'

'Mmhmm,' Haniya mumbled through lips pressed together as the make-up artist started doing her make-up.

Reshma made her way through the villa, trying to spot one of her cousins. Uncle Jawad was watching TV, so she asked him where they were and he told her they'd both gone to get some last-minute bits and pieces for Auntie Ruqayyah.

'Did you need something?'

'Yeah, I left my bag of accessories at the villa. I'm just going to go and grab it.'

'I can go?'

'No, it's fine. Won't take me long.' She was feeling restless anyway, maybe some fresh air would do her good. She would also get to see if Zafar was getting ready for the reception or to go to the airport, though she didn't know what she'd say to him.

She knew she probably looked very strange walking around the complex dressed up like she was, but she needed to clear her head. She took the long way back, walking almost the entire perimeter of the complex before finding herself back on the path towards her villa.

The best thing for her to do would be to speak to Zafar. There was no sense working herself up into a tizzy without having all the information. It could well amount to nothing. And if not . . . well, at least she'd know for sure then.

She was about twenty metres away when she saw Zafar pull the front door of the villa closed, dragging his small suitcase behind him. He made his way purposefully towards the gate and got into a car. The engine started up and before she could take a step in his direction, the car moved off.

He'd gone. He'd left her.

Without so much as a goodbye. Without looking back even once.

Reshma felt the breath she had taken lodge in her chest and when the edges of her vision went hazy, she pulled in a shuddering breath.

He'd left her. He'd gone.

She had thought she'd felt pain when she'd found out that he'd come here under duress, but that was nothing compared to the pain now unfurling in her chest and spreading its poisonous tentacles throughout her body until she felt it in every single cell, in every fibre of her being.

She staggered a few steps towards a low wall on the side of the path and lowered herself onto it, careless of the fact that it might dirty her clothes.

He'd left her. He'd gone.

She shouldn't have let him suck her into a false sense of security. When she'd found out the truth behind his arrival, she should have stuck to her guns and kept her distance from him. But she hadn't and now she was paying the price for it. He'd proved, beyond all doubt, that she was not, and never would be, his priority.

She didn't know how long she sat there for. It couldn't have been that long because no one had come across her while she'd been sitting there in a daze as her reality crashed over her with each breath she took and she was very grateful for that. She wasn't sure what she might have said or how she would have explained why she was sitting there like that, short of the fact that Zafar had left.

Slowly, Reshma got up and, on leaden legs, she went back to her aunt's villa. Uncle Jawad was standing outside on the phone and when he saw her, he frowned. She walked past him and into the villa, which was a hive of activity. Her aunts were running to and fro and she spotted Daadi sitting in the garden through the patio door with Uncle Imtiaz's mother.

Reshma lowered herself onto the sofa, her head pounding and her hair feeling too tightly arranged. She reached up to see if she could loosen some pins, only to find the mass of it was in loose waves and not in an updo. The only pins in her hair were the ones holding her maang tikka in place.

'What do you think?' She looked up and found Haniya standing in front of her, showing off her hair and make-up.

Reshma tried but couldn't muster a smile for her.

Haniya was instantly on high alert. 'What is it? What's happened? I thought you went to grab your things.'

'I did. That is, I went to go and get my things, but on the way there I saw Zafar leaving with his suitcase. He's gone,' she said numbly.

'What?! Did he say anything?'

Reshma shook her head. 'No. I heard him on the phone yesterday. Ibrahim called him to tell him about a problem at work and then later I heard Zafar saying he needed to get back to London as soon as possible. So, he's gone.'

'Without saying anything to you or anyone else? Just gone?'

Reshma nodded as Haniya shook her head.

'I find that hard to believe.'

'It's not that complicated, Niya. He's focusing on what's important to him and I need to focus on what's important to me.' Impatience laced her voice.

Yes, she was heartbroken. Yes, she felt like each breath she took was like a fresh cut to her heart. The sense of abandonment and rejection which she was so familiar with surrounded her again and she felt weighed down by it. But she wouldn't let it drown her. She would get up, get what she needed to so she was ready and then make her way to Saleema's reception with her family.

She wasn't angry with Zafar as much as she felt livid with herself for letting things get to the point where she'd opened herself up to being in such a position yet again. It seemed to her that she didn't learn and each time she put herself out there, she would face such heartbreak. Though nothing would ever hurt her the way Zafar had today.

She made her way back to her villa after persuading Haniya to finish getting ready and assuring her that she was fine, at least enough to go and get the things she needed. Her bag was sitting where she'd left it on the floor beside the kitchen island. She cast a glance across the kitchen and dining table and saw evidence that Zafar had been here. The sink was half-filled with dishes, and there were used mugs and an empty plate on the dining table. She was surprised to find her phone still charging on the island and looked at the screen, only to find it still switched off. She looked at the socket and realised that she hadn't actually switched the power on, so her phone hadn't charged at all. Maybe Zafar had . . . no. He could have come to speak to her directly or called any one of her relatives and asked to speak to her.

She took the charger and phone with her and after putting her jewellery and sandals on, she went back to Auntie Ruqayyah's villa, where everyone had gathered outside.

Daadi came towards her. 'I was looking for you, darling. Ready?'

She nodded as she swallowed the lump in her throat.

'Jawad told me about Zafar. Honestly, that boy.' Daadi shook her head blithely, no sign of frustration or annoyance with her grandson and Reshma stared at her open-mouthed.

Daadi knew? So did Uncle Jawad?

And they seemed to be fine with it. There was no outrage on anyone's face and they all seemed to take it in their stride, as though it were perfectly acceptable for him to have just left her.

'Auntie Mumtaz, you come in the car with us, and Reshma, you go with Niya, Sho and Khalil.' Auntie Bilqis was directing everyone towards the cars, ready to make their way to the hotel where the reception was due to take place.

Reshma followed, her mind completely blank. She was too tired to think. All she really wanted to do was . . . nothing. But she knew that wasn't an option.

She got into the car and, blocking out everything around her, she stared out of the window as Khalil drove them to the reception, his loud music drowning out any conversation that was going on around her. Haniya kept shooting worried looks her way, but she didn't say anything.

Half an hour later, they got to the venue, where Nomaan's family were waiting at the entrance to greet them. There was a great deal of noise and laughter as they met and hugged each other, as though they hadn't all been partying together two days ago after the nikah ceremony.

The thought brought a lump to Reshma's throat as she thought about sitting with Zafar during the nikah. The closeness she'd felt with him.

She felt a prickling in the corners of her eyes and the dull ache in the region of her heart intensified. She wouldn't cry, she couldn't, and certainly not right now.

Steeling herself, she greeted Saleema's mother-in-law as she moved past her and into the foyer. Saleema and Nomaan were standing at the next set of doors which led into the hall the reception was to be held in and Reshma managed to hold herself together as she hugged her cousin and then her husband.

Saleema looked absolutely stunning, her face glowing with happiness as she stood beside Nomaan, their hands linked as they greeted guests. There was this aura about Saleema and Nomaan, which seemed to hold them apart from everything. Even when she was speaking to someone and he was speaking to someone else, you couldn't miss the connection between them, it had a presence of its own. She couldn't stop herself from reflecting on the fact that she'd thought she had that connection with Zafar these last few days but how wrong she'd been. It had all been an illusion.

Reshma moved with Haniya towards the tables reserved for their family and found the seat with her place card. She was putting her clutch down when she saw Zafar's name card on the seat beside hers. The seat that would be empty for the reception.

She felt her throat close up and knew that she wouldn't be able to hold back the tears that were now threatening to flood her eyes. She told Haniya she was going to the ladies' but didn't wait for her to acknowledge her before she weaved her way through the tables and went through a smaller set of doors in the corner of the hall and came back out in the foyer. Reshma moved through the melee of people still making their way into the hall and walked out of the hotel, following the path away from the main entrance.

She stopped several metres away, where she could see the main entrance but was at enough of a distance that people wouldn't see her, and then she let the tears fall.

27

Zafar

Zafar watched as Reshma came through the doors, her head bowed and her shoulders hunched and, as she made her way to the other side of the building, he saw Haniya follow after her. Neither of them had spotted him and as he stood there staring after them, he saw Haniya put her arm around Reshma's shoulders as his wife seemed to break down into tears.

What on earth had happened?

Zafar hurried in their direction, walking past the entrance to the hotel and the line of guests making their way inside for the reception. The turnout looked just as big as it had been for the wedding.

He was almost directly behind Reshma when he heard her sobbing into her hands as Haniya rubbed her hand over her back, soothing her.

'He left me, Niya.' She sucked in an audible breath and he heard the depth of emotion in it. 'After all that, he just left me. He said nothing. He didn't bother telling me he was going. He didn't suggest I go back with him. He didn't even bother to say bye or see me before he left.' Her voice broke as she covered her face with her hands.

'Aww, Reshma, honey, please stop crying. I don't know what's happened or why you think Zaf would leave—'

'Because that's what happens to me. People don't stay. They leave. They don't want to be with me. I always say or do something that makes them want to leave and for Zafar nothing comes above his dedication to his work. Certainly not me. He didn't want to be here, remember?'

This was about him?

Zafar didn't know what to make of what he was seeing and hearing. What on earth had happened since this morning to make Reshma think he'd left her without a word?

'Reshma?'

She jerked her head towards him at the sound of his voice, her tear-filled eyes wide and her lips parted in an O. Haniya turned to look at him too, surprise clearly etched on her face.

The three of them stood there staring at each other for a long moment until Haniya recovered her ability to speak. 'You're here?'

Zafar looked at her and raised his eyebrow in question. 'Where else would I be?'

'I thought . . . we thought that you might have . . .' She looked at Reshma and then back at him. 'Umm, I think there may have been a bit of a misunderstanding.'

'You think?!' Zafar asked incredulously, the sight of Reshma's tear-stained face making his heart sink, but as her words and their implication slowly registered in his brain, he felt a flicker of annoyance at her lack of faith in him. 'Can you give us a minute please, Niya?' he asked with more calm than he felt. He'd had a day from hell and now this.

'Sure.' She smiled at him and gave Reshma a final pat on the back before quietly walking away.

Zafar didn't move from where he was standing and Reshma didn't either. Thankfully, her tears seemed to have stopped, but they'd left her eyelashes spiky and tracks down her cheeks. She had dark smudges under her eyes where some of her make-up seemed to have smeared. But she still looked bloody gorgeous to him.

'I don't even know where to start, Reshma. What the hell is happening here?'

'I thought you had left. What are you doing here?'

'Uhhh . . . correct me if I'm wrong, but we have a reception to attend right now. I don't make a habit of putting on a tux every day. And where exactly am I supposed to have gone?'

She sniffled and rubbed the back of her hand under her nose. When she spoke, her voice was little more than a whisper. 'London.'

'London? Because . . .?'

'You said you had to go back as soon as possible because your hotel deal had some issues. You said that last night. On the phone. And then . . .' She swallowed, her voice a bit clearer but with a hint of confusion in it. 'I saw you getting into a car and you had your suitcase with you. I thought you were leaving to go back to London because of your work.'

'Without telling you?'

She looked at him for a moment without responding and just as he was about to repeat the question, she jerked her head once in a nod.

Zafar closed his eyes as he pinched the bridge of his nose. 'Jesus. Reshma.' He could hear the growl in his voice. How could she doubt him like that? Granted, he'd been pretty focused on the hotel situation since they'd left the restaurant yesterday – though it felt like it had been days ago – but he couldn't believe that she thought he'd have just left her without so much as a *'I'm leaving, see ya.'* Especially after the way they'd connected in recent days.

'You didn't go to the airport.' She said it like she was testing the words out.

He lowered his hand from his face and saw her looking at him, her expression still one of disbelief but with a hint of confusion and now sheepishness there.

'I didn't go to the airport.'

He was tempted to hold her. Take her in his arms and comfort her, reassure her that he hadn't left and was still there. With her. But he had to clear this up first. He had to try to understand how she had got it so wrong to the point of breaking down like that. He put his hands into his pockets.

'I did say yesterday I need to go to London and I also said I needed to do it as soon as possible. But it was my immediate reaction to the problem. It's what I would have done if I gave no thought to anything – or anyone – else.'

She swallowed and he saw the misery gradually disappear from her face and posture as her shoulders relaxed a bit. 'But I saw you get into the car with your suitcase.'

He nodded. 'That's because I did get into a car with my suitcase. I didn't have a laptop bag or rucksack, so I emptied my suitcase and loaded the laptop and bits I needed into it and made my way to a nearby hotel because I had no internet after the power cut.'

Her eyebrows furrowed. 'What power cut? There was no power cut.'

He raised his eyebrows at her outright denial. 'There *was* a power cut. Just before you saw me leaving the villa, there had been a power cut. I called you, but when you didn't answer, I messaged you and then called Uncle Jawad. He said all the villas had lost power. Weren't you at Auntie Ruqayyah's villa?'

Her forehead didn't clear as her lower lip slowly curled in to sit between her teeth. God, that habit of hers . . .

Zafar cleared his throat and tried to bring his attention back to the moment.

'I wasn't at the villa. I had gone for a short walk. It must have happened then.'

'It didn't last long, but it threw the internet out for long enough that I didn't bother hanging around. I packed what I needed and went to a hotel to use the internet and finish off what I was doing so that I could make it in time for Saleema's reception.'

She stared back at him, and he saw the moment the penny dropped with her that he hadn't actually walked out on her without a word. The only thing she said, though, was a softly voiced, 'Oh.'

'Yes. *Oh.*' Zafar shook his head. 'I don't even know what to say, Reshma. I didn't realise you had so little faith in me. What is it you need from me to reassure you that I'm here? With you. I'm not going anywhere.'

She watched him intently and he watched her back. Her lower lip trembled and her eyes filled with fresh tears and in the next moment she took the few steps between them and wrapped her arms around him, resting her cheek against him. She held him so tight, she had both his tux and his shirt in her grip.

'I thought . . .' She turned her face into him and he gave up holding back and wrapped his arms around her, holding onto her just as tightly as she held onto him. Zafar could see the depth of Reshma's insecurities and her doubts stemmed from the way she'd been treated in the past. It would take time for her to shake them off, so he could understand why she had reacted the way she had.

'I think I can take a guess what you might have thought, love. But I'm here. With you, Reshma. And when we go back to London, we'll go back *together*. We just need to remember to take my menace of a grandmother back with us. We need to have some sympathy for the Kenyan citizens. Can't leave her behind.'

She giggled softly, just as he'd hoped she would, but her hold on him was as firm as before and he continued to hold her. He'd do it for as long as she needed and he was quite happy to do so, inhaling her scent as they stood there.

'I do need to apologise to you, though.'

She lifted her head and looked up at him questioningly, her face clear of the despair that had clouded it a little while ago.

'I'm sorry. I said some things that I shouldn't have said. I let my frustration do the talking instead of being rational and patient. I can see why you might have thought I'd want to get home immediately because that's how I behaved. But once I'd calmed down and looked at the problem logically and like I should have without getting worked up, I saw what needed doing and the fact that I could manage it well enough remotely.'

'So the problem's fixed?'

Zafar pursed his lips. 'It should be. We'll find out in the morning for sure when the guys have a chat with the seller, but we've done everything we could. If it's meant to be, it'll be.' He watched her as she took a deep breath, feeling her relax in the circle of his arms. 'Is my apology accepted?'

She looked up and smiled, her first full smile since the waterfall of tears he'd witnessed. Her nose wrinkled ever so slightly as her nose stud twinkled. 'It is. I'm sorry too. I . . . I completely misunderstood everything and let my fears take over. Everything seemed to point in that direction and with Ibrahim calling you when he did and then everything today. . .'

'Yeah, his timing does leave a lot to be desired, doesn't it? He cut me off from saying one of the most important things I've ever said to someone.' He paused, taking in every dear feature of her face as she looked at him questioningly. 'I love you, Reshma. Actually, I was going to say I love you too yesterday, but since there's been a severe lag on my part, I believe adding the "too" is unnecessary. I think just "I love you" is the important part, right?'

She didn't say anything, just looked at him with an inscrutable expression. 'You're not just saying it because I said it, are you? Because you don't have to do that. Maybe you should wait till we're back in London and you're sure. It could be the time and place that's—'

Zafar didn't let her finish her sentence, cutting her off in a way he found thoroughly pleasurable, even if there was a risk of them getting caught by a relative. He moved his hands from around her to cup her cheeks and angle her face to his. He kissed her languorously, as though he had all the time in the world, and she didn't take long to respond, opening up to him and taking entry into his mouth and allowing him entry into hers, her hands tightening their grip on him.

They kissed until he felt pressure building within him to take in air. Reluctantly, Zafar eased away from her, dropping soft kisses around her mouth and on her face in between taking breaths and interspersing them with a softly voiced 'I love you' after each kiss.

He looked down into her bright eyes. 'I do love you, Reshma. Your bright and beautiful light has filled my life in a way it's taken me too long to realise and appreciate. You mean more to me than you know and while I'll accept that our match was arranged by our families, don't for a minute think that I don't choose you. I do. And I will, each and every time. Ah, please don't cry again. As it is, I'm not sure you'll want to go into the reception with your make-up looking slightly. . . um. . .' He circled his finger around her face, refusing to elaborate verbally.

She sniffled and cuddled up to him again, as though snuggling into a duvet. 'I love you too, Zafar. So much.' Her words reached deep inside him, warming his heart in a way he'd never thought possible and he knew he'd never tire of hearing them.

He kissed the top of her head as he heard someone clearing their throat behind him.

He turned and found Safiya standing there, a broad smile on her face.

'Hey, Saf.'

'Sorry to interrupt, but Daadi's worried that she's misplaced the pair of you. Would you like to come and reassure her? She sent your cousins to look for you, Reshma. One of them said he saw you here with Zafar and what he saw had him turning back and needing to wash his eyes out, so I came to get you instead, being a mature adult and all.'

Zafar barked out a laugh as he saw Reshma's cheeks go pink. At least there was colour in them now.

Safiya caught sight of Reshma properly and her gasp had him wincing and Reshma's eyes widening. 'What? What is it?'

'Wait here. I'll bring my bag. I've got some powder and lipstick. Hopefully they'll do the trick.'

28

Reshma

Saleema and Nomaan's reception was as spectacular as the rest of their wedding events had been. Though she and Zafar had missed Nomaan's father's welcome speech and part of Nomaan's speech – thanks to Safiya doing a quick fix of her make-up after insisting that she wanted no details about why it was needed in the first place – they'd caught the end of it, where he'd asked everyone to toast his new wife.

When they'd joined the others at the table, Haniya had given her a relieved smile when she'd squeezed her hand in silent communication and Shoaib had handed her back her mobile phone – sixty per cent charged. She'd given it to him and asked him to charge it in the car for her on the way to the reception. She looked at her list of notifications and bit her lip at the number of messages from Zafar and the few voicemails he'd left. He saw her screen but didn't say anything, he just raised that imperious eyebrow at her and shook his head, a smile teasing his lips as she looked back at him sheepishly.

The bride and groom had then cut a huge three-tiered wedding cake before dinner was served and they were now on the dance floor, their heads together as they moved in time with the music.

The romance of the moment had Reshma suppressing a deep, contented sigh. Or maybe it was the deep sense of love and romance she was feeling towards the man who had maintained some form of contact with her throughout the evening, and now held her in his arms in a corner of the dance floor.

He hadn't gone and he hadn't left her.

He could have, but he hadn't. He'd stayed and she knew without a shadow of a doubt that he'd stayed for her.

Because he loved her.

Mentally, she did a little jig. Her fear of being left had led her to forming her own narrative about what had happened and had caused her nothing but misery in the last twenty-four hours as she'd immediately believed that Zafar had done something when he'd made a conscious effort to do the opposite.

She felt his thumb rub the skin just above her eyebrow, smoothing it. 'Stop thinking so hard. Everything is fine. All in order. Shipshape.'

She smiled.

It would take her time to shed her insecurities, but she would do it. There was no place for them in her life going forward. She needed to have faith and confidence in Zafar and her marriage. And, most importantly, she needed to have confidence in herself. Confidence that she was worthy of being important to someone, worthy of being someone's priority but also worthy in herself, without any validation from another.

She wasn't defined by her relationships or who stuck by her and who didn't. Being true to herself had enabled her to move forward with Zafar, something she hadn't necessarily done from the start with him. She needed to stop letting her fear call the shots and take control of life and how she navigated it herself. Of course, having Zafar along for the ride was a particularly delightful bonus.

The song came to an end and she eased away from him, though he didn't let go of her hand for the rest of the evening.

When they got back to the villa later that night, and Daadi was in her room, they made their way to the pool. Reshma went down the steps into the cool water, while Zafar dived in smoothly, coming up for air halfway down the pool's length. Feeling more relaxed than she had in a long time, she flipped onto her back, watching the stars in the sky, the distant sound of the waves mixing in with the sound of the water as it lapped over her body.

She felt movement to her side and, a moment later, Zafar held her hand as he floated on his back next to her. She wished she could bottle the sense of peace she was feeling. It made her feel like postponing their departure and staying in their bubble for a little longer. But she knew they had to get back to normal life. She had work to get back to, as did Zafar.

'This is going to sound crazy given the circumstances of my arrival, but I don't think I'm ready to go back.'

She turned her head, regarding his side profile. 'Same.'

They stayed there for a bit longer, savouring the tranquillity of the moment and their closeness, not needing to say anything, though the hum of energy around them was palpable to both.

Two days after the reception, it was time for them to leave.

Reshma had spent the previous day with Auntie Ruqayyah and the rest of the family, knowing that it would be a while before the whole family would be together like that again. Her father and his family were also there, but the situation between them and Reshma was exactly how it had been before. There was no change there and, to be fair, she didn't feel all that bad about it. You couldn't really miss what you'd never had, especially when she was surrounded by others who loved her and cared for her so much more than her father ever had.

Zafar had spent the earlier part of the day with Safiya and had been in a bit of a sombre mood thereafter because she had left to go back to Nairobi with her husband and mother-in-law.

'At least you're going to be in touch with her now. That should make you feel better. And we can always come out and see her or vice versa.' She knew it wasn't enough, but she hoped, going forward, things would improve on that front. She had more optimism in her than she would have had a few weeks ago and she wanted to hold onto it.

They were on the same flight home as Uncle Jawad and his family and when they landed back in London, they were greeted by sunshine and showers, literally and figuratively. Harry and Ash were waiting in arrivals for them.

She and Zafar didn't take long to fall into their usual domestic routine. He hit the ground running with his work, as did she. The hotel deal still hadn't been concluded, but she knew Zafar was much calmer about it now and didn't attach the success of it to his happiness or his relationship with his grandfather. In fact, since their return, Zafar was more mindful about what he did and what he now delegated, as he told her one evening when he'd asked Harry to accompany their father to a dinner being hosted by a business associate.

'I need to learn the art of delegation, it's healthy for me and the others. As for skipping tonight's dinner invite, I think it's good for Harry to do some of these gigs. He can decide whether he wants to play more of a role in the business and these events make up a big part of it. Besides, I really didn't fancy spending an evening listening to Mr Gervais sharing his life story for the hundredth time. I'd much rather keep my date night promise to you.'

'So, I'm preferred company to Mr Gervais? That's good to know,' she said deadpan, though she was pleased that they'd managed to keep the connection they'd forged, and it was getting stronger by the day.

'You are no competition for Mr Gervais. His level of dull is unparalleled. Ask Harry when he gets home.'

She scowled at him as he gave her a lopsided grin, his dimples coming out to say hello.

'You're preferred company to everyone else, my love. Always.'

He reached across the table and linked his fingers with hers but had to pull away a moment later when their waiter brought their starters. Zafar had brought her to a seafood restaurant in Mayfair for their first date night since they'd come back from Mombasa as a nod to their thwarted date out there.

'I have to say, I'm impressed, Mr Saeed. Mombasa to Mayfair. Not shabby at all.'

'I'm glad you approve, Mrs . . . Ms . . . What did you decide?'

'I'm Mrs Reshma Mir-Saeed. I'm me and I'm also married to you.'

'I like that. It's perfect.'

They tucked into the starters.

'Guess who messaged me today?' she asked as she broke off a piece of bread.

'Umm, Saleema?'

Reshma shook her head. 'Habib. My father's younger son.'

Zafar looked at her wide-eyed, his expression one of surprise.

'What did he say?'

'He said he's been wanting to reach out to me since Mombasa. Asked if we'd be up for meeting for a coffee.'

'And?'

Reshma smiled at Zafar as she shrugged a shoulder. 'I said I'd think about it and get back to him. What do you think?'

Zafar chewed thoughtfully for a moment before swallowing. 'I'm happy to follow your lead, Reshma. If you want to meet him and see how things go, then I'm happy to do that, and if you don't, then I'm happy with that too. But something tells me that you're open to seeing him, yes?'

She tilted her head slightly, her soft smile still in place. 'I am. I don't know how our relationship will evolve, but if we can have some connection, then I'm open to that.'

Zafar held her hand in his across the table. 'Then let's go with that.'

They shared a scrumptious meal and then took a walk through Hyde Park, slowing down by the Serpentine. She'd come to the conclusion that she and Zafar liked being by the water, be it the Indian Ocean or a recreational lake in a park.

'We should have a water feature—'

'I want a pool—'

They looked at each other and burst out laughing and Reshma sent up a silent prayer of thanks at finally being able to have moments with Zafar that she'd thought of as impossible dreams before.

He shook his head and she stopped walking and manoeuvred them off the path and onto a patch of grass. As she faced him, she looped her arms around his waist. She looked up at him as his hands rested around her lower back.

'I love you.'

He looked at her as though cataloguing each and every feature on her face before lowering his forehead against hers. 'And I love you.' He turned his head enough to place a lingering kiss on her cheek and she felt a sense of both connection and contentment fill her.

She slowly moved away, certain that her sense of peace and joy were radiating off her like the rays of the sun and she could see the reflection of them on Zafar. She linked her arm with his and they made their way back onto the path and carried on walking.

They didn't need to say anything more to each other. Those three words encompassed everything there was to say, all the promises there were to make and all the feelings there were to convey.

And Reshma knew, without any doubt, that even though marriage had come first, their love for each other was strong and enduring and they would always choose each other.

Credits

Laila Rafi and Orion Fiction would like to thank everyone at Orion who worked on the publication of *First Comes Marriage* in the UK.

Editorial
Sanah Ahmed

Copyeditor
Jade Craddock

Proofreader
Jane Howard

Audio
Paul Stark
Jake Alderson

Contracts
Anne Goddard
Dan Herron
Ellie Bowker

Design
Rashmi Tyagi
Nick Shah
Joanna Ridley

Editorial Management
Charlie Panayiotou
Jane Hughes
Bartley Shaw
Tamara Morriss

Finance
Jasdip Nandra
Nick Gibson
Sue Baker

Production
Ruth Sharvell

Sales
Jen Wilson
Esther Waters
Victoria Laws
Toluwalope Ayo-Ajala
Rachael Hum
Anna Egelstaff

Sinead White
Georgina Cutler

Operations
Jo Jacobs
Sharon Willis

Don't miss the next irresistible and
achingly romantic second-chance
romcom from Laila Rafi . . .

THE LOVE DETOUR

**Two broken hearts. Could this be
their second chance at love?**

*Don't miss Laila Rafi's irresistible and hilarious
fake-dating romcom . . .*

**One fake relationship. Two complete strangers.
And love was *definitely* not part of the plan . . .**

Jiya and Ibrahim are a perfect couple. Except they're not
actually together, just faking it to get their families off
their back.

Jiya wants to complete her MBA and get her dream job
in the city. So being perfect wife material and finding
the right guy is the last thing on her mind . . .

And Ibrahim certainly doesn't want to end up like his
older, dutiful brother by being pressured into a marriage
not of his choosing!

Their plan is perfect, until the attraction they're faking
starts to feel all too real . . .